Sea Change

By Aimee Friedman

Sea Change

AIMEE FRIEDMAN

Point

For my grandmothers,
Margaret Smouk and Civia Friedman,
who have always been so generous with their gifts

Copyright © 2009 by Aimee Friedman

Library of Congress Cataloging-in-Publication Data

Friedman, Aimee.
   Sea change / Aimee Friedman. — 1st ed.
      p. cm.
   Summary: When her estranged grandmother dies and leaves her mother the family home on
Selkie Island, seventeen-year-old Miranda meets her mother on the Georgia island, where she
discovers mysterious family secrets and another side to her logical, science-loving self.
   ISBN-13: 978-0-439-92228-9 (alk. paper)
   ISBN-10: 0-439-92228-3 (alk. paper)
   [1. Islands—Fiction.   2. Secrets—Fiction.   3. Social classes—Fiction.   4. Southern states—
Fiction.   5. Mermen—Fiction.]   I. Title.
   PZ7.F89642Se 2009
   [Fic]—dc22

2008046959

ISBN 978-0-439-92230-2

12 11 10 9 8 7 6 5 4 3 2 1   10 11 12 13 14 15/0
                    Printed in the U.S.A.   40

First POINT paperback printing, June 2010

The display type was set in Opti Cits.
The text type was set in Sabon.
Book design by Becky Terhune

OF HIS BONES ARE CORAL MADE:

THOSE ARE PEARLS THAT WERE HIS EYES:

NOTHING OF HIM THAT DOTH FADE,

BUT DOTH SUFFER A SEA-CHANGE

INTO SOMETHING RICH AND STRANGE.

— WILLIAM SHAKESPEARE, *THE TEMPEST*

THE CURE FOR EVERYTHING IS SALT WATER —

SWEAT, TEARS, OR THE SEA.

— ISAK DINESEN

One

MONSTERS

*T*he waiting ferryboat — ivory-colored and two-tiered — resembled a slice of cake. Or maybe I was just hungry, I reasoned as I hurried across the dock, my duffel bag bumping my hip. The name *Princess of the Deep* was stamped across the boat's side, and the American flag hanging from its bow whipped and snapped in the salty wind.

I took a deep breath. I was really going.

As I joined the boarding line, I wished I'd covered my head, like the other, wiser travelers in their Atlanta Braves caps and floppy straw hats. Sweat slid down my back, and my vintage round sunglasses were no match for the glare off the ocean. I hadn't had much time to prepare for this trip.

"Next!" called the ticket taker, a large, silver-bearded man in a white T-shirt. He motioned to me and I stepped forward, the dock's wooden slats hot beneath my sneakers. When I handed him my ticket, his bushy eyebrows shot up so high the sailor hat on his head wobbled.

"You're headed to Selkie?" he asked. In his thick Georgia drawl, he pronounced the word *Sayl-kee* — all long syllables. "Selkie Island? You sure about that, darlin'?"

I hesitated. I certainly hadn't planned on traveling to Selkie Island, a place I knew next to nothing about. My summer, like most things in my life, had been all mapped out: As soon as school ended, I was to start my dream internship at the Museum of Natural History in New York City. But then the grandmother I'd never known passed away, setting in motion a chain of events that brought me to where I was on this late June afternoon. For a second, disorientation swept over me, and then I shook it off.

"Positive," I replied, lifting my chin. I was eager to complete the last leg of my draining journey; that morning's flight from New York to Savannah had been delayed, and the cabdriver who'd taken me to the harbor had meandered through the shady streets at a speed that matched his speech.

"All *right*," Sailor Hat sighed in an unmistakable it's-your-funeral tone. As he tore my ticket in two, he gave me a look that was equal parts amused and worried. "It's the last stop, sugar snap."

"I know," I said tartly, to show how little sugar there was in me. I'd seen on the map inside the ferry terminal that *Princess of the Deep* made stops at several of the Sea Islands — which shimmer like small gems in the Atlantic, draping all the way from the coasts of South Carolina to Florida — before reaching Selkie.

"And it's Miranda," I added, marching around him and toward the boat. Unfortunately, *Miranda* isn't too far removed from *sugar snap* on the Sweet, Girly Name List. I've never felt it suited me.

"Well, Miranda," Sailor Hat called after me as I followed the passengers clanking up the gangplank. "You must be plenty brave, a young thing like you setting off for Selkie all by her lonesome."

I had no idea what Sailor Hat was talking about, and I didn't really care. Still, his words struck at one chord of truth: I couldn't wait to meet my mother at the Selkie dock. During the past four days I'd spent by myself back home, I'd missed her steady presence.

The bottom level of the ferry was dark, dank, and packed with howling children. Orange life vests were fastened to the low ceiling, and though still tethered to the dock, the boat rocked roughly on the waves. I figured it would be pleasanter to stand in the open air, so I climbed the metal staircase to the top deck, where the breeze toyed with my ponytail, and the view was a dazzling blue sweep of water and sky. Most people stood at the railing, but I remained by the stairs, near a group of golden-haired girls who looked to be about my age.

The girls were huddled together, laughing, and I felt a pang. They all wore tiny shorts and platform flip-flops, the better to show off their long, bronzed legs and perfectly formed toes. I pictured myself beside them — a pale, thin, dark-haired girl in a red-striped shirt, jeans, and black Converse — and smiled wryly. We may as well have been different species.

Growing up, I had zero interest in lip gloss or slumber parties. My idea of fun had been mixing Mr. Clean and baking powder in water glasses and writing down the results. "Miranda's concocting her potions," my friends would tease, and I would correct them: I was doing *experiments*. My weirdness made sense; both my parents are surgeons, so I was born with science in my blood. It was no surprise that, at fourteen, I got accepted into the Bronx High School of Science, where I'd just finished up my junior year, earning A's in Advanced Placement Biology and Chemistry (but eking out C's in English and History).

With a great, unladylike belch, *Princess of the Deep* loosened herself from the dock and lurched out to sea. Immediately, my knees buckled and, unthinking, I reached out to grab the arm of the girl nearest me.

"You okay, hon?" she asked. Her eyes were hidden behind wraparound sunglasses but I could sense the judgment in her stare. "Bless her heart," she said, turning to her friends. "She hasn't gotten her sea legs yet!" The other girls exploded into giggles, a pack of pretty piranhas.

I drew my hand back, my cheeks scalded with embarrassment. *Sea legs.* Such a strange expression, as if humans could sprout fins to adapt to life on water.

True, I'd forgotten how tricky it was to stay balanced on a ship. I'd grown up not quite landlocked, but close; home was Riverdale, a small, serene pocket of the Bronx, which, of New York City's five boroughs, is the only one that is part of the mainland. The last time I'd been on a ferry, I was nine. It was right before my parents' divorce, and my father, perhaps warding off his impending guilt or acknowledging his impending freedom, had taken me and my older brother, Wade, to the Statue of Liberty. The ride to Liberty Island had been choppy, and I'd fought back my seasickness by leaning over the railing in search of marine life.

Which, at the moment, once again seemed like an appealing activity.

Carefully, I maneuvered away from the Southern princesses, who were now squealing over someone's purchase of a new bikini. When I reached the railing, I positioned myself beside a blond boy, who must have been about seven, and his tired-looking parents. The spray cooled my flushed face, and I placed my duffel bag between my feet.

Seagulls screeched and swooped overhead, and the ocean was a shining sheet of aquamarine that rippled out in all directions. Wakes left behind by smaller, faster boats made indentations in the water, like tangles in a girl's straight hair. I let out a breath I didn't even know I'd been holding. School, and friends, and the ghost of my unhappiness seemed immeasurably far behind me. I felt a lightening in my chest. Maybe getting away from home was what I needed, after all.

"What's *that*?" the blond boy cried, breaking into my thoughts. Eyes enormous, he jabbed a pudgy finger through the boat's slats while tugging on his mother's arm.

I glanced down at the waves that frothed and slapped against the ferry. There was a long, dark shape swimming close to the surface of the water, which was soon joined by three matching shapes, all of them silvery and sleek. I gasped and my pulse began to pound.

"Dolphins!" the boy cried, jumping up and down. "Mom, there are dolphins in the ocean!" Quickly, a crowd amassed around the railing, everyone exclaiming, snapping photos, and jostling for a better look.

I grinned. Honest-to-goodness bottlenose dolphins. I'd been fascinated by the funny, smart sea mammals ever since watching a documentary about them. In the womb, dolphin fetuses sprout these leglike limb buds, which hint that, many evolutions ago, the creatures had lived on land. That is what I love about science: the surprises, the secrets, the discoveries that make your head spin a little. Now, watching the dolphins play and arc up out of the water, their dorsal fins glistening, I again felt there was something half fish, half man about them. Maybe because they seemed to be smiling.

The dolphins kept pace with the ferry, even as we made stops at bustling harbors that boasted cafés and pastel hotels. After we left the third dockside — where the giggling girls disembarked — the dolphins dispersed, swimming off to unknown depths in search of fresh entertainment. I was sorry to see them go.

"Do you suppose something frightened them off, Miranda?"

Startled, I spun around to see Sailor Hat — the ticket taker — standing behind me, wearing an elusive smile. I'd been so focused on the dolphins that I hadn't noticed him appear on the top deck. As I glanced around, I saw that the boat had emptied out considerably. The only people who remained were the boy and his parents, who were now digging through their luggage for sandwiches, and, at the far end of the deck, a strikingly handsome man with salt-and-pepper hair, and his equally good-looking teenage son, who was texting on his iPhone.

I faced Sailor Hat again and shrugged.

"Like what?" I asked, figuring I'd humor him. "Sharks?"

Sailor Hat chuckled, shaking his head. "You won't find a

lot of sharks out here. Most likely it was the kraken. Surely you've heard of it? The sea beast with tentacles long enough to consume a ship whole?" He dropped his voice an octave and raised his brows.

I bit back a laugh. "I suspect *he's* the right age for that story," I said, nodding to the blond boy, who was busy devouring a sandwich.

Though, come to think of it, my first, only — and now ex — boyfriend, Greg Aarons, had been obsessed with the kraken, and he was seventeen, not seven. Back in April, we'd even downloaded the second *Pirates of the Caribbean* movie off iTunes and watched it on his laptop (that same night, Greg had also tried to get me naked, and I'd insisted on keeping my socks on, which understandably killed some of his ardor). But I had little tolerance for magic; everything had a logical explanation, a root of reason.

"You don't believe in the kraken?" Sailor Hat asked, his smile widening. His tanned skin had the leathery, wrinkled texture that spoke of too much time in the sun.

"I don't," I replied flatly, crossing my arms over my chest. I bristled whenever anyone tried to take me for a fool. "It's a myth. Ages ago, some drunken sailors saw a giant squid in the water and decided it was a monster."

"Ah, I understand," Sailor Hat said, taking a step toward me. I flattened myself against the railing, wondering if I should jump overboard if he tried something sketchy. I was, thanks to early childhood lessons at the Y, an excellent swimmer. "You've never been to Selkie Island before," he continued with confidence. "Otherwise, you'd be familiar with the many, many strange creatures that fill these waters."

He gestured toward the ocean, and despite myself, I felt a chill tiptoe down my spine. The ferry went over a big swell that made my stomach jump.

"Look, sir," I said, keeping my voice firm. "My mother is originally from Savannah. She spent every summer on Selkie Island when she was young, and she's never mentioned any —"

I paused, frustrated. The fact was, my mother didn't like to speak of her past. I'd heard only snatches about her summers on Selkie, where her family owned a grand vacation home. And the Google-Wikipedia research I'd done before leaving New York hadn't revealed much besides the island's map coordinates and weather patterns. So I knew that Selkie was six miles long and often stormy, but that was all.

"Well, then," Sailor Hat said, stroking his beard, "you should be informed of the sea serpents that swim in the surf off Siren Beach. It's believed that, in the seventeen hundreds, they helped liberate a slave ship by devouring the captain and crew. They're a prickly bunch. And," he added, sidling up next to me and resting his elbows on the railing, "rumor has it that mermaids and mermen populate the sea around Selkie, but live on land as humans."

"Good to know," I muttered, checking my watch. We were scheduled to arrive in two minutes. Thank God.

"Naturally, all of Dixieland is rife with legend," Sailor Hat added as if I hadn't spoken. He squinted out at the water. "But Selkie lore carries the whiff of truth."

His tone was so haunting, his choice of words so deliberate, that I suddenly got it — he'd given this speech countless times before. The man had a gift! The visitor's center of Selkie Island probably dispatched him to ride the ferries and lure in tourists with such tall tales. Maybe there was even a folklore museum on the island that profited from Sailor Hat's smooth talk.

I was getting ready to extricate myself from the conversation once and for all when Sailor Hat stretched out his arm and pointed. "Ah!" he said. "There she is now."

I turned and saw nothing but fog. It was a clear, bright afternoon, so the thick haze seemed to have materialized out of nowhere. The oddest blend of foreboding and anticipation washed over me.

"Most boats can't even find Selkie," Sailor Hat explained as we passed through the fog, which felt like damp smoke. "It's as if the island is hiding in a shawl of mist."

I hated to admit that his fanciful description was accurate.

Behind the mist there lay a lush, loamy sliver of land dotted with trees and houses. In the forefront, there was a sun-bleached dock with a sprinkling of miniature-looking people. Above the dock, hoisted up on two wooden stilts so as to appear like a gate, was a large, ancient-looking sign. On it, in bold black calligraphy that resembled writing I had seen on old maps, were the words:

Sailors, beware of Selkie Island! Here Be Monsters!

I rolled my eyes. Sailor Hat himself probably made that sign. I thought of the red double-decker tour buses that snaked through the streets of Manhattan, and the miniature Empire State Buildings that were hawked on Broadway. The shops on Selkie Island must have been bursting with eye patch–wearing rubber ducks that said *"Yarr!"* when you squeezed them, and sexy mermaid costumes complete with seashell bras. Everything thrived on the tourist trade; it was a simple law of economics.

"Heed that warning, Miranda," Sailor Hat said as he started toward the staircase. "Be careful of whom you meet, in and out of the water."

I ignored him, scanning the harbor as it loomed larger. I couldn't find my mother among the faces, but my eyes fell on a patch of land beside the dock — a crude crest of green that sloped down to the sand and tall sea grasses. The slice of nature was so pure, so primitive, so far removed from any civilization. I realized it must have remained unchanged for centuries; maybe the first sailors to come to Selkie — those same sailors who might have invented the kraken — had landed on that very spot.

The ferry began to dock, and it occurred to me that scientists and sailors are somehow similar; they both want, more than anything, to explore. I felt a sailorlike stirring in me as I picked up my duffel bag. There was, of course, nothing to beware of on Selkie Island. But I couldn't shake the sense that there would be plenty to discover.

Two

GIFTS

So you made it," Mom declared, waving to me as I stepped off the ferry on the heels of the little boy and his parents.

"I'm here," I replied, half in disbelief. Tall, spiky-leaved palmetto trees were everywhere, giving the harbor a subtropical feel. Sea salt hung thick in the steamy air.

Though my mother and I had never been very demonstrative, we exchanged a quick hug, and I breathed in her familiar scent: rubbing alcohol and Kiehl's moisturizer. But as Mom pulled back and took my bag from me, I realized why I hadn't been able to make her out from the boat. She looked . . . different.

The Mom I knew, the harried surgeon, was always in wrinkled green scrubs with her hair tied back and shadows under her wide gray eyes. This Mom wore an orange tunic over a long, flowing skirt. Her soft, light-brown waves tumbled down her shoulders, and her face — oval-shaped and pretty, a face that led some people to think I was adopted — had a healthy glow.

"What happened to you?" I blurted. I had a secret fear that when I went away to college and began coming home for holidays, I'd find my mother white-haired and stooped — abruptly old. But seeing her now felt like the opposite experience; since leaving New York, Mom had gotten younger.

Mom chuckled. "You've just never seen me with a real tan. The sun finds me. Trust me, it's not like I've had time to go to the beach." She cupped my chin in her hand, regarding me fondly. "I bought *you* buckets of Banana Boat yesterday, Ms. Alabaster — SPF forty."

I could tell from the lilt in her usually businesslike voice how glad Mom was to have me with her. Two days ago, she'd called me from Savannah, where she'd flown to attend the funeral of my grandmother, her mother, Isadora Hawkins. It was there that Mom had learned of her inheritance: the summer home on Selkie.

Mom's siblings, Aunt Coral and Uncle Jim, who both lived near Isadora in Savannah, had been up in arms. Mom and Isadora hadn't spoken in almost thirty years; they'd had a falling-out in Mom's youth, the details of which were murky to me — something about Mom marrying my dad, a poor Yankee from Brooklyn — so nobody could believe that Isadora had left Mom such a legacy. Mom was equally mystified, but mainly aggravated that she had to take a leave of absence from work, sail out to Selkie, and try to sell the old house.

"I could really use your help," Mom had told me over the phone. "I want to sort through Isadora's personal effects as fast as possible, and you, my love, are extremely talented when it comes to organizing."

I'd felt a warm flicker of flattery as I stood outside my high school, having just taken my disastrous English final. I was curious about the unknown strands of DNA that linked me to the South. And although I had my internship lined up, part of me had longed to escape what was shaping up to be a lackluster, lonely summer. My nineteen-year-old brother, Wade, was with our father in Los Angeles, and I sort of enjoyed the idea of the genders being divided across the country, like the Union and the Confederacy.

So after several e-mails to the museum, my internship was deferred until July fifteenth, and I was buying tickets on Travelocity.

"How's everything going so far?" I asked Mom now as

we stood facing each other under the azure sky. The water's rhythmic lapping against the dock was soothing.

She groaned, putting a hand to her forehead. "Don't ask. Aunt Coral keeps calling me, hollering her head off about how the house should be *her* birthright, and . . ."

Mom paused midrant, and her jaw dropped as her gaze fell on something behind me. Her face blanched beneath her tan, and for one crazy second I wondered if she'd seen the kraken unfurling from the ocean.

I looked over my shoulder to see Sailor Hat loading luggage onto a rolling cart. The man with salt-and-pepper hair from the ferry stood at his side, nodding and handing him a few folded dollar bills. The man's dark-haired son was walking off the boat, his head still bent over his iPhone. A few other ferry workers tramped around them, preparing *Princess of the Deep* for its return voyage.

"Who are you looking at?" I asked as I turned back to my mother, intrigued.

"Nobody," Mom replied, and she took hold of my arm. "Come on, you must be starving, and we have a ways to walk. They don't allow cars on the island."

I threw one last glance back at the ferry, then hurried after my mother. We headed off the dock, cutting through swaths of scratchy yellow grass, and then started up a pebbly path that snaked away from the water.

More questions bubbled on the tip of my tongue; the solid land of questions and answers was where I felt most comfortable. I wanted to ask Mom for more details about my grandmother's funeral, which had been a lavish affair; apparently, a mountain of magnolias had been fashioned into Isadora's likeness, and a gospel choir had sung "Michael, Row Your Boat Ashore." I also wanted Mom to elaborate on the Aunt Coral drama. But when we emerged onto a paved road called Triton's Pass, I was struck silent by the strange beauty of our surroundings.

Massive live oaks lined the road, their green leaves forming a canopy overhead, and lacy, pale-gray Spanish moss dripped from the trees' branches, creating a ghostly effect. Slimmer, white-trunked trees — "crepe myrtles," Mom told me as we passed — bloomed with brilliant purple flowers that filled the air with a ripe sweetness. A shiny, lumpy armadillo lumbered right past us.

Though the island's flora and fauna looked wild and untouched, it felt as if Mom and I were walking along an elegant, old-fashioned promenade. There were columned houses behind the trees, and men tipped their hats to us as they passed. Two girls in white dresses, sailing by on bicycles, offered cheerful "good afternoons." If I was one to believe in time travel, I might imagine that the ferry had carried me into the past.

"This is us," Mom said as we rounded a corner and stopped in front of a wide lawn. The house — the biggest I'd seen yet — was painted a pale blue, with four columns and a wrought-iron wraparound porch. The lawn was weed-choked and overgrown, and the screens on the bay windows were torn, but it was clear that the house, like a delicate-featured elderly woman, had once been a stunner.

"No, it's not," I replied automatically. The facts did not compute. I peered around, half expecting to find the barrel of a shotgun pointing at us for trespassing.

Logically speaking, how could Mom and I possibly be connected to this . . . *mansion*? A mansion in which to shoot a Civil War movie, not a place for regular people like Mom and me.

"Take a look," Mom said, guiding me over to the rusted mailbox. On its side, in chipped white paint, were the words:

THE MARINER
MR. AND MRS. JEREMIAH HAWKINS
10 GLAUCUS WAY
SELKIE ISLAND, GEORGIA 31558

I felt a flush of recognition. Jeremiah Hawkins was my grandfather, who had passed away when my mother was still in high school. But . . .

"Who's 'The Mariner'?" I asked, angling my head to better study the writing.

Mom let out a small laugh. "Oh, *that* was your grandmother being pretentious. She named the house after her favorite poem, 'The Rime of the Ancient Mariner.'" When I looked at Mom blankly, she added, "You know, 'Water, water, every where / Nor any drop to drink'? Samuel Taylor Coleridge? The albatross?" I shook my head, and she nudged me in the side. "Oh, Miranda. You should read something other than your biology textbooks once in a while."

I sighed as I followed Mom up the curving path to the house. Somehow, in between her surgeries and medical conferences, Mom always found time to read novels or poetry collections. I simply found works of fiction too . . . fictitious.

We climbed the crumbling porch steps, and as Mom dug in her purse for the keys, I studied the blue-and-white life ring that hung on the door like a wreath, now yellowed with age.

"When was the last time anyone stayed here?" I asked. Mom herself had only arrived the day before.

"About two years ago," Mom said, unlocking the door. "When I was around your age, after my father passed" — she cleared her throat — "Isadora decided that the family shouldn't summer here anymore. She'd come out by herself now and then, but when her health started failing, she locked up The Mariner and stayed in Savannah for good."

The mingled scents of mildew, dust, and Lemon-Fresh Pine-Sol floated toward us as we stepped into the large foyer. A tingle of eagerness raced through me. Then the toe of my sneaker caught on a loose floorboard and I tripped. *Sea legs,* I thought. To steady myself, I grabbed hold of a flat cardboard sheet that was propped against a wall, waiting to be turned into a box.

"It's a wreck," Mom warned me, shutting the door. "Everything's ancient and falling to pieces. There's no TV, no Internet, and it's a miracle there's cell reception." She tutted as she set my duffel bag on a claw-footed chair. "Some gift!"

I usually shared Mom's taste for sleek, modern design — our apartment in Riverdale was all glass and steel gray — but there was something beautiful about the foyer's dark wood paneling and the frayed lace curtains over the windows. Gilt-framed seascapes hung on one wall, and another wall was covered in peeling blue wallpaper patterned with tiny sea horses. History seemed to breathe in each corner of the house, from the twisting wooden staircase to the cut-glass chandelier.

I was reminded of how I often felt when I walked into my high school. Over the entrance hung an enormous color mural featuring scientists through the ages: Galileo, Copernicus, Marie Curie. School legend had it that the money used to pay for the mural was supposed to go toward a pool. I would have loved being able to swim every day, but I loved the mural more: It made me feel like I was part of something bigger, a tradition of inventors who'd inherited the lessons of those who came before them.

"Welcome to The Mariner, Miranda," Mom said softly as she flipped a switch to turn on the ceiling fans. Her gaze was on me, and I wondered if she was a little bit amazed to see me standing there — her new life suddenly inserted into her old one.

As I walked up to a coatrack in the shape of an anchor, I felt a surge of wonder. Was this really the house where Mom had slept and eaten back when she was just Amelia Blue Hawkins, and not my mother? Had an adolescent Mom strolled down this very hall, her sandals skimming over the faded green compass painted onto the floor?

I shivered. What was I doing, conjuring phantoms? I never let my imagination roam so freely. When Mom set her hand on my back, I started violently, and she laughed.

"Whoa, there! I was just going to ask you if fresh fish sounds good for dinner. I got grouper at the market and was going to grill it up with corn on the cob."

"Sounds great," I answered truthfully, my stomach growling. I was surprised that Mom was going to cook; at home, we were all about Thai takeout.

"In the meantime, I'll prepare some sweet tea to tide us over," Mom said. "Why don't you relax on the back porch and I'll meet you out there?"

I nodded. "Sweet tea" was what Mom called iced tea with two heaping spoonfuls of sugar; it was one of the few Southernisms that lingered in her speech. Most of the time, Mom sounded like a clipped, crisp Northeasterner; she said that she'd shed her Georgia accent as soon as she walked into her freshman dorm at Yale, which was also where she met Dad.

Mom pointed me in the direction of the living room, where a pair of French doors faced the ocean, and then she bustled off toward the kitchen, which was past the stairs.

I padded into the living room, passing antique sofas, the stuffing bleeding out of their backs. I could feel myself starting to unwind from the day. I wandered over to the marble mantelpiece and studied the two framed photographs that were perched there.

The first one showed a family grouped outside The Mariner: a shapely brunette woman — Isadora; a distinguished-looking bald man — Jeremiah; two girls; and a boy. My heart thrummed when I realized that the littlest girl in a starched pink dress, holding a parasol over her light-brown head and scowling, was none other than Mom. Which meant that the other girl — grinning and frizzy-haired — was Aunt Coral, and the boy — crossing his eyes for the camera — was Uncle Jim.

Although Mom and I never went to Savannah to see them, my aunt and uncle had both visited us in New York. Coral, with her frosted-platinum bob and Neiman Marcus charge card, had complained about the filthy subways. Uncle Jim, a clone, I now saw, of his father, had complained about the shameful quality of grits in restaurants. After her siblings left, Mom had complained about *them*.

When I moved on to the next picture, my breath caught. It was a solo shot of Isadora, taken when she must have been no older than me. I'd never seen a photograph of my grandmother so young; in the handful of photos Mom had of Isadora back home, my grandmother was middle-aged. Here, the teenage Isadora reclined on a porch swing, her coy dark eyes glinting from under the brim of a beribboned hat. She wore a strapless pear-colored sundress, her jet-black curls spilling over her porcelain shoulders, and her ruby-stained lips parted in a smile. She and Mom didn't resemble each other at all.

"You look like her, you know."

I whirled around to find Mom in the doorway, holding two glasses and a pitcher of iced tea on a silver tray. She gave me a small smile and nodded toward the photo. "Can't you tell?"

"Mom, are you kidding?" I shook my head, a little bit dazed. I may have inherited Isadora's coloration, but her beauty gene had clearly skipped me, like a stone over water.

"You'll have other opportunities to check out Isadora's image while you're here," Mom said as she ushered me through the French doors and onto the back porch. The cooling air swept toward us, carrying the smell of the sea. I sat down on the cushioned bench, taking in the startling view. Frothy waves rolled onto the sand, chasing away twittering sandpipers, and the mellowing sunshine turned the water into diamonds.

"She essentially made The Mariner a shrine to herself," Mom went on as she tipped the pitcher over a glass; a waterfall of amber-colored liquid poured forth, along with a cascade of lemon slices and shards of mint. "Lord, was that woman a monster," she concluded with a sigh.

I flinched as I accepted the drink. Mom had referred to Isadora in similar terms over the years, but now, it felt wrong to speak ill of the dead. Plus, I couldn't quite imagine the luminous creature from the photo as cruel.

Then again, what did I really know about my grandmother? On occasion, when I was growing up, Wade and I would receive a Christmas or birthday card signed *Isadora Beauregard Hawkins* in looping, stylized script. I'd always been vaguely amazed that she even knew of our existence.

As Mom sat down beside me, I glanced at her profile,

wondering how she had come to feel so harshly about her mother. A week ago, when Aunt Coral had called us with the news of Isadora's death, Mom's eyes had turned stormy with tears and her face had gone all splotchy. The sight had rattled me; Mom never cried. But when I'd inquired about the cause of death — I like diagnoses — Mom had snapped back to her usual sardonic self, blowing her nose and saying that complications from being eighty and drinking peach juleps every day had probably done Isadora in.

"What's wrong, my love?" Mom asked now, pulling me out of my thoughts. She poured iced tea into her own glass, then faced me, her brow furrowed. "I know you're always pensive, but, lately, you've seemed . . ." She paused, biting her lower lip.

I froze. Mom couldn't have failed to notice how, over the past month, I'd retreated from the world like a hermit crab into the sand. I used to go to my best friend Linda Wu's house after school, or have Greg over to the apartment for "tutoring sessions." But since May I'd been coming home alone and taking long, restorative baths before curling up on the sofa to watch the Discovery Channel.

"I'm fine," I replied quickly, and sipped my drink, but discomfort stained my cheeks red. I wanted to tell Mom, I did, but I was a little bit frightened that if I started to talk, I'd break down.

"Okay," Mom said, regarding me carefully. "But here's something that might cheer you up: Tomorrow, there's going to be a party on the boardwalk. We should stop by."

"What kind of party?" I asked, chewing on a piece of mint. My stomach tightened briefly at the memory of the last party I had attended.

"It's called the Heirs party," Mom said, swallowing her tea.

"Airs?" I echoed, thinking of the colorless gases that comprise the atmosphere. I pictured a faintly pagan ceremony on the shore involving billowing robes and kites. I couldn't begin to imagine my mother — or myself — at such an affair.

Mom tipped her head to one side, smiling. "As in, heirs and heiresses. You know . . ." She twirled her wrist for emphasis, the ice cubes in her glass clinking. "The descendants of those who've summered on Selkie forever. The LeBlanc family, one of the most prominent on the island, started the tradition at the end of the nineteenth century. The last week in June, all the summer people meet and toast one another's wealth." She rolled her eyes, but there was no mistaking the nostalgia in her tone.

"So we were invited?" I asked, a little bewildered by all the pomp and tradition. I did feel a spark of interest; after the past month, it might be nice to socialize with people again. Not that I had anything to wear to a party; amid the T-shirts and jeans I'd packed was a sole drawstring cotton skirt with a hole in its hem.

"There was an invitation sitting in the mailbox when I arrived last night," Mom confirmed, crossing her legs. "Intended for Isadora; she always got one automatically."

"But do *we* belong there?" I asked, finishing my drink.

"We do," Mom said quietly, meeting my gaze, and I realized she must have attended the party many times before. "For better or worse, you *are* an heir, Miranda. And so am I."

My skin prickled and I looked back at the ocean. None of us ask for the things we inherit; they are thrust upon us, willy-nilly. Like The Mariner, I suddenly understood. Mom and I *weren't* trespassing. This house was ours. This view was ours. And that seemed as absurd and unreal as the stories Sailor Hat had spun for me on the ferry.

Three

TALES

*R*ight after dinner, I decided to go for a swim. The nearness of the ocean was too tempting to resist, so I hurried upstairs to change into my bathing suit.

The room I'd be staying in was the bedroom Mom and Aunt Coral had shared back in the day. It seemed stuck in time: the wallpaper with its rosy seashells, the pink quilts covering the two twin beds. I was not a fan of pink, and I envied Mom, who was settling into the blue-and-green master bedroom down the hall.

I plunked my duffel bag on one of the beds and began removing my neat piles of clothes, transferring them to the drawers of the wooden bedside dresser. Nothing calmed me more than creating order. It was no wonder that, in my room back home, Dmitry Mendeleyev's periodic table of the elements hung above my desk, a sort of inspiration. I was probably the only living sixteen-year-old with that decoration.

Once I'd unpacked, I stripped off my clothes and wriggled into my black one-piece swimsuit. I hesitated for a second before kicking off my Converse. There probably wouldn't be any other swimmers out at this hour, so I could remain barefoot.

I was born with the toes on both my feet webbed — "like a pretty little duck," Dad would say. Since my parents are both plastic surgeons, they had a colleague operate on me as early as possible, and the webbing was removed. But my feet still look undeniably odd; scars run like needlework along the skin between my toes, and the toes themselves are slightly curled. *Syndactyly* is the proper name for the condition; I'd done plenty of research on it, reading about babies' development in the womb. I was the only one in my family with this strangeness, which doctors aren't sure is genetic. *I* was just sure that I preferred flats to flip-flops.

Wrapping a towel around my waist, I glanced out my window, which faced Glaucus Way. Blush-colored stripes were appearing in the sky, and blinking fireflies danced between the rooftops. A young mother was quickly pushing a stroller under the shadowy branches, and the Spanish moss looked like the spidery beards of old men. I didn't relish the idea of swimming in the dark; I had to get a move on before night fell.

I called to Mom that I'd be back soon, then raced down the creaky stairs, through the living room, and onto the back porch. I rubbed my arms, shivering in the evening chill. The porch steps were cold beneath my feet, but the sandy slope that led to the water was warm — perfectly sun-toasted.

And so was the ocean. I waded in up to my shins, my toes sending up small clouds of sand. Coils of seaweed brushed my ankles, and a sense of peace settled over me. I gazed around at the open expanse of dark turquoise. There was a sailboat in the distance, and if I squinted, I could see a fishing trawler chugging toward the island. Other than that, I had the sea all to myself.

What was it Mom had said earlier? *Water, water, every where / Nor any drop to drink.* I'd never been in the position of dying of thirst, but I could relate to such longing. It was how I'd felt for years before I got a boyfriend, when my high school seemed to be a sea of guys, all of them kissable, all of them datable, but none of them wanting me.

I shook my head, pushing away those memories. Then I eased farther into the Atlantic and, holding my breath, submerged completely.

I loved the gray-blue shade of the world underwater, the way the sea grasses seemed to sway in slow motion. As I came up for air, I stretched out my body and slowly began scissoring my legs. Only swimming afforded me such grace and freedom; not even acing a science test felt as good. And there was something thrilling about floating in the ocean, something primal and natural about the warm caress of water.

For most of my life, I'd had to make do with pools; Mom didn't like seaside vacations, so when she was able to get off work, we'd travel to cities like Chicago, or to the upstate New York mountains. My father was always up for taking me to the beach in L.A., but I didn't see him often. Now, I wondered if Mom avoided the ocean because it reminded her of her childhood, of Isadora.

When I felt something slimy brush my leg, my heart skipped a beat. I no longer felt so alone in the water, and, to my annoyance, Sailor Hat's words about dangerous creatures resounded in my head. Ridiculous. Still, I began paddling back to shore, telling myself that it was time to go inside anyway. The sky was morphing from orange to purple to navy blue.

I toweled off, my ponytail sopping and water running down my arms. It was funny how a swim could transform one so much; I knew I looked very different from the dry Miranda I'd been minutes before. My teeth chattering, I rushed up the porch steps and slipped into the house. The living room was dim, the foyer enveloped in blackness. Save for the constant shushing sound of the ocean and the whir of the ceiling fans,

The Mariner was silent. Mom had told me she might go to bed early, so I took care to tiptoe. Unlike me, Mom was a light sleeper; she said that becoming a mother had made her that way.

I wasn't ready for bed; the swim had refreshed me, made me just shy of restless, and also thirsty. I began creeping toward the kitchen to see if there was any sweet tea left over. I remembered the kitchen as being behind the stairs, but I navigated incorrectly in the darkness. Somehow I found myself in a tight corridor — and face-to-face with a haggard old man.

I clapped my hand over my mouth to stifle my scream an instant before I realized I was looking at a painting. It was a portrait of a white-maned, wild-eyed man in a tattered sailor's uniform, tattoos on both his arms and a bottle in his fist. He was hideous. Slung around his neck was a thick rope, and from the knot at its end swung an enormous white bird — *an albatross*, I realized, shudders running down my back.

So this was the mariner of the poem, the presiding spirit of the house. Maybe Mom was right; had I been at all familiar with literature, I might have recognized the portrait right away and spared myself my minor coronary.

As though the house had read my mind, a draft in the hallway caused the door next to the painting to open slightly. I pushed the knob and peeked into what looked like a small study. Flicking on the light, I walked inside. There was an antique wooden writing desk with a high-backed chair, a crimson love seat, and mahogany bookshelves lining the walls. The single slice of wall not covered in books showed off another watercolor portrait, but this one did not scare me.

It was of Isadora, resplendent in a silky green gown. She was posed on the staircase of The Mariner, her bearing regal. The portraitist had added whimsical flourishes: peach blossoms dangled above her head, and she held a fur-lined wrap in her arms that no one south of the Mason-Dixon Line would ever need. The whole look was sort of hilarious, and screamed Scarlett O'Hara. Not coincidentally, the bookshelf beneath the portrait held a copy of *Gone with the Wind*.

I scanned the rest of the shelf, curious as to what else my grandmother had considered good reading material. The books weren't arranged alphabetically, or by subject; the lack of order made my head hurt. There was *Marion Brown's Southern Cook Book* beside *Romeo and Juliet*, which was nestled next to the *Collected Poems of T. S. Eliot* and a book of Andersen's fairy tales. Nothing called to me. But when I saw the phrase *Selkie Island* on the lower half of a torn, dark blue spine, I pulled the book out.

The cover nearly came off in my hands, and I did a double take when I saw it bore a reproduction of the warning sign that hung above the Selkie dock. The book's title, *A Primer* on the *Legend and Lore of Selkie Island,* was emblazoned across the top, and the author's name, Llewellyn Thorpe, was written out in script across the bottom. Turning the book over, I wiped the film of dust off its back cover and read the paragraph that was written in gold leaf:

Many are drawn to Selkie Island. Few know why. Selkie's essence of mystery surrounds the isle like its famous shroud of fog. But the island's varied legends — of beasts, of freaks, of shipwrecked sailors — have an undeniable lure. The tome you hold in your hands, gentle reader, is a compendium of these legends. Proceed with care.

I smiled. More tall tales? Maybe Sailor Hat was Llewellyn Thorpe.

I cracked the book's flimsy spine, and a musty scent rose up toward me. The frontispiece was a grainy map showing Selkie's location in the Atlantic, but the island was surrounded by drawings of winged fish, krakens, and mermaids. I turned the slippery, yellowed pages until I reached the back of the book. There, I found a pen-and-ink drawing of a reed-thin man wearing spectacles and a suit. Beneath this image it said:

Llewellyn Thorpe was born in 1873 in Savannah, Georgia, and died in 1913, shortly before the publication of this volume. A professor of anthropology, he devoted his life to researching the folklore of Selkie Island.

Okay. So not Sailor Hat.

Holding the book open, I walked backward to the writing desk. I spread my towel on the high-backed chair and sat, thumbing through the book more slowly now. Why was I hooked? Why did I care?

I flipped past chapters entitled "Side-Shows and Cabinets of Curiosity," "The Sharp-Toothed Serpents of Siren Beach," "Stories of the Gullah People," and "Cryptozoology." Finally, I came upon a chapter called "A Brief Historie of Selkie Island," and I paused, wondering if this might offer something resembling solid fact. I set the book down on the desk, moving aside a pad of paper and a black oblong box to make room. Then I began to read.

It was the high summer of 1650 when Captain William McCloud, a Scottish pirate sailing to the Caribbean, discovered what is today known as Selkie Island.

The book went on to explain that Captain McCloud's crew had mutinied and dropped him in a dinghy off the coast of Georgia. The pirate was half mad from starvation when a beautiful green-eyed mermaid with a red-gold tail steered him to land. There, the mermaid, named Caya, shape-shifted into a woman. Captain McCloud promptly fell in love with her, married her, and named the island Selkie — the Scottish word for a creature capable of transforming from a seal into a human. Captain McCloud and Caya had several children, who, like their mother, became merfolk when they submerged themselves in the ocean, but lived as humans on land. And, according to Llewellyn Thorpe, these merfolk descendants still populated the island.

I laughed to myself, amused, but I kept on reading.

Merfolk such as Caya have been a universal element of lore. The ancient Assyrians told of Atargatis: half-woman, half-fish. And in his Metamorphoses, *Ovid gave us Glaucus, the lovelorn merman. Many dismiss mermaid sightings as a sailor's misinterpretation of a manatee or a dugong swimming beneath the waves. But in his journals, Christopher Columbus wrote of spotting Sirens off the coast of Hispaniola, and Henry Hudson swore he witnessed a woman with the tail of a porpoise swimming by the side of his ship. It is on and around Selkie, however, that the greatest evidence of merfolk life exists. The native Selkie merfolk are as much a part of the island as the Spanish moss and the marshes.*

Selkie merfolk are usually recognizable by a few key features, such as: a lush, sensitive beauty; a predilection for the colors red and gold; kindness toward visitors and explorers; and homes close to the shore. They can sometimes be spotted at night, when venturing out to —

A sudden, shrill scream came from outside the house. I jumped in my chair, knocking the book off the desk, and leapt to my feet, my pulse thudding in my ears, louder than the ocean. Every inch of my skin was awake, my nerve endings on alert.

The scream came again, and I pressed a hand to my damp collarbone, taking a deep breath. *Calm down.* I recalled the Sea Islands Wildlife website I'd skimmed before leaving New York. I was probably hearing the call of an American oyster-catcher, a bird native to the area. That was all.

What is with you, Miranda?

I glanced at where Llewellyn Thorpe's book lay, several of its pages loose and scattered. It was the silly book that was spooking me. I looked up at the portrait of Isadora, who stared back at me — her foolish granddaughter, shivering in a swim-suit. Who else, besides me, had come into the study late at night only to find *A Primer on the Legend and Lore of Selkie Island*? Had Mom? Had her siblings? Had Isadora herself? Had any of them fallen for Llewellyn Thorpe's words?

There was an irrational part of me that wanted to continue reading, to find out more. But I knew that was a bad idea, that there was nothing useful to be learned from the book. And I needed to get some sleep; Mom had said we'd have a big day of cleaning and sorting tomorrow, and there was that Heirs party.

I stuffed the pages back into the book and returned it to its place on the shelf, feeling my usual rationale return as well.

As I shut off the light and left the study, I felt my heartbeat slowing down. Even the mariner seemed benign as I hurried past him now. I made my way to the kitchen, got a glass of water, and carried it upstairs, hoping the moaning of the steps wouldn't wake Mom.

In my room, I drew the drapes and quickly changed into a blue tank top and my favorite pajama bottoms: They were white and printed with miniature blue whales. I'd purchased them at the Museum of Natural History when I'd interviewed there back in March. My friend Linda, who'd been with me at the time, had laughed at the pajamas and called them "absolutely adorkable."

I glanced at my cell phone, which I'd placed on the dresser earlier, and I almost reached for it, the muscle memory of my fingers wanting to text Linda, to tell her about The Mariner and Llewellyn Thorpe's book. But I couldn't. I shouldn't. Things weren't the same anymore. At all.

With a sigh, I slid into bed, my head full from everything that had happened that evening. I thought of the night deepening outside, of my swim in the ocean, of lost pirates and helpful mermaids. Then I burrowed my head into the pillow and hoped I'd dream about sensible things, like in which box tomorrow I'd pack away *A Primer on the Legend and Lore of Selkie Island*.

HEIRS

"I slept like a stone last night," Mom remarked the next morning as we struggled onto the front porch, carrying heavy cardboard boxes. "I haven't done that in ages. It must be the fresh sea air."

"Too bad it didn't work its spell on me," I said through a yawn. I'd slept fitfully in the narrow twin bed. And now the sea air felt soupy and sticky — not ideal weather for manual labor.

For the past half hour, Mom and I had been lugging broken lamps, threadbare throw rugs, and cracked vases out onto the street. According to Mom, on Thursday afternoons, garbage collectors came by in golf carts to sweep people's junk away.

"Probably because you saw that mariner painting," Mom huffed, setting her box down on the corner. "He used to give me nightmares as a child."

Over breakfast, I'd filled Mom in on my run-in with the old seafarer in the hall. But I hadn't mentioned my discovery of the study, or of Llewellyn Thorpe's tome. The experience seemed even more embarrassing in the light of day, and I figured I'd feign ignorance whenever Mom and I tackled Isadora's book collection.

As Mom took a box of cutlery from my aching arms, I heard a female voice cry out behind us.

"Amelia? Amelia Blue Hawkins! As I live and breathe!"

I whirled around to see a skinny woman about Mom's age trotting up the road and waving. She wore gigantic sunglasses, a purple head scarf, a tight sundress, and high-heeled sandals.

I glanced back at Mom, whose expression was both stricken and resigned. I felt a sympathetic twinge of dread, but my curiosity was definitely piqued.

"Speaking of nightmares . . ." Mom muttered under her breath. Then she pasted on a smile, waved, and called back, "Hello, Delilah!"

"Well, well, well!" Delilah sang, snapping off her sunglasses as she neared. "Felice Cunningham said she spied the lights on in The Mariner, and Teddy Illingworth swore he spotted you by the docks yesterday, so I *had* to come see for myself!"

She stopped in front of Mom and gave her a peck on each cheek as I backed up a few paces, crossing my arms over my chest. "Amelia Blue Hawkins," Delilah repeated, shaking her head from side to side.

"Actually, it's Merchant," Mom corrected gently. "Amelia Merchant. I kept my married name after I got divorced. For professional purposes."

"Oh," Delilah replied, looking flustered. "Of course. Anyway." She patted Mom's arm. "You're as gorgeous as you were at eighteen. I thought being a big-city doctor would have shriveled you up by now!" Delilah let out a high laugh, then swung around to observe me. "And this *must* be your daughter. Why, she's the spitting image of Isadora — may she rest in peace," she added hastily, lowering her head.

I wasn't prepared for the quick rush of pleasure I felt at the comparison. "Thanks," I mumbled, shifting from one foot to the other.

"Amen, darling," Delilah instructed, widening her heavily lined blue eyes at me. "You say 'amen.'"

"Yes, this is Miranda," Mom spoke up, coming to my rescue. "Miranda, this is Delilah LeBlanc Cooper of Atlanta." I recognized the last name LeBlanc; Mom had said that family had started the Heirs party. "Her summer home is just down the road."

"Has been for generations," Delilah drawled, draping an arm around Mom's shoulder; her long crimson-painted nails resembled talons. "Growing up, your mother and I were inseparable. It's such a shame we drifted apart." I did my best not to meet my mother's eye; I doubted she mourned this loss.

"You have a son, too, don't you?" Delilah asked Mom, who quickly explained that Wade was in Los Angeles with his father.

"Well, it's more fun for mothers and daughters to spend time together, anyway," Delilah said, grinning first at Mom and then me. "You can swap lipstick and jewelry, and shop together."

This time, Mom and I couldn't help but exchange a glance. Neither of us wore much makeup or jewelry, and Mom never had time to go shopping. In the Mother and Daughter Olympics, it seemed, we would have finished last.

"Oh, speaking of which!" Delilah exclaimed, clearly capable of keeping a conversation going all on her own. "Miranda, I *have* to introduce you to my daughter, Cecile. Everyone calls her CeeCee. She's fifteen and absolutely precious, and the two of you will get along like a house afire."

Once again, Mom and I looked at each other, and Mom appeared to be holding back a laugh. We both knew that if CeeCee was anything like her mother, our friendship prospects were very slim.

"And," Delilah was saying, "y'all can meet CeeCee this afternoon at the Heirs party. I assume you got an invitation?"

When Mom nodded, pursing her lips, Delilah grinned at me again. "Every summer, Amelia and I got dressed up together for the Heirs party. And how the boys would *stare* when we entered the restaurant! It was no wonder that your mother won the affections of the most eligible —"

"Is it almost noon already?" Mom interrupted, taking my wrist and studying my watch. Her face was suddenly flushed. "Miranda and I still have a lot of work to do in the house. . . ." Mom trailed off, looking at Delilah pointedly.

No! I almost cried, my heart thumping with delayed suspense. I wanted Delilah to keep going. I'd never thought of my mother as having had a love life; she hadn't really dated anyone since she and Dad split up.

But the moment had changed, had taken on a charged quality. Delilah looked miffed as she removed her arm from Mom's shoulder and slid her sunglasses back on.

"I need to pick out my outfit, anyway," she sniffed, glancing disdainfully at our cleanup gear: Both Mom and I wore cutoffs, ratty T-shirts, and sneakers. "I'll see you ladies later." She waggled her fingers at us, but before walking off, added in a teasing tone, "And there are others who will be pleased to see you, Amelia."

I wanted to ask Mom what Delilah had meant — and also how the two of them had ever been close — but I felt dazed by the human hurricane that had just swept over us.

"It's amazing," Mom said once Delilah was out of earshot. Her face had returned to its normal shade. "That woman hasn't changed a bit. I'm exhausted just thinking about spending time with her at the Heirs party."

"Should we skip it?" I asked reluctantly. Delilah *was* crazy-making, but I wondered what else she knew about my mother, or even about Isadora.

"You should go, my love," Mom said, wiping perspiration off her forehead, "but I'm afraid I may have to conveniently come down with a headache."

⌁

However, after two hours of cleaning and mowing the lawn, Mom was ready to get out a little bit. So was I. As we left The Mariner, freshly showered and dressed — Mom in a linen shift and Grecian sandals, me in my red drawstring skirt and black tank top — I felt a jumpiness, an excitement in my stomach. The afternoon smelled of fresh-cut grass and flowers, and possibility hovered in the air along with the seagulls.

Mom led me through the town, which was comprised of a gourmet food market, a swimwear shop, a store dedicated entirely to hats, and a beauty parlor. Everything was clustered around a lush green square with a fountain at its center. As

Mom and I walked through the square, we passed two women in long, colorful skirts, weaving grass baskets before a small crowd. When we turned onto the boardwalk that ran along the beach, I felt I'd been more or less oriented to the island's layout.

The boardwalk offered an ice-cream stand and a store called Selkie Sandbar that had bobblehead pirate dolls and shark-shaped surfboards in its window — exactly the kind of touristy shop I'd envisioned on the ferry. There was also a clam shack called A Fish Tale, and a restaurant called The Crabby Hook, complete with an inflatable red crab on its roof. The restaurant was our destination, but before we walked inside, Mom squeezed my hand, something I couldn't recall her ever doing before.

A mass of bodies filled the large, airy space, everyone chattering and cheek-kissing. Silver streamers and blue balloons tickled the tops of our heads, and from the open kitchen came the sizzling sound and delicious scent of frying food. Along one wall was a buffet table laden with fried chicken, lobster tails, and plantains, and against the opposite wall was a bar. Those armed with drinks and plates of food were making their way out onto the sunny back deck, where a 1940s-style swing band was playing.

Mom and I had taken maybe two steps toward the

buffet when I heard someone say, "She's here!" and we were swarmed. Leading the charge was Delilah, on the arm of a pudgy, mustachioed man who bore an eerie resemblance to a walrus — Mr. Cooper, I assumed. An emotional woman in a diamond necklace embraced Mom, almost spilling her glass of golden-brown liquid on me, and an elderly man in a panama hat tried to pinch Mom's cheek. On the fringe of the throng stood the man with the salt-and-pepper hair from the ferry, looking dapper in slacks and a jacket. He was watching Mom with a wistfulness that made me uneasy.

I was about to subtly point him out to Mom when someone tapped my shoulder.

"Miranda?" the someone inquired excitedly.

I turned around and faced a petite, pretty girl in a white dotted swiss sundress and wedge espadrilles. Her long red tresses, big blue eyes, and sprinkling of freckles across her nose instantly gave her away as Delilah's daughter. I stiffened.

"CeeCee?" I ventured.

"Oh, my gosh, Mama told me all about you!" CeeCee cried, clapping her hands together. The charm bracelet on her wrist jangled. "You don't understand! I feel like we're sisters or something!" And with that, she swept me into a hug of surprising force.

Trying not to choke on CeeCee's voluminous hair or

the scent of her flowery perfume, I wondered if Mom was witnessing this encounter. CeeCee was right; I *didn't* understand. The fact that our mothers had been friends in another lifetime — something my own mother now appeared to regret — did not remotely make us relatives.

"I've always wanted a sister," CeeCee sighed, finally releasing me. "Are you an only child, too?"

"I have an older brother, but he's in California for the summer," I managed to reply, smoothing my ponytail. I was rattled, but I had to admit there was something refreshing about CeeCee's warmth.

"Ooh, is he cute?" CeeCee squealed, her eyes shining. "I bet he's real cute."

"He's all right," I replied, thinking that Wade — reckless, witty, and a lothario at Yale; in other words, Dad 2.0 — would have probably appealed to a girl like CeeCee. My brother and I couldn't have been more different. While Wade was constantly getting grounded in high school, I always toed the line. I never even *thought* about crossing it.

"It's so cool that you're from New York," CeeCee bubbled. She pronounced *York* in a songlike way, breaking the *o* into two syllables. "I've only been there once, and I could *not* stop shopping! Daddy practically had to drag me and Mama out of Henri Bendel's before we bought more handbags. How do you do anything else?" she asked me. But her slightly critical gaze, as it traveled down my outfit, seemed to answer her own question.

"Somehow, I find a way," I replied dryly. When I did go shopping, it was mostly in vintage stores, where Linda and I were pros at finding cheap jeans and cardigans. And while Linda and I shopped, we talked — long, winding talks about gender and birth order and astronomy. Linda was undeniably brilliant, with a thirsty mind. CeeCee's mind, on the other hand, seemed to have been thoroughly watered by the fountains of Fendi and the streams of Sephora. The thought of her as my sole companion on Selkie filled me with a kind of emptiness.

If CeeCee picked up on my reticence, she didn't show it; instead, she brightly asked for my cell phone number, and then announced she wanted to meet Mom, who was still surrounded by a circle of admirers. As CeeCee flung her arms around my mother, I shook hands with Mr. Cooper, the walrus (CeeCee had certainly dodged that genetic bullet), and Delilah kept winking at CeeCee and me, as if she'd set us up on a successful blind date. Then CeeCee suggested that the two of us head out onto the back deck so I could meet her friends.

I was torn; though it would be a relief to escape the close, sweaty crowd, I suspected CeeCee's friends were replicas of the girls on *Princess of the Deep* — cool confections of female perfection. Plus, I didn't want to abandon Mom, who at the moment was listening to a coiffed elderly woman ramble on about the price of oysters. But when I glanced questioningly at my mother, she leaned close, whispered, "We'll be out of here in ten minutes," and waved me off.

Stopping to get sodas from the bar, CeeCee and I maneuvered our way out onto the deck, which smelled of suntan lotion and beer and faced the beach. I gazed at the striped umbrellas, the creamy sand, the figures bobbing in the surf like sleek seals, and felt a prickle of envy. Maybe I could go swimming later.

CeeCee steered me past the band and the swing-dancing couples over to two girls who were sipping sodas, charm bracelets dangling from their wrists. One was a curvy blonde wearing a halter dress printed with small cherries, and the other was model-tall, with skin the color of dark chocolate, and she wore a short yellow dress cinched with a belt. Like CeeCee, they both appeared to have been cut out of a *Teen Vogue* spread.

They don't know the properties of helium, I told myself. *They don't know what Newtonian mechanics are, or who discovered penicillin. They will not make you feel insecure.* Still, I tugged discreetly on the hem of my skirt, hoping the hole wasn't visible.

Oblivious to my discomfort, CeeCee made introductions — the blonde was Virginia, the brunette Jacqueline — and Jacqueline smiled, linking her arm through mine.

"Delilah was raving about you earlier," she said, her voice soft.

"Jackie's my best friend from Atlanta," CeeCee explained, taking my free arm. "She's been coming out and staying with us for the past three summers."

As I stood sandwiched between CeeCee and Jacqueline, I was surprised to feel a warm rush of belonging. I'd forgotten how comforting it was, the casual intimacy that could exist between girls.

"And Virginia's from Charleston," CeeCee added, nodding toward Virginia, "but she's been my best Selkie Island friend since we were babies. Right, Gin?"

"Uh-huh," Virginia replied. Her cunning hazel eyes were trained elsewhere — on a group of attractive guys standing a few feet away.

"Have you seen the fountain in the town square yet?" CeeCee asked me. When I nodded, she went on, her tone proud. "It was built one summer by Virginia's great-granddaddy, Colonel Cunningham."

"That's . . . nice," I answered hesitantly. It was funny how, on Selkie, every family's history seemed connected to the island in some way. Llewellyn Thorpe's book came to mind, but I brushed the thought away.

"Well, he didn't *actually* build it himself," Jacqueline pointed out with a knowing grin. "I'm sure he had someone else do that for him."

"Blah-blah-blah," CeeCee said, and Jacqueline stuck her tongue out in response.

"Girls, stop bickering!" Virginia commanded. Her drawl was even thicker than CeeCee's. "Can we focus, please? We need to figure out our summer picks."

"Picks?" I echoed. Feeling naïve, I followed Virginia's gaze to the boys, who were laughing and bantering, seemingly unaware of the attention she was paying them. A blush started around my collarbone. *Oh.*

"It's a tradition we started two summers ago," CeeCee told me as the crowd around us broke into applause for the band, "when we realized that the boys who'd been summering here forever were suddenly becoming . . . hot."

"It must be something in the water," Virginia remarked, grinning wickedly and twining a blonde curl around one finger.

"Maybe," I said. In truth, everyone mingling and laughing on the deck bore the beauty and grace that came from generations of careful breeding.

"I think I'm going after Macon," Jacqueline murmured, nodding toward a stocky, ruddy-faced boy with a buzz cut. "Remember how much he was flirting with me last summer, right before he went back to Chapel Hill for school?"

"Not as much as Rick was flirting with me," Virginia countered, motioning with her drink to a guy with close-cropped dark curls who was wearing a vest over a button-down blue shirt. He glanced in her direction, and she smiled, lowering her lashes.

"I'm deciding between Lyndon and Bobby." CeeCee sighed dramatically, as if this were a heart-wrenching choice. She gestured to two boys who were practically indistinguishable: Both had longish white-blond hair and sported neckties. "I guess I'll have to make out with both of them to see which one I prefer!" At this, she, Jacqueline, and Virginia broke into gales of laughter.

I was stunned speechless. Was this how some girls were about boys? Selecting them as if they were no more than fish to be shot in barrels? I was especially surprised by Jacqueline, whom I'd figured for a shy kindred spirit. I wished I had the confidence to assume such control over my romantic destiny. Not that there'd been anything romantic in my life of late.

"Wait!" CeeCee said breathlessly, sounding truly alarmed. "I forgot!"

Virginia snorted, and she and Jacqueline exchanged a

glance. "CeeCee, you'd forget your own firm little behind if it wasn't attached," Virginia sneered.

"Oh, shut up," CeeCee giggled. "I forgot about Miranda!" She faced me, her enormous eyes sparkling. "We have to snag you a boy, too!"

The blush crept northward to my neck. This insanity had to be nipped in the bud. "Look, CeeCee," I said firmly, in a tone similar to the one I had used with Sailor Hat on the ferry. "I appreciate the offer, but I don't need a summer pick. I promise."

"Why not? Do you have a beau back home?" CeeCee asked. I could feel her, Jacqueline, and Virginia holding their respective breaths, watching me in disbelief. *Miranda? Has a boyfriend?*

"Um, no," I sputtered. "I mean, I did, but —" I bit my lip, commanding myself not to think, or speak, of Greg. The last thing I wanted to do was tread into such personal waters with CeeCee and her cohorts. "No," I finished lamely.

"Then how about Archer Oglethorpe?" Jacqueline suggested, shrugging her slender shoulders. "He's cute, and single —"

"Taken!" Virginia cut in before I could say that the boy's name alone was a deterrent for me. "He and Kay McAndrews were all over each other on the ferry two days ago, which is *so* tacky, by the way."

"But it wasn't tacky when you stuck your tongue down T.J.'s throat at the fireworks last summer?" Jacqueline teased. Virginia promptly gave Jacqueline the finger, the sun glinting prettily off her dark pink nail polish. It unsettled me how deftly these girls could seesaw between kindness and cruelty; it had never been that way between me and Linda, at least not until —

"Wait, that's it!" CeeCee exclaimed. "T. J. Illingworth." She lowered her voice and spoke directly into my ear. "He's standing next to Macon. In the striped shirt? See?"

I saw. And realized that T. J. Illingworth was the dark-haired boy from the ferry. The son of the salt-and-pepper guy who had been staring at Mom back in the restaurant. At the thought of Mom, I looked around the deck to see if she'd come out to get me, but I couldn't find her amid the dancing and drinking mob.

"Isn't he dreamy?" CeeCee said, and I turned back to study T.J. "His family's filthy rich," she whispered conspiratorially. "The Illingworths funded most of what's on this boardwalk."

"Yeah, like that new marine science center T.J.'s father kept bragging about at dinner last night," Virginia chimed in with a groan.

My ears perked up. "What science center?" I asked, more interested in this development than I was in finding a summer pick. "Where is it, exactly?"

But nobody was listening, and CeeCee had continued with her praise of T.J. "He's completely sweet," she was saying, "and he's, like, a golf champion. Oh, and he's starting Duke in the fall. He's perfect."

"Hang on," I said, suspicious, as I disentangled myself from her and Jacqueline. "If he's so wonderful, why isn't he *your* summer pick, CeeCee? Or yours?" I added, looking at Virginia and Jacqueline.

"Simple," Jacqueline replied, using her pinkie to smooth the gloss on her bottom lip. "The three of us made a pact: no boy sharing. It's too incestuous."

"I dated T.J. last summer," Virginia explained, rolling her eyes. She said *last summer* as I might say *grade school*. "But don't worry, Miranda. You have my full blessing. I lose interest in boys the minute I have sex with them. It's like magic! We do it, and poof! They become boring to me." She smiled placidly.

"I'm so jealous of that," Jacqueline sighed. "I get totally attached."

"Same," CeeCee said.

I cleared my throat, the blush now settling in my face. I had nothing to contribute to this particular discussion. I looked down at my black flats.

"So what are we waiting for?" Virginia was saying. "Shall we head over?"

Oh, God. Where was Mom? Hadn't it been ten minutes by now?

"Hang on," CeeCee said, reaching out to tug lightly on my ponytail. "Miranda, do you want to take your hair down first?"

I shook my head vehemently. "It's too humid," I replied. My hair is naturally curly but I always brushed it back and tied it up so it wouldn't frizz out. Besides, I knew it was a slippery slope; if I gave in to CeeCee on this point, in seconds she'd be all over me with mascara wands and foundation.

"All right," CeeCee pouted. She must have sensed that I was prepared to bolt, because she took my arm again.

Walking four abreast, CeeCee, Virginia, Jacqueline, and I crossed the uncharted gulf that had separated us from the boys. My palms grew clammier with each step. I hadn't been social for a month; what if I no longer remembered how to carry on a conversation?

The young lords of Selkie Island stood framed against the beach, their hands in their pockets and their smiles easy. When we reached them, Macon grinned and jabbed Rick in the arm, and Lyndon and Bobby smirked, but T.J. nodded solemnly at us. With his neat dark hair slicked back, wearing khakis and a navy blazer that accentuated his broad shoulders, he looked even more classically handsome than he had on the ferry. Was

CeeCee insane? In what parallel universe was this boy in my league?

"Ladies," he said, in a low, mature-sounding drawl. "Lovely afternoon, isn't it?"

Seriously? I swallowed down a laugh. I didn't know any guys my age who spoke like that.

But CeeCee and Co. seemed enchanted by T.J.'s words, smiling up at him, cocking their hips, and tossing their hair. I bit my bottom lip and wished I could be someplace, anyplace, where I'd feel more at ease.

"Who's the newbie?" Rick demanded, jerking his chin toward me as Virginia drifted ever so casually to his side. Jacqueline, meanwhile, made her way over to Macon, who gave her a hug that lifted her feet off the boardwalk.

"This is *Miranda*," CeeCee pronounced, giving me a poke in the back that sent me stumbling forward. "She's visiting from New York, but her roots are in Savannah. Hey, just like yours, T.J.!" she bubbled in mock surprise.

CeeCee's glee in playing matchmaker sort of made me want to kick her. Wasn't she supposed to be busy choosing between Lyndon and Bobby?

"Fascinating," T.J. said, focusing his big brown eyes on me, which made my blush deepen. Having fair skin is a curse. "What's your family's name?"

"Merchant," I said automatically, before realizing that T.J. would in no way know or care about my dad's side of the family, who hailed from ever-glamorous Brooklyn. "Hawkins," I corrected myself as CeeCee went over to talk to either Lyndon or Bobby.

An impressed smile split T.J.'s chiseled face. "Of course," he replied. "I grew up hearing about the Hawkins family! My mother would practically genuflect if she met you — she says that every Southern lady should aspire to be like Isadora Hawkins."

"Trust me, I'm not worth any sort of curtsying," I laughed, trying to wrap my mind around the fact that I was *talking* to this boy. Though my face was still warm, my heart wasn't racing; T.J.'s impeccable manners were definitely keeping me calm. Suddenly, I felt a small thrill at standing in the thick of this group, the crackle of flirtation passing between the girls and boys and back again. Could it be that I really fit in here?

"I beg to differ," T.J. replied smoothly, and my stomach jumped. I couldn't tell if his apparent interest in me was only because of our Savannah connection or if CeeCee's Cupid act was actually, shockingly, paying off. "In any case," he continued, "my mother's not here. She summers on Tybee Island with my sister now that she and my father are . . . divorced." He dropped his voice on this last word, as if it were dirty.

"My parents are divorced, too," I blurted, surprised that T.J. and I had something else in common.

"That's too bad," T.J. replied, tapping out a brief beat with his tan loafer. "I guess happily ever after isn't such a reality anymore."

"I've never believed in happily ever after," I replied truthfully, and T.J. squinted at me as if I'd spoken a foreign language.

"Hey, you girls have good timing," one of the boys announced, and I looked away from T.J. to see Lyndon or Bobby smiling, his arm around CeeCee's waist. "T.J. was just about to open his package," he added.

My heart skipped a beat. "Um, what?" I asked, and looked at T.J., who grinned.

"No Heirs party would be complete without the package," T.J. intoned; it was clear he was referring to a tradition not unlike the summer picks. Then he swung open one side of his blazer, revealing two silver flasks tucked into the inside pocket. The others exploded into cheers, and a few partygoers glanced at us, amused.

"Theodore Illingworth, Junior," Virginia pronounced as she turned away from Rick, her hands on her hips. "You always come through for us." Her eyes glinted and I wondered if she really was as over T.J. as she had said.

"Gather around, gentlemen, ladies," T.J. said, removing

one of the flasks and obviously enjoying the attention, "for the finest rum north of Cuba."

I hung back, feeling foolish for believing that these pampered kids would be content with drinking straight soda. I'd never been drunk, never had more than a sip of beer, not even at Greg's parentless pregraduation party in May. I was sure I wouldn't enjoy the sensation of being out of control.

As everyone, including CeeCee and her girlfriends, held out plastic cups to be filled, I took several more steps away from the glowing group. I noticed then that they were all equally matched, the girls with their thick hair and the boys with their strong jaws. T.J. swiftly uncapped the flask and poured clear liquid into a cup, and Jacqueline laughed and kissed Macon on the cheek. What had I been thinking? Yes, I was technically an heir, but I was not a part of this crew.

"Where are you going, Miranda?" T.J. asked, glancing up at me midpour. He seemed insulted that I was walking out on his moment of stardom.

"Aren't you going to drink?" Virginia asked, judgment in her voice.

"I'll be back," I fudged, determined now to track down Mom. I wanted to ask her why she hadn't come to rescue me yet.

When I turned around, I got my answer. Mom was standing near the band, holding a glass of white wine. She was laughing, and her face had a rosy tinge. And the person who was standing at her elbow and making her laugh was none other than T.J.'s father, Mr. Illingworth. I drew in a big breath, suddenly remembering how Mom had fled the docks yesterday. And then Delilah's coy remarks today. Was there something my mother wasn't telling me?

I couldn't stand the kind of chaos that was happening in my head. I turned back and looked beyond the young heirs toward the beach, at the waves that swelled and broke onto the shore. The beach, I reasoned, was where I belonged — among the seashells and barnacles that neither laughed nor flirted nor judged. I could return to the party once my whirling thoughts settled.

So, as the wind billowed my skirt up, I made my way down the boardwalk steps and started across the sand. And the human sounds of glasses clinking and conversation were swallowed up by the ocean roar.

Five

DISCOVERIES

I wasn't expecting to see the boy.

I had been walking along the beach for longer than I'd intended, trying to make sense of my interaction with T.J. and the image of Mom talking to Mr. Illingworth. The kids building sand castles and the couples frolicking in the water barely registered. I only noticed the shards of seashells and the cawing seagulls, and before long, that was all there was to see. As the water grew rougher and slammed into jagged rocks, the beach grew less populated, and I realized that The Crabby Hook and the boardwalk itself were quite a way behind me.

Which was why I was startled by the sight of a tall, tanned guy with dark blond hair striding toward me from the opposite end of the beach. He was carrying a bundle of rope and a fishing rod, the muscles in his arms visible under his faded red T-shirt. He wore ragged carpenter pants that had been hacked off at the knee, and his sun-browned legs were as muscled as his arms. I guessed him to be around my age, but he did not look like someone the kids at the Heirs party would know.

For some reason, I stopped walking, my flats sinking into the sand. Behind the boy, the beach seemed to disappear into a well of fog, and I realized how alone I was. I felt a quick twist of fear and considered turning and racing back to the boardwalk. Then I chided myself; why was I getting so irrationally spooked lately?

"You lost?" the boy called, waving one arm at me.

"Not at all," I replied defensively, squaring my shoulders. "I was just exploring."

The boy came closer. "It's not a great idea to go exploring by yourself on Siren Beach," he said. His voice was deep but a little raspy, and his Southern accent was different from CeeCee's and the others' in a way I couldn't quite define.

"Why?" I demanded, suddenly annoyed that this boy had appeared out of nowhere to break into my thoughts. I could feel my patience running low, like an uncharged battery. "Because of the 'sea serpents'?" I asked, making air quotes.

"You know about the sea serpents?" He was standing before me now, a smile tugging at his full lips. His eyes were a clear, brilliant green, unmuddied by traces of brown or gray.

"I know they're nonsense," I replied, crossing my arms over my chest.

The boy swept his gaze over my face, and my heart flip-flopped. What was he thinking? First T.J., now him. Trying to figure out the inner workings of boy-heads was a daunting task; *two* boys in one hour felt impossible for a novice like me.

But, back on the boardwalk, T.J. hadn't studied me as intently as this boy was studying me now. Almost against my will, I remembered the funny looks Greg — shaggy-haired, bespectacled, chess-team-captain Greg — used to sneak me back in February, when I was no more than his physics tutor. Then, one night, as I'd been explaining the principles of electromagnetism, he'd kissed me, and I'd understood what those glances had meant. And it had seriously freaked me out.

"It's your first time on Selkie, right?" the boy asked, his tone slightly teasing. For some embarrassing reason, the phrase *first time* made my skin catch fire.

"Is it that obvious?" I asked, giving a nervous laugh.

"Well, I would have recognized you," the boy replied, his smile widening.

"Miranda! Miranda, what are you doing?"

Relieved and disappointed, I turned toward the sound of

my mother's voice. She was jogging across the sand, holding her sandals in one hand and the bottom of her dress with the other. Her face was flushed, as it had been at the party.

"Like *The Tempest*," the boy said behind me, so softly that I almost didn't hear him over the crashing waves.

"Excuse me?" I asked, glancing back at him.

"Miranda is a character in *The Tempest*. The Shakespeare play," he explained with a slow smile. He had a dimple in each cheek.

"I try to ignore Shakespeare as much as possible," I replied, surprised that a boy who looked so rough-hewn would know anything about fusty literature.

"That's a mistake," he said as Mom came to a stop at my side, out of breath.

"Miranda, what's gotten into you?" she snapped, sounding frantic and unlike her usual even-keeled self. Her eyes were very big. "Why did you disappear like that? You had me so worried. One of the boys with CeeCee told me he saw you start off this way."

T.J.? I wondered.

"Sorry," I said, unable to look at my mother full-on. I knew it was irrational, but she suddenly seemed like a stranger to me, a stranger who laughed with handsome men. "I wanted to take a walk."

"A walk?" Mom repeated, arching one eyebrow at the boy standing next to me. Suspicion darkened her gaze. "Were you planning to tell me?"

"You don't tell *me* everything," I muttered, wishing we weren't having this conversation in front of this boy.

Mom seemed to feel the same way. "Pardon us," she told him, her tone brisk, and she tugged on my arm, pulling me in the direction of the boardwalk.

I looked back to see the boy hoisting some of the rope onto his shoulder and watching us, his expression unreadable. Then I faced forward again.

"This isn't like you," Mom declared, her feet kicking up sand as she all but dragged me along the shore. She didn't bother to push her windswept hair out of her eyes. "Wandering off, talking to some strange boy on the beach, catching an attitude with me."

"We weren't *talking*," I protested, my blush coming back for a second. "We exchanged, like, two words."

"You were fine when we got to the party," Mom went on as the first sunbathers came into view ahead of us. "What happened?"

I sidestepped a strand of seaweed, wanting to ask Mom about T.J.'s father. But my bubbling resentment stilled my tongue. How could Mom accuse *me* of acting oddly when she wasn't being herself, either?

Instead of speaking, I glanced over my shoulder again, but the boy was gone. I couldn't see him walking inland toward the dunes, nor could I spot him wading into the water. Had he disappeared into the fog? Jumped into a speeding fishing boat? Or had I — in a truly un-Miranda-like fashion — imagined him entirely? But no, Mom had seen him, too. I shook my head, dismissing him from my thoughts.

We were nearing The Crabby Hook. From what I could see, the Heirs party was dwindling; the band had stopped playing, and only a few people milled about on the deck. I felt fatigue wash over me.

"I guess the party got to be a bit much," I finally told Mom. "Actually, do you think we can head back to The Mariner now?" The thought of returning to the crowd, of having to explain my absence to CeeCee, T.J., and the others, made me want to crawl inside a clamshell and remain there, pearl-like.

Mom's face softened, and she gave me a sheepish smile. "Sure we can," she said. "And forgive me, my love. I didn't mean to freak out. I think I'm still on edge from being back here, seeing all the folks I used to know. . . ."

Like Mr. Illingworth? It was the perfect opening, but I didn't take it. I sensed that if I broached the topic with my mother right then, she'd only grow uncomfortable. Or, worse, she'd reveal something illicit, something I wouldn't want to know. There is always that danger in research.

So I nodded. "Maybe we can just avoid everyone else for the rest of the time we're here," I offered. Mom and I lying low in The Mariner, away from all the gossip, seemed like a logical solution. I could already feel the two of us reverting to our regular selves as we bypassed the party.

Mom chuckled. "That's not a bad idea. But good luck trying it out with CeeCee."

Sure enough, I was awoken the next morning by a cheery rapping on my door.

"Five minutes, Mom!" I groaned, rolling over onto my back. A glance at the clock on the dresser told me it was ten o'clock.

I was usually an early riser, and I was eager to tackle our tasks for the day, but I'd again had trouble falling asleep. I'd tossed and turned in the oppressive heat, wishing for air-conditioning and entertaining the notion of going downstairs for more of Llewellyn Thorpe's tales. Thankfully, I'd drifted off before I could act on that plan.

"Silly! It's me!"

With that, CeeCee flounced into the room, a bright-eyed, bushy-tailed belle. She was clad in a floral sundress and holding a covered tray.

"CeeCee, what are you *doing* here?" I asked, scrambling

to sit up while pulling the sheet tighter over my rumpled pajamas.

"Bringing you breakfast," CeeCee replied breezily, lifting the lid off the tray. "Mama was concerned that you and Amelia didn't have proper food in the house, so we came to deliver some down-home delicacies." With a flourish, CeeCee gestured to the strips of bacon, golden-brown hush puppies, and bowl of grits.

"You know what? I'm great," I said, rubbing the sleep out of my eyes. Breakfast was always whole-wheat toast and a strawberry yogurt. I'd never tried grits, but their off-white mushiness didn't appeal to me.

"Mama says that a true Southerner always has stone-ground grits in the house," CeeCee pronounced, marching over to my bed and ceremoniously setting the tray in front of me. "You eat up, and I'll fill you in on everything you need to know."

"What are you talking about?" I asked. I was still half in my dream — something about a green-scaled fish swimming between my hands.

"Well, first off, T. J. Illingworth wants to see you again," CeeCee said, plopping down on the edge of the bed and beaming. "Before I left the party, he asked me if you were staying at The Mariner. You realize that means he wants to come and visit?" She widened her already huge eyes at me.

"He does?" In my cotton-mouthed, sloppy-haired state, I couldn't comprehend how a member of the opposite sex would find me attractive. Still, my stomach leapt at the thought that a boy like T.J. had asked about me.

"Yup," CeeCee said, pushing the bowl of grits closer to me. "Didn't I say you two would hit it off? And that was a smart move on your part, sneaking away like that in the middle of everything. Boys love *nothing* more than mystery."

"Um, I didn't —" I paused, picking up a spoon from the tray. CeeCee wouldn't understand why I had left the party yesterday, but there *was* a chance that she knew about Mom's past with Mr. Illingworth. Before I could raise the subject, CeeCee spoke again.

"It seems all the summer picks are taking off!" she exclaimed, then began counting on her fingers. "Once the rum started flowing, Virginia and Rick couldn't keep their hands off each other, and after the party, Jacqueline and Macon snuck off to Macon's house. And let's just say Jackie wasn't in the guest room this morning." CeeCee winked at me, then plucked a strip of bacon off my tray.

"Really?" I asked. Once again, I was innocently, immaturely surprised by Jacqueline and Virginia's effortless conquests. "What about you?"

CeeCee shrugged. "Lyndon and I kissed on the beach during sunset, and he was an awful kisser, so now I know

Bobby's the one for me," she replied, flipping her hair over one shoulder.

"But . . . what if Bobby's a bad kisser, too?" I asked, genuinely curious as I dipped the spoon into the grits.

Not that I would know a good kisser from a bad one; all I had to go on for reference was Greg. I briefly wondered what it would be like to kiss a boy on the sand as the sun sank into the water, and my legs tingled. At sunset yesterday I'd been sorting through Isadora's filing cabinet while Mom prepared dinner.

"You're so negative, Miranda!" CeeCee observed, pouting at me.

"Just realistic," I corrected her, and tried the grits. They were soft and buttery, and surprisingly tasty.

"You mean bo-ring," CeeCee retorted, giggling.

CeeCee's opinion wasn't of great importance to me, but all the same I felt a pang of hurt. *Was* I boring? I'd always prided myself on the fact that I hadn't changed much over the years, maintaining the same style and interests with little regard for trends. Maybe that only made me . . . predictable. Ordinary.

"Oh, I was kidding, Miranda!" CeeCee cried. Her mouth turned down at the corners. "I'm sorry, I say whatever pops into my head. Can I make it up to you today?"

I shook my head, swallowing a big mouthful of grits. *You can, by going away.*

"Come on, we'll do something fun," CeeCee wheedled. "We can get pedicures in town, or . . . whatever *you'd* like to do!" she finished graciously, smiling at me.

"I have to help my mother sort through the study," I said, and immediately thought, *bo-ring*. "And, you know, other things," I added, taking my hair band off my wrist and looping my hair back into a ponytail.

"Well, I'm sure if you ask Amelia, she'd let you take a break." CeeCee shrugged, getting to her feet. "I'll wait downstairs with our moms, 'kay?"

Mom would be impatient to get rid of our morning guests, so I quickly finished my grits, wondering if my Southern background made me predisposed to liking them. I threw on jeans and my yellow-and-green Bronx Science T-shirt. When I arrived in the kitchen, however, I found Mom sitting at the table, talking animatedly with Delilah. Their breakfast — a duplicate of mine — was spread out before them, and CeeCee, also at the table, was texting on her BlackBerry Pearl. Sunshine spilled through the lace curtains.

"You're awake, my love!" Mom said, smiling and swinging one foot, clearly relaxed. After the party yesterday, she'd been quiet and tense as we split up and tackled various chores around the house. "Wasn't this a treat from Delilah and CeeCee?" she added, spearing a hush puppy with her fork.

"Our pleasure," Delilah drawled, patting Mom's hand, and

Mom shot her a grateful look. "What's a treat is to sit here and chat with you, Amelia."

I hovered at the entrance to the kitchen, bewildered. What was *up*? In no way did Mom appear as if she wanted Delilah to leave.

"So Virginia and Jackie are both too hungover to play with us," CeeCee announced, setting her BlackBerry on the table, and Delilah made a *tsk-tsk* noise. "What?" CeeCee asked, blinking at her mother. "*I* know how to hold my liquor."

"That you do," Delilah confirmed proudly, raising her glass of orange juice to CeeCee in a toast. "You're a LeBlanc, after all!"

I tried — and failed — to imagine having the same conversation with Mom. Or with anyone's parent. But Mom only chuckled and rolled her eyes.

"Amelia," CeeCee was saying, "Miranda wanted to be sure you'd be all right with her joining me today for a girls' outing. I know you have to paint the study and all. . . ."

"We don't have to paint." Mom chuckled, and glanced at me. "You know, the repairmen are coming to look at the roof and the plumbing, anyway. You girls go and have a good time! Just be sure to call me if you'll be out past dark."

I stared at Mom, attempting to eye signal to her that I didn't *want* to spend the day with CeeCee, but she had already returned to eating her hush puppy. Great.

"What are you two beauties up to, then?" Delilah asked, taking a sip of juice.

"It's Miranda's call," CeeCee said, fixing the strap of her dress. "But I was just thinking how pathetic it is that we don't have more shops on the boardwalk."

"Don't let the Illingworths hear you say that," Delilah advised, and Mom laughed — sort of nervously, I thought. "The boardwalk is their pride and joy."

At the mention of the Illingworths and the boardwalk, I remembered something Virginia had said at the party yesterday, and my spirits buoyed.

"The science center!" I exclaimed. "Isn't there a marine center on the boardwalk?" I asked CeeCee, whose face fell.

"There is?" Mom asked, and Delilah nodded. "Who knew? I thought nothing had changed on this island, but I guess there are always new additions." She smiled at me, her expression encouraging. "That sounds right up Miranda's alley!"

"What do you think, CeeCee?" I asked, leaning against the doorjamb and grinning. "Too *boring*?" Swinging by this science center while simultaneously irritating CeeCee seemed like the ideal Selkie Island activity.

CeeCee heaved a great sigh, pushing her chair back from the table. "Okay, okay, you're the boss. The science center it is. But afterward we're getting popcorn shrimp at A Fish Tale and laying out on Siren Beach."

Siren Beach. Without warning, I thought of the strange boy from yesterday, and I felt my cheeks flush. Would he be there again?

But why did it matter? There was another boy to focus on, after all.

"Deal," I said, walking over to CeeCee. "And later we can try to meet up with our . . . picks," I added boldly. CeeCee's lips parted in surprise, and I raised my chin, pleased. Who was boring now?

The Selkie Island Center for Marine Discovery was located in a modest, pale green house on the edge of the boardwalk, several doors down from The Crabby Hook. A gleaming plaque on the center's side announced that it was A GIFT OF THE ILLINGWORTH FAMILY. As CeeCee pulled open the screen door, I glanced at the handmade flyers taped to the windows. One flyer stated that the center's hours were from noon to six, Mondays, Wednesdays, and Fridays. Another flyer advertised sea creature beach walks, and a third announced an exhibit on baby alligators. Nothing fancy, but I hadn't been expecting the Museum of Natural History.

The air-conditioned foyer was full of little kids and chitchatting parents. On the wall was an underwater photograph of coral reefs, alongside a sign that read DISCOVER OUR

COLLECTION OF POLKA-DOT BATFISH! I sighed contentedly, feeling more at home in the center than I did at The Mariner. At least here, there was a distinct lack of legend or lore.

CeeCee and I walked over to the desk in the corner, which was being manned by a teenage girl with pretty rows of dreadlocks and wire-framed glasses.

"Two, please," CeeCee told the girl in an imperious tone, handing her a five-dollar bill; when we'd left The Mariner, CeeCee had insisted that this visit be her treat.

As I watched the girl punch the keys on the register, her expression studious, I realized she reminded me a little of . . . myself.

"This must be a cool place to work," I mused out loud, studying the brochures stacked on the cluttered desk.

"It's my summer job," the girl said flatly, shooting me a look of confusion. It occurred to me that she was a resident who lived on the island year-round — a local — and couldn't grasp why I was talking to her. I wanted to mouth, *I'm not one of them!*

"What's there to *do* in here?" CeeCee asked, wrinkling her freckled nose as she accepted the two tickets from the girl.

"We have our aquarium room, featuring snapping turtles, puffer fish, and the Atlantic octopus," the girl replied in a rote tone, handing me one of the brochures. "And Leo is actually about to give these kids a tour of the center starting" — she glanced at her watch — "now."

"Lord help us," CeeCee murmured, looking at the gaggle of children in panic.

"Who's Leo?" I asked, skimming the brochure and thinking that a tour sounded like fun.

"He's the other summer intern," the girl responded, then pointed over my shoulder. "There he is. Hey, Leo!" she shouted. "Can you take two more on your tour?"

I turned around and my heart flew into my throat.

Leo was the boy I'd met on the beach.

He looked different — cleaner — than he had yesterday; he now wore a white polo shirt with a name tag that read LEO M., navy blue board shorts, and flip-flops. But it was inarguably the same boy, with the same straight, burnished gold hair, high cheekbones, and bright green eyes. It didn't make sense; I'd assumed he was a young fisherman, or some sort of nomadic beach wanderer.

"Of course I can," Leo replied in that deep, scratchy voice. He was addressing the girl, but he was staring directly at me. "The more, the merrier."

I felt CeeCee pinch the skin above my elbow. "Eye candy alert," she whispered. "Let's take the tour!"

"Oh, I don't know," I faltered, feeling heat spread across

my cheeks. Would Leo say something to me? Would we both pretend we hadn't met yesterday? I had no precedent for this particular situation.

"Coming here was *your* idea, missy," CeeCee said, steering me toward Leo, who was now clapping his hands and asking people to gather around him. "We're doing it."

Six

EXPLORERS

"Welcome to the Selkie Island Center for Marine Discovery," Leo said, his eyes sparkling as he faced the crowd. "A gift of the Illingworth family," he added in an ironic kind of baritone, and I felt a smile playing on my lips.

"Cute, but he's got to be a local," CeeCee whispered disdainfully. "Total Fisherman's Village type."

I started to ask CeeCee what she meant, but the woman standing ahead of me shot us an irritated glance. This wasn't the time to gab. Behind us stood — I'd done a double take to confirm — the excitable little blond boy from the ferry and his parents.

"We are much more than an aquarium," Leo continued, spreading his large, tanned hands. "This center is involved in wildlife preservation and does a great deal of research both in Selkie's marshes and on Siren Beach."

I felt my breath catch. I couldn't get over how boyish Leo had seemed on the beach yesterday, when he was now so official. Professional. He also had not glanced at me again since CeeCee and I joined the group, so I wondered if he even remembered me.

"This," Leo said, leading us into a dimly lit room that smelled of salt, "is our aquarium where you can meet — and sometimes touch — a few of Selkie's most interesting inhabitants."

I gripped the brochure in my hands, barely noticing the illuminated, sand-bottomed tanks full of crabs, jellyfish, and the famous baby alligators. Why, *why* did Leo speaking the word *touch* make my whole face flame? I was grateful for the darkness of the room, but I peeked at CeeCee to make sure she hadn't noticed my blush. Thankfully, she was checking her BlackBerry.

"Feel free to roam around on your own," Leo announced. "The placards next to each tank will tell you a lot about each little buddy inside, but if you have any questions, just holler. And for those of you who want to befriend a baby alligator, follow me."

There was promptly a stampede toward the baby alligators, while a handful of kids admired the tank of spider crabs.

"I'm going to step outside for a minute," CeeCee murmured with a grimace and a toss of her hair. "Call me if this gets fun, okay?" she requested. And before I could tell her that I hadn't brought my cell phone, she blew me a kiss and trotted out of the room.

Inexplicably, my heartbeat sped up. Tucking the brochure into the back pocket of my jeans, I found myself wandering toward the alligator tank, and Leo. When I got there, I stood a bit away from the crowd that *oohed* and *aahed*.

Leo's right arm was outstretched and on his hand sat a small alligator, its tail thumping against Leo's wrist and its ancient, reptilian eyes blinking steadily. The boy from the ferry daringly stroked the alligator's scaly body.

"You're doing great," Leo encouraged, nodding at the boy. "I think he really likes you. Maurice — that's his name — Maurice can be a little wary of strangers."

I can relate, I thought with a small smile. I was impressed by Leo's ease around kids. If I were in his position, I would have been dolefully reciting facts about the anatomy of cold-blooded animals.

"Now," Leo said, glancing around at the circle of saucer eyes, "can anyone tell me the only two places in the world where alligators are natives?"

"North America and China." The answer shot out of me automatically, and then I bit my lower lip. Why did Studious

Miranda have to show up *now*? "Um, I DVR basically every show on the Discovery Channel," I added awkwardly, avoiding the stares of parents and children.

Leo's eyes crinkled at the edges as he smiled. His dimples emerged.

"Thank you, Miranda," he said. "That's right."

He remembered me.

Why did that fact make my stomach somersault? Twice?

I decided that now would be a good time to go check out the snapping turtles, but something kept me rooted to the spot. And as the kids pushed past me, heading toward the other displays with their parents in tow, I realized that only Leo and I were left standing by the alligators.

Leo's gaze met mine briefly. He glanced at the neuron symbol — my school's logo — that was printed on my T-shirt. Then he looked down at the alligator in his hand.

"Hi, again," I ventured, my voice uneven. When Leo didn't answer right away, my breath stopped. Why did this boy have such a strange effect on me?

"What's that, Maurice?" Leo finally spoke, addressing the alligator. "You think she's the smartest girl we've had in the center so far?"

My heart fluttered, but I felt a spark of irritation. People who blurred the lines between animals and humans irked me.

"Do you always pretend that alligators can communicate with you?" I asked, folding my arms over my chest.

Leo glanced back up at me with a lazy half smile. "I'm not pretending."

"Oh, really?" I shot back. "What other things does Maurice over here tell you?"

Leo raised one eyebrow mischievously. "Can you keep a secret?" he asked. When I nodded, he took a step closer to me. Despite myself, I drew a deep breath. Leo smelled fresh and sharp, like rainwater and sand. Incongruously, I recalled the scent of Greg's Mitchum deodorant.

"He wants out," Leo whispered as Maurice blinked patiently at me. "All his buddies do. They want to run free."

I shook my head, a laugh escaping my mouth. "You don't need to talk to animals to guess that. A natural habitat is always preferable."

As he had yesterday, Leo rested his eyes on my face for a long moment, so long that I knew my cheeks turned crimson. The voices of other people milling about the room sounded faint and distant.

"If that's how you feel," Leo said at last, turning away and gently placing Maurice back in the tank with his brethren, "you should come on one of our sea creature beach walks. I'm giving one today at six o'clock, right when the center closes."

I thought of standing on Siren Beach with Leo again. Only

this time we were exploring, looking for sand dollars and seashells on the shoreline. A smile I couldn't control crossed my face.

"I'll take that as a yes?" Leo said as he brushed his hands on his shorts.

I nodded, then tried to force my lips back into a straight line. "Is that where you, um, were headed yesterday?" I asked, tightening my ponytail. "To give a beach walk?"

Leo shook his head, scratching the back of his browned neck. "The center's closed on Thursdays, so that's when I help out my dad — he's a fisherman. When you saw me yesterday, I was going to meet him on his boat."

I remembered CeeCee's remark, something about Fisherman's Village.

"I see," I said, choosing my words carefully. "I, um, I wouldn't have pegged you as someone who works at a science center."

Leo grinned and the wicked glint reappeared in his eyes. "I'm full of surprises."

I swallowed hard and was preparing a response when Leo clapped his hands and called, "All right, everyone! It's time to resume the tour!"

I looked down at my Converse. I couldn't. I couldn't continue the tour. Maybe it was a combination of my hot cheeks and my pounding heart, or maybe it was the knowledge that

I'd be going on a better tour later. In any case, as the visitors swarmed back around Leo, I glanced at him, mouthed "See you at six," and turned to go.

As I walked through the lobby and out into the sunshine, I felt my breathing even out. I stared at the crystal blue of the ocean, which washed white and foamy onto the sand. Two guys in swim trunks were wading into the surf with their boogie boards, and a tugboat sliding past the horizon honked its horn. The air was thick as always.

CeeCee was sitting on the wooden steps that led down to the beach, her ever-present BlackBerry in her hands. "I hate boys," she moaned when I sat down beside her.

"Why?" I asked, thinking of Leo. Had she seen us talking and disapproved?

CeeCee scowled down at her BlackBerry. "I texted Bobby about hanging out tonight, but supposedly he's got some sort of a family dinner. My *gosh*." She rolled her eyes. "If he seriously wanted me, he'd skip the stupid dinner, don't you think?"

"I have no idea," I replied honestly. What did I know about male creatures?

CeeCee gave me a *you're hopeless* look, then glanced at her BlackBerry again. A seagull strutted by the boardwalk, pecking at a discarded hot dog bun. "The good news," CeeCee spoke, smiling up at me, "is that I texted T.J. and he *is* free this evening. You should definitely meet up with him, Miranda!"

My stomach jumped. I'd forgotten that, in the flush of my earlier bravado, I'd suggested hanging out with the summer picks, a plan that didn't jibe so well with the beach walk I'd just agreed to attend. Plus, the prospect of spending the evening one-on-one with T.J. felt distinctly . . . datelike.

"Don't look so scared!" CeeCee laughed, squeezing my arm. "T.J.'s too much of a gentleman to make a move on you right away."

Adrenaline raced through me. Did T.J. *want* to make a move? A piece of me suddenly yearned to experience it: the warmth of T.J.'s breath, surely freshened by mints. The scent of whatever expensive cologne he must have dabbed on every morning. The chance to discover what another boy kissed like. T.J. seemed so suave, so experienced, that I was certain he would be good at whatever he did.

But why did a bigger piece of me still want to go on that beach walk?

"I'm not scared, I just don't think I'm ready to hang out with T.J. alone," I replied, hugging my knees to my chest. "I'd rather hold out for a double date." *Or nerd out on a sea creature walk.*

CeeCee sighed. "If you're sure . . . " she drawled, and dutifully began texting again. "I'll tell T.J. that you have other plans. You know," she said, shooting me a grin, "it's clever to play hard to get and all, but you need to be careful. You don't want T.J. slipping through your fingers. Otherwise you'll end up with Mr. Townie in there as your summer pick." CeeCee jerked her thumb back toward the center.

I set my chin on the tops of my knees, a shiver going down my spine.

"Yeah," I said softly. "That would be awful."

For obvious reasons, I refrained from uttering a word to CeeCee about the sea creature walk. So, over a lunch of popcorn shrimp at A Fish Tale, I let her prattle on about the importance of moisturizer and whether or not Virginia had gotten a boob job. I tried to drop in a few questions about our mothers, in case CeeCee had absorbed any information about Mom's past from Delilah. But her response was always a carefree shrug and a blithe, "I don't really remember."

In the vain hope that CeeCee would eventually remember something she'd been told, I agreed to a trip to the beauty parlor for "mani-pedis." A pedicure was out of the question — the idea of baring my toes for examination was mortifying — but I succumbed to my first-ever manicure, which turned out to be fairly pleasant.

At six to six, I was studying my buffed, clear-polished nails as I hurried back down the boardwalk to the marine discovery center. CeeCee had wanted us to browse in the swimwear shop in town, but I'd made up a hasty excuse about needing to get home for dinner.

I was surprised not to see a group forming outside the center; I had figured the beach walks would be a popular draw. Plus, the day was turning into a beautiful evening, the oppressive heat giving way to a soft breeze, and cotton-ball clouds — *cumulus*, I thought automatically — drifting across the eggshell blue sky. A few beachgoers were still lolling about, soaking up the last hours of sunshine. But when I reached the screen door, I saw just one person standing there, his arms folded across his chest and his eyes trained on the water.

Leo.

Instantly, I felt woozy, almost as if I were seasick.

Get a grip, I told myself sternly.

"I thought I was late!" I said in my most casual voice, strolling over. "Where is everyone else?" I peered through the center's window into the empty foyer.

Leo turned to me, and for an instant it looked as if his face turned red. But it must have been the rose-colored glow of the sun. I watched his Adam's apple move up and down as he swallowed. He no longer wore his name tag.

"We don't usually get a big turnout for these after-hours walks," he replied, glancing down at his flip-flops. "Most people are heading to The Crabby Hook for happy hour, or having barbecues with their families."

"Right," I said, feeling a pang of guilt and wondering if Mom did, in fact, expect me home soon for dinner. Knowing my perfectionist mother, though, she was probably still giving directions to the repairmen. Besides, I'd return to The Mariner before dark.

Leo looked back up at me, and I realized, with a jolt, that I'd been spaced out staring at him, at the dark blond hair that the wind was sweeping across his forehead

"Oh, I'm sorry!" I exclaimed, reaching into my jeans pocket. "How much is the walk?" Where had my head gone?

"No, no," Leo said, holding up his hands and laughing. "This one's on the house."

"Okay . . . thanks," I said slowly. Something — a suspicion — flickered inside me, but I dismissed it as utter silliness.

"So let's get going," Leo said, kicking off his flip-flops. He lifted them up in one hand, the muscles in his arm moving fluidly, like water. "You should take off your sneakers," he advised. "We're going to be walking right where the tide hits the shore."

"Oh, I — I don't mind," I stammered. I had no desire to show Leo my toes. Most of the time, people didn't even notice, but in my mind, the freakishness was magnified. Last summer, when Wade and I had gone to see Sideshows by the Seashore at Coney Island, I'd felt as if the bearded ladies and sword swallowers were long-lost siblings.

"You will," Leo promised with a crooked smile, and his eyes — which turned an even more iridescent green in the sun — searched mine for a second. "You can't fight the ocean." Then he shrugged and began walking again, and I followed, relieved.

But as soon as we passed the sunbathers and hit the damp hillock of sand that sloped down to the sea, I realized Leo was right. The unrelenting tide retreated and advanced with ferocity, and my beloved Converse were quickly soaked. Leo strode along easily as the water enveloped his long, browned feet.

"All right, all right, I admit defeat," I sighed, stopping in my tracks. How could I consider myself a true explorer if I couldn't even, well, get my feet wet? And something about Leo's relaxed vibe told me that he probably wouldn't care that my toes were weird. Maybe it was time to quit being such a baby about my imperfection.

I eased off one sneaker with the toe of one foot, but then I staggered, losing my balance. Leo was immediately by my side, extending his hand for me to grab.

I took it.

His fingers closed around mine, warm but rough and slightly callused. I looked down at my small, smooth, pale hand in his much larger one, and I felt my head spin. I was suddenly glad that I'd gotten a manicure.

"Better, right?" Leo asked as I kicked off my other sneaker. The comfortably warm water rushed up to swirl around my ankles. To my horror, I caught Leo looking directly at my bare feet, and my chest seized up.

"Yes," I mumbled, withdrawing my hand and scooping up my Converse. My toes wiggled in the water of their own volition, as if astonished to finally be free.

"Then let's dive in," Leo said with a grin.

"You mean, swim?" I asked, confused. Our brief bout of hand-holding, along with my toe-baring, had disoriented me.

"No, I mean, let's start the tour," Leo laughed as a fresh wave slammed into the shore, depositing coils of seaweed around our feet. "And here we go," he added, crouching down and picking up a flat circle dotted with small slits. "Ever seen a live sand dollar before, Ms. Aspiring Marine Biologist?"

"What makes you think that's what I want to be?" I challenged. The fact was, I wasn't sure which branch of science I wanted to follow in life — often, the laws of physics and the structures of chemistry spoke to me more than the rawness of biology.

"Well, your eyes were shining at the center today," Leo replied matter-of-factly as he rose. I could feel him observing the side of my face. "You seemed . . . passionate."

The seasick feeling returned, and I hoped Leo wouldn't notice how my fingers trembled as I carefully touched the sand dollar. I was never completely relaxed around boys, but at least when talking to T.J. yesterday I'd been somewhat composed. Why was Leo's presence making me feel so unmoored?

"No, I haven't ever seen one up close, and it's very cool," I responded at last, pretending to be fully absorbed in the sand dollar.

"I'll show you something even cooler," Leo said, clearly enjoying himself; his eyes were dancing as he set the sand dollar back down where he had found it. "See those tiny holes in the sand?" He pointed, and I looked down to see the mysterious pinpricks. "Ghost shrimp," he explained. "Funny little guys. They burrow into the sand so they can eat and hide out."

"That doesn't sound like typical shrimp behavior," I said, smiling and getting back into the swing of things. Leo's enthusiasm, *his* passion, for the ocean world was contagious. And incredibly attractive.

My heart thumped.

"We just call them shrimp," Leo said, drawing a circle around the hole with his toe. "They're really relatives of lobsters. Surprising, huh? It's like, did you know that Spanish moss isn't really moss?"

"But — yes, it is," I protested, thinking of the moss-heavy trees on the island.

"It's related to *pineapple*," Leo told me, widening his stunning eyes. "I swear. You can look it up. Isn't that wild? Names can be so misleading."

As I gazed back at Leo, I understood that he, this strange boy from an island in the middle of nowhere, loved science for the exact same reasons I did. Now *that* was wild. I felt like we were two explorers, partners, out there on the empty beach, with everything open for discovery.

"What's in a name?" I said with a small laugh, and then, feeling brave, nudged Leo in the ribs with my elbow. "See, I know *some* Shakespeare."

"Nice," Leo said, nudging me back. "I like *Romeo and Juliet*. Forbidden love. Tragic ending. All the good stuff."

"I'm with you there," I said as we continued walking, wishing I hadn't blushed at his use of the word *love*. "Happy endings never feel real to me." I kept my head down; now that Leo had pointed out the ghost shrimp's holes to me, I couldn't stop seeing them in the sand.

"Well, it all depends," Leo replied, crouching low again, "on what one considers a happy ending. Aha," he said, lifting from the sand a small red bulb attached to a purplish stem.

"For you, ma'am. A sea pansy. I know it's not a dozen roses, but it's the best I could do on such short notice."

What did *that* mean? The blush that spread across my face now put my earlier flushing to shame. Was Leo implying that we were on a date? Had I dodged a date with T.J. only to wind up on another one? And since when was I the kind of girl who had these kinds of problems?

He's kidding, I decided, accepting the sea pansy and watching its round, brainlike bulb wobble in the wind. "Thank you, kind sir," I replied, rolling my eyes.

"You're welcome," Leo replied, standing up. He came closer to me, closer than he had been in the center when he'd told me about Maurice. He was beautiful, I realized, studying the planes of his face — the straight line of his nose, the fullness of his mouth. Over his head, the sky was transforming from pale gold to pale red, and the soft texture of the air made me feel almost beautiful, too.

Something overcame me then — something stronger than sense or reason — and I felt my hand reach out. I wanted to touch Leo's cheek, to feel its rough smoothness. Leo inclined his head toward me, and I was holding my breath, and then an enormous, swelling wave crested onto the shore.

The force of the current was so great that it lifted my feet and sent me tumbling backward. I landed hard, on my butt, on the sand. I managed to hold on to my Converse, but the sea pansy was ripped from my hand.

"Oh, no, are you okay?" Leo asked. Gripped with shame, I looked up to see his eyes sparkling and his mouth twitching. He wanted to *laugh*.

"It's not funny!" I cried, scraping bits of gravel off my palms as I scooted backward onto drier sand. The seat of my jeans was sopping wet. I felt jittery and shaky, wondering what would have happened between us had nature not intervened. "And I lost the sea pansy," I added mournfully.

Leo sat down beside me, putting his flip-flops in the sand. "We'll find you another one," he said reassuringly, a laugh still in his voice. "Don't get angry with the current," he added, watching me. "Just go with it. There's this quotation I always think about: 'Life is like the surf, so give yourself away like the sea.' Isn't that true?"

"Who said that?" I asked, still feeling petulant about my spill. "Shakespeare?"

"No," Leo said, and I could see him smiling in my peripheral vision. "It's from a movie I saw once."

The sea was waxing and waning at our feet, and the sun was beginning its descent into the horizon. Seagulls cried out as they flew by, and I felt the warmth of Leo's arm near mine. If a moment in my life had ever felt like a movie, this was it. I turned my head to look at Leo, wondering if he was thinking the same thing. He was looking back at me, his expression now serious.

"Miranda," he said. Never before had my misbegotten name sounded so lovely, never had its syllables been pronounced with such care. "I'm really glad you came to Selkie this summer."

"I think I am, too," I said, or started to say, because suddenly Leo was leaning toward me, and I couldn't differentiate between the scent of the sand and his skin.

Just go with it, I thought.

And let him kiss me.

The kiss started slow, his salt-licked lips lightly brushing mine, his sweet, clean breath tickling my own. Every inch of me was poised, waiting, tingling. I didn't think. I didn't question. As Leo deepened the kiss, I closed my eyes. I felt his sandy hand caress my cheek, his fingers tracing, exploring, and I reciprocated eagerly, touching his face.

Leo kissed languidly, a kiss like he had all the time in the world, a kiss as hot and slow as the summer itself. So different from Greg's kisses, which seemed hurried and clumsy by comparison. I felt Leo's warm tongue in my mouth, and I understood why people sometimes went crazy, risked everything for a kiss.

We ended the kiss at the same instant, drawing back and opening our eyes. My head was swimming and I couldn't stop smiling. Had that really just happened? Had it really been me?

"I've been wanting to do that ever since I saw you yesterday afternoon," Leo remarked, smiling, too. "Right on this beach."

I glanced around at the quiet sand and the empty dunes, on which shadows had started to form. Abruptly, I was aware of the hour. My old, reliable common sense returned, and I got to my feet. My lips still felt tender from Leo's kiss, and I was grateful that my knees were stable enough to hold me up.

"I don't have my cell phone," I told Leo, shaking my head at my forgetfulness, my lapse in logic. I attempted to brush off the damp sand that clung to my backside, growing flustered. "My mom will worry if I'm out after dark without calling. We're from New York, you see, and she — she worries."

Even if I'd had my phone, though, what would I have said to Mom? *Sorry, but remember that boy you saw me talking to yesterday? Yeah, we've been making out on the beach. No worries.*

Never.

"Is that where you're from?" Leo asked, jumping to his feet so quickly I could barely blink. He reached for my arm, his eyes bright with curiosity. "Tell me about it. Tell me about you."

"I can't now," I said, backing up a few paces even as my heart strained for me to stay put. "My mom —"

"Okay, okay," Leo laughed, holding up his hands. "I get it. You're a good girl."

A taunting tone had crept into his deep voice, and his mouth curved up in an enigmatic smile. I felt a flash of ire at being cast in such a narrow role — even if it was an accurate one.

"Maybe I am," I replied, cramming my feet back into my wet Converse and leaning over to tie the laces tight. "Is that so wrong?"

"Of course not," he said. "I wish I could be a good boy more often. Can I at least walk you home?"

"How good boy of you," I shot back, but I could feel my annoyance dissolving as I glanced up into his green eyes. "But no, thanks," I added, softening. "I know my way."

I hesitated, wanting him to ask me to stay, wanting him to kiss me again, and at the same time overwhelmed, unsure of how to proceed. Wasn't this when most people exchanged phone numbers or e-mail addresses?

"Listen, I'm — when —" The words *should we meet up sometime?* seemed to stick to the roof of my mouth like taffy.

"Come find me," Leo put in, his gaze full of understanding. "Whenever you want. I'll be here."

I wasn't sure how that was possible, but I didn't want to ruin the moment by asking. So I lifted my hand in a half wave, turned, and hurried along the heavy sand, my ponytail swinging from side to side. When I reached the boardwalk, I paused outside the brightly lit, noisy Crabby Hook and glanced over my shoulder at the dark beach.

I couldn't spot Leo anywhere on the sand. There was only the ocean storming the shore and leaving a trail of bubbles in its wake. If I squinted, though, I could make out a pale shape bobbing on the whitecapped waves. It was moving too quickly to be a person, so maybe it was a dolphin, or a dinghy, or a harlequin duck. Maybe it was a ghost shrimp. A sand dollar.

Or maybe it was the sea pansy Leo had given me, carried away by the current like a memory I longed to grab on to and hold for as long as possible.

Seven

MISTAKES

*S*urreal.

That was the only way to describe the experience of returning to Siren Beach in broad daylight.

It was Sunday, July first, two days after my beach walk with Leo. I was lying on a towel, a few feet from where he and I had shared our knee-weakening kiss. Every time I thought of that kiss — approximately every five seconds — my whole body flushed. Beside me, CeeCee, Jacqueline, and Virginia were stretched out silently in bikinis, their faces turned worshipfully toward the sun. Behind us, Mom, Delilah, and Virginia's mother, Felice, lounged on beach chairs, chatting. So there was absolutely no one with whom I could discuss my tumbling emotions.

Not that I was really in the mood to talk. In my black swimsuit, Converse, and oversized sunglasses, I felt somehow disguised. Incognito. I'd put in my iPod earbuds but left the music off, an old trick that allowed me to listen in on conversations while being left alone. I loved observing.

"The repairmen were a disaster," I heard Mom moan, and Delilah clucked her tongue. I allowed myself a glance back; Mom's white caftan and matching head scarf fluttered in the wind and made her look almost identical to Delilah. "They left plaster all over the floor," Mom went on, "and the faucets spit out brown water."

Fortunately, Mom had been so preoccupied with the repairmen's shoddy work that she hadn't batted an eye when I'd walked into The Mariner on Friday evening late, wet, and covered in sand. And the day before, while I'd roamed uselessly around the house in a daze of disbelief and joy, Mom had been busy making phone calls — to the real estate lawyer, to Aunt Coral, and then to Delilah, who'd been the only person able to calm her down. At night, Mom had made one last, whispered call on the back porch, closing the French doors behind her. But I hadn't asked her about it — I'd been too busy staring out the kitchen window and wondering if I'd really see Leo again.

Which was why, on the beach now, every tanned, blond boy who passed my towel made my heart skip and my head turn. One particularly pathetic false alarm had been Virginia's younger brother, who'd stopped by to snag one of the peach smoothies Virginia's housekeeper had packed in a cooler.

Come find me, Leo had said, after all. But so far I hadn't.

"Poor Amelia," sighed Felice, whose face was frozen in eternal youth by the magic of Botox. "It truly *is* hard to find good help lately."

I was so shocked that she had actually — without irony — uttered those words, that I let out a small sputtering laugh. I looked at Mom, waiting for her to laugh as well, but to my surprise, she simply took a sip of her smoothie.

Sighing, I rested my head back on the towel and looked up at the cloud-speckled sky. A Frisbee whizzed by overhead. I heard Felice announce to Mom and Delilah that she was going for a quick dip, and I watched from behind my sunglasses as she flip-flopped past my towel toward the ocean, her straw hat bobbing.

It was indefinable, but ever since the Heirs party, Mom had seemed different. She'd stopped making snarky remarks about Delilah, and this morning, she'd happily forgone sorting through Isadora's things and accepted Delilah's invitation to go sunbathing with "the ladies."

Suddenly, CeeCee, Jacqueline, and Virginia squealed in unison. I'd been so focused on Mom that I hadn't realized the girls were speaking.

"You *love* him," Virginia pronounced, and for one second, I wondered if she was addressing me. Could she have known about Leo?

I turned my head toward the girls, who were now propped up on their elbows, and Jacqueline was rolling her eyes and blushing. Virginia must have been referring to Macon.

"And you're going to get *married*," CeeCee chimed in, giggling and licking peach foam off her straw.

"I don't love him," Jacqueline replied sensibly, slathering sunscreen onto her long dark legs. "It's a summer thing. The novelty's fun, but in a few weeks, we'll both go back to our separate lives."

Normally, I would have cheered on Jacqueline's levelheaded declaration, but hearing those words now made a strange sadness well up in me.

"Jackie, since when are you such a pessimist?" CeeCee groaned. A group of shrieking girls in bikinis raced by, chased by bronzed boys in swim trunks, and they sprayed sand onto CeeCee's towel. She scowled.

"Well, Macon's not all that," Virginia said, and took a sip of her smoothie. "Any boy who suggests a date to Fisherman's Village loses points in my book."

"He claimed he was trying to be *inventive*." Jacqueline started laughing, and the others joined in.

Curiosity nipped at me. CeeCee had referred to Fisherman's Village in relation to Leo. I sat up, taking out my earbuds and taking off my sunglasses.

"What's Fisherman's Village?" I asked.

Three made-up faces turned toward me, six flawlessly plucked eyebrows shot up.

"Miranda! We thought you were napping!" CeeCee exclaimed.

"Well, now that you're up, is there any T.J. news?" Virginia asked, adjusting the top of her green polka-dot bikini to better showcase her bust.

"Fisherman's Village is that way, I think," Jacqueline replied. She pointed her smoothie cup toward the craggy rocks where I had first seen Leo walking on Thursday. Once again, all I could make out was mist. "I've never been, but I know it's where the Selkie Island locals live."

"Don't worry, Miranda," CeeCee said, unscrewing the cap off her tube of sunscreen. "T. J. Illingworth would never dream of taking you there!"

"Exactly. So what's the T.J. news?" Virginia repeated, zeroing in on me.

I bit my lip. After my evening with Leo, I hadn't thought about T.J. once. I felt mildly guilty for forgetting about him.

"Nothing, really," I said, shrugging. "I haven't heard from him —"

"That's because he and Mr. Illingworth are in Savannah for the weekend," CeeCee put in. "There's some big golf tournament or something." She mimed yawning and her friends cracked up.

"What's this about Mr. Illingworth?" Delilah called from behind us. I glanced back to see Mom swat Delilah with her copy of *Vanity Fair*. My stomach tightened.

"We're trying to set Miranda up with his son!" Jacqueline replied cheerily, and Mom choked on her smoothie. She coughed into her fist before regaining her composure.

A grin spread across Delilah's face. "Miranda and T. J. Illingworth? How . . . intriguing." She snapped off her sunglasses and raised one eyebrow at Mom. "It's like history repeating itself, isn't it?"

Mom's sunglasses hid her expression, but I saw her jaw clench as she intently turned the pages of *Vanity Fair*. Normally, she read *Scientific American*. "Delilah," she said in a warning tone. My stomach constricted again.

"Oops." Delilah brought her fingers to her lips. "My mistake," she said, but her eyes were dancing.

"What do you mean, Mama?" CeeCee asked, spinning around on her towel. Virginia and Jacqueline rolled over, too, and we all stared at Delilah.

But it was my mother who answered.

"It's not a big deal," she replied in a clipped tone, pushing her sunglasses onto the top of her head. "Mr. Illingworth and I used to date, back when we were kids. *Ancient* history," she added, and met my gaze for a second before looking back at her magazine.

I'd suspected there had been something between Mom and Mr. Illingworth, but to hear her speak the words was startling. And if it *was* no big deal, why hadn't Mom simply told me? And why was her face so pink?

"Oh, my gosh, can you say *destiny*?" CeeCee cried while Jacqueline grinned and Virginia looked stone-faced. "I swear I didn't know that when I decided Miranda and T.J. should get together. Maybe I'm psychic!"

"You mean *psycho*," Virginia muttered, flopping down on her back.

Delilah settled into her chair, clearly pleased. Just then, Felice reappeared, dripping wet in her age-inappropriate gold lamé bikini.

"The water was too cold for my taste," she said, wrapping a towel around herself. Glancing at our little group of mothers and daughters, she clearly noticed the hovering tension. "What happened?" she demanded. "What did I miss?"

No one answered.

"CeeCee!" Mom spoke up loudly, flipping the pages of the magazine with force. "Was T.J. the young man I spoke to at the Heirs party? The one who told me where Miranda had gone?"

"Yup," CeeCee replied, bouncing up and down a little. "Isn't he divine?"

"He is very good-looking," Mom concurred as Felice sat down beside her again. "Extremely polite, too." Mom's eyes flicked up toward me again, full of meaning.

My head spun. Was my own mother getting in on the matchmaking scheme? Not only was she suddenly involved in my romantic future, she apparently had a romantic *past* with my intended's father. This was too weird.

"I have to pee," I announced, setting down my empty smoothie cup and standing. I'd seen a restroom near the ice-cream stand on the boardwalk.

"Miranda!" Delilah exclaimed, slapping a hand to her bosom, and Mom shook her head at me. Felice looked outraged as well — or at least tried to look outraged.

"That's not proper language for a young lady," Mom told me, knitting her brow. "You can excuse yourself, but we don't need the details."

I heard the soft titters of CeeCee, Virginia, and Jacqueline, and I bowed my head. I felt like a five-year-old who'd been sent to the corner for talking in class. I'd never known Mom to admonish me in such a manner. Then again, I'd also never known her to have dated Theodore Illingworth the first.

"Excuse me," I muttered, before turning and jogging away. As I went, I heard Virginia ask, "And *why* is she sunbathing in her sneakers?"

In the bathroom, I splashed water on my face and tried to calm down. Still, when I emerged, I didn't feel prepared to rejoin Mom and the others.

The wind whipped through my hair as I walked down the boardwalk, drawn inexorably toward the marine center. I knew it was closed on Sundays, but I paused hopefully outside the screen door. My eyes traveled to the flyers on the window, and when I read one of them, my heart flipped in my chest.

Don't Miss Our Sea Creature Beach Walks,
Wednesdays! Meet Intern Leo at the center
at 6 P.M. to purchase tickets.

Wednesdays? Leo had taken me on the beach walk on Friday. I remembered how he hadn't wanted to accept my payment, and the suspicion that had crossed my mind. Now, comprehension descended. There *had* been no beach walk on Friday. Leo had fabricated it as a way for us to meet one-on-one.

I sucked in a sharp breath, at once flattered and freaked. No boy had ever gone to such lengths for me. On the other hand, I wondered if I had made an error in judgment, trusting Leo — *could* I trust a boy who was capable of lying with such ease? Would T.J. have done something similar? I doubted it.

I returned to my towel more confused than when I'd left.

Fortunately, the three moms had moved on to discussing where to find the freshest lobster in town, and Virginia and Jacqueline were splashing in the ocean while CeeCee lay on her stomach, texting Bobby.

I reapplied my Banana Boat, stretched out, and put in my iPod earbuds again, but now I turned the music way up, filling my eardrums in hopes of clearing my head. T.J. and Leo ping-ponged around in there, competing for space with Mom and Mr. Illingworth. Even Greg, who I thought I'd pushed into the recesses of my mind, cropped up.

Were CeeCee and her friends — not to mention Mom and *her* friends — infecting me? Or was it Selkie Island? Maybe being so far from home was turning me into the kind of girl who could think only about boys, dates, and ancient history.

When the wind turned rougher and the tide began creeping farther up the sand, all the moms agreed it was time to pack up. As Virginia and CeeCee whined about uneven tans, I threw one last look around the beach. I was starting to won-der if Leo's remark that I could find him anytime had been another fabrication.

Besides, I thought as I shook out my sandy towel, what would I have realistically done had I actually spotted Leo on the beach? Kissed him in front of everyone?

My limbs tingled at the thought.

As we headed up the boardwalk toward town, Mom and I lagged behind, our shared beach bag dangling from my shoulder. I knew why *I* was lingering, but it seemed odd that ever-efficient Mom was dragging her feet.

I glanced at her, thinking how quiet she'd been since the Mr. Illingworth revelation. There were two pink spots on her cheekbones — not a sunburn.

"So . . . I have a question," she spoke after a minute, her voice low enough so that Virginia, Virginia's brother, and Felice, who were ahead of us, wouldn't hear.

"I thought I was the one with the questions," I joked, trying to ease what felt like a blossoming hostility between us.

Mom gave me a perfunctory smile. "This T.J.," she began, and my pulse instantly sped up. "Maybe he's someone you'd like to get to know better? So you could have, you know, another friend on Selkie, besides CeeCee and the girls?"

And Leo, I thought, looking down at my Converse.

"He, um, seems nice enough," I managed to say, realizing why I had never discussed boys with Mom — it was possibly the most awkward conversation one could have with a parent.

I breathed in the scent of boiled corn from The Crabby Hook as we passed by, recalling the Heirs party. T.J. seemed cast in a different light now that I knew our parents were linked — he was at once more familiar and more distant.

"Well, I was considering inviting him and his father over for tea tomorrow," Mom said in a rush, and it was clear to me that she'd been pondering this proposal all afternoon. The pink spots on her cheeks darkened.

"You were?" A small knot formed in my stomach. Was Mom arranging this tea so I could hang out with T.J.? Or did she have other motives? I thought of her secretive phone call the night before. "Mom," I went on haltingly, avoiding her gaze, "I know you and Mr. Illingworth used to — whatever, but . . ." I trailed off, and my face colored. Maybe *this* was the most awkward parent topic ever.

Mom nodded, her eyes distant. "It has been some time since Teddy — since Mr. Illingworth — and I were acquainted. But now that I'm back on Selkie, I've been giving a lot of thought to the importance of mending fences. I suppose I made a few . . . mistakes in my youth." Then she pursed her lips, as if worried she'd said too much.

"What mistakes?" I asked as I searched her face. Mom didn't make mistakes. She was an accomplished plastic surgeon — she perfected people's appearances for a living. And she was equally controlled and orderly outside the operating room. She did the *New York Times* Sunday crossword puzzle with a pen. She was *Mom*.

"That's not the point, Miranda," Mom said briskly, quickening her pace. "The point is . . ." She seemed to grope for her next words. "I wanted to be sure you were all right with us having company over."

"I guess," I replied, excitement and anxiety washing over me in tandem. T.J., in The Mariner? With me? I tried to picture it: his big brown eyes surveying the chaos of boxes, his pressed blazer hanging on the anchor coatrack.

"All right," Mom said, sounding much more relaxed as we entered the town square. "I'll call Mr. Illingworth and extend the invitation."

As Mom hurried to catch up with the others, I frowned at the strangeness of the scenario. When I'd told CeeCee that I'd wanted to go on a double date with T.J., this was not the kind I'd imagined.

⁓

"So then the caddy asked, 'Sir, is that your son?' and all I could say was, 'I sure hope so!'"

Theodore Illingworth the first chuckled at his own story, and I cringe-smiled as I stood beside T.J., who was grinning modestly. Mom, stirring mint into the pitcher of iced tea, murmured something about T.J.'s talent, and I envied her social skills.

Monday afternoon — teatime — was here. The elder and younger Illingworths had arrived at The Mariner only ten minutes before and we'd already been regaled with two golf stories. I didn't know how many more I could take.

In his sharp seersucker suit, smelling of Scope and cigars, T.J.'s dad cut a dashing figure as he stood in our kitchen. But I had yet to grasp what Mom had seen in him, even all those years ago. My dad, who wasn't as classically handsome as Mr. Illingworth, came off as much more charming, if only for the fact that he told jokes well.

"This house is amazing," T.J. said to me, gesturing to the marble counters. "I've heard about it, naturally, but visiting it is something else entirely."

What was amazing, I reflected, was how smooth and shiny T.J.'s hair looked, how neatly he combed it back off his tanned forehead. After not seeing him for three days, I found his handsomeness almost jarring. And the fact that he was standing near me, so near that I could study the weave of his blue button-down shirt, made my neck prickle.

"It's in disarray right now," I replied, borrowing an apologetic phrase I'd once heard Mom use. I sounded weirdly . . . ladylike. Across the kitchen, Mr. Illingworth opened the refrigerator door for Mom and she murmured, "Why, thank you, Teddy."

"It could use some sprucing up," T.J. allowed, tapping a finger against his square chin. His gaze skimmed over me for a moment before he nodded toward the curling edges of the aquamarine wallpaper.

My belly turned over. Was I paranoid, or was T.J. implying that *I* could use some sprucing up, as well? I glanced down at my white V-neck, green capri pants, and black flats. Mom and I had spent the morning cleaning, and I'd barely had time to shower and throw together an outfit. I was now the most underdressed person in the room; Mom wore heels and a pale pink, full-skirted sundress that I didn't even know she owned.

"I was shocked when my father told me you were planning to sell The Mariner," T.J. went on, running his palm along the countertop. "True, you could earn a thick wad of cash, but a place like this is essentially a historic landmark."

I shrugged, wondering how I could steer the conversation away from real estate. "Our lives are back in New York," I explained, realizing how far off New York seemed then. How far it was from Leo. "Trying to keep up this house would be like —"

"An albatross around your necks?" Mr. Illingworth boomed. I'd had no clue that he'd been listening. He chuckled, rocking back and forth on his heels, and added, "Just like in that painting of the old mariner that hangs in the corridor off the study."

I frowned. How did Mr. Illingworth know about the painting? We hadn't passed by it when we'd gone from the foyer to the kitchen.

"Sort of," Mom laughed, kneeling by the stove and checking on her blueberry cobbler. I couldn't get used to the fact that Mom suddenly appeared to relish cooking and baking. She'd even asked me to help her with the cobbler that morning, but I'd declined; food preparation held no appeal for me.

"Say it ain't so, Amelia Blue!" Mr. Illingworth said, putting his hand to his chest while T.J. chuckled appreciatively. "I'm not sure Selkie Island could bear you leaving again." He paused, adding soberly, "I already let you get away once."

Okay. No. I fought the urge to clap my hands over my ears. I glanced at T.J. to see if he, too, was squirming in embarrassment, but he was nodding at his father earnestly.

"Who's ready for cobbler and sweet tea?" Mom asked, her voice coming out high-pitched. She held the baking dish in her oven-mitted hands, wobbling in her pumps while her face got progressively pinker. She shot me a sheepish smile.

I wished The Mariner's kitchen had a secret trapdoor that I could fall through.

Mr. Illingworth reached for the pitcher of iced tea. "Let's carry everything onto the back porch. It's cloudy out, but it probably won't rain until later."

I shrank back against the counter. The golf stories had been one thing, but the thought that Mr. Illingworth might throw out another flirtatious, too-much-information remark while we were on the porch wracked me with fear. No matter what Mom had said yesterday, it seemed that, to T.J.'s dad, their courtship *had* been a big deal.

Then T.J., my unlikely savior, spoke.

"Daddy, what were you saying before about a painting?" he asked. "Is there fine art here?"

"The finest," Mr. Illingworth replied, lifting the pitcher. "I believe Roger St. Claire did the painting of Isadora that hangs in the study, did he not?" Mom nodded, and Mr. Illingworth said, to me, "St. Claire is one of the South's best-known portraitists."

"Oh, Miranda!" Mom trilled, her voice still sounding funny. "*I* know! Why don't you show T.J. the portrait in the study? And the mariner painting, too, of course. Wouldn't that be fun?" She peeked at Mr. Illingworth, who gave her an understanding smile. My heart began to pound. Was Mom taking lessons from CeeCee?

"That sounds wonderful," T.J. said warmly, turning to me.

"Yes, you kids run along, and we'll save you some cobbler," Mr. Illingworth said, shooing us toward the kitchen door while winking at T.J. "Enjoy yourselves."

"Shall we?" T.J. asked, offering me his arm.

I hesitated. Taking T.J.'s arm seemed like a big step — like a commitment of sorts. Greg and I had hardly ever held hands — which, in retrospect, probably should have been a warning sign. But there *was* something heart-fluttering about assuming such an old-fashioned pose with a boy like T. J. Illingworth. And Mom was watching me so encouragingly that I somehow felt I couldn't let her down.

Taking a breath, I slid my hand around T.J.'s elbow, and together we left the kitchen, and our parents, behind.

Eight

KISSES

You make a great hostess," T.J. told me as we walked toward the painting of the mariner. My hand — clammy — was still on his arm and I was wondering when it would be appropriate to let go. I could feel a hint of T.J.'s muscles under his sleeve, which made me think of Leo, which made the backs of my knees grow warm.

"Um, thanks," I replied, my lips twitching at T.J.'s overly polite manner of speech. "I haven't really done much," I added as we passed the staircase.

"A good hostess makes her guests feel comfortable," T.J. said, sounding as if he were quoting from a book on etiquette. "I really feel so . . . at home here," he went on, sweeping his arm through the dust particles in the air.

T.J. did look as if he belonged in The Mariner, I reflected, taking in his ramrod posture and the noble slant of his profile.

It wasn't much of a stretch to imagine him as the young master of a grand Southern estate.

Too bad the lady on his arm was wearing capri pants and a T-shirt.

"Well, here is the mariner," I said as we arrived in the small corridor where I'd had my nighttime scare. I took the opportunity to casually lift my hand from T.J.'s arm and point to the painting. In the gray afternoon light that fell through the front windows, the old seafarer seemed spooky once more.

T.J. ran his eyes over the painting, his expression critical. "Excellent craftsmanship," he declared. "Nice use of sfumato."

I had no idea what T.J. was talking about. "He gives me the creeps," I said.

T.J. laughed. "Nah. Head into Fisherman's Village any day of the week and you'll see hundreds of geezers who look just like him."

"Really?" I asked, my face becoming hot. Fisherman's Village. Where Leo probably lived. I shifted from one foot to the other, suddenly uncomfortable with T.J.'s haughty tone.

"Not that a girl like you should go to Fisherman's Village," T.J. amended with a quick shudder, then smiled at me. "Hey. Would I be too much of a nuisance if I asked to see the study?"

"No," I replied distractedly, pushing open the door. In the

prerain gloom, the bookshelves sat in shadows. The window was open, and a cool breeze fluttered the pages of an old *Town & Country* magazine on the writing desk.

I'd been in the study earlier that day; in her cleanup frenzy, Mom had asked me to start putting books into crates. I'd only made progress on two of the shelves and had purposefully avoided the shelf that contained *A Primer on the Legend and Lore of Selkie Island*. Though I wanted the book gone, I'd worried that if I picked it up, even to pack it away, I'd start reading again.

"Wow," T.J. murmured, walking in a slow circle. He stopped at the writing desk and ran his fingers over the gold-buckled black box that rested on its surface. Then he glanced up at the bookshelves. "Very impressive collection." He smiled at me as if I'd had something to do with the room's impressiveness. I shrugged.

Then T.J. stopped and stared straight ahead at the portrait of Isadora. "Wow," he said again, his chiseled jaw going slack. "My father was right. You do resemble her."

I blushed. When Mr. Illingworth and T.J. had arrived on our doorstep earlier, bearing brandy and chocolates, Mr. Illingworth had taken one look at me and said, "Isadora!" I'd felt both rattled and flattered and had wondered if I'd ever get used to — or believe — the comparison to my grandmother.

Now, I shook my head. "I'm not sure," I said, glancing up

at the painting. Isadora seemed to smirk down at me, as if she knew something I didn't. "She was *so* . . . elegant. Put together. I don't think that trait can be inherited."

T.J. swiveled away from the painting so that he was studying me. He cocked his head to one side, and I felt like a work of art he was appraising.

"You could be elegant," T.J. declared. He reached out and gently touched the end of my ponytail, and I tensed up. "You could try wearing your hair like that." He motioned to the painting. "Or even a dress like that!" He laughed. "I bet you'd look great."

I crossed my arms over my chest, bristling slightly. I couldn't tell if I'd been complimented or insulted.

"Look, T.J.," I said, walking backward and plopping down onto the high-backed chair I'd sat in the night I'd read Llewellyn Thorpe's book. "That isn't *me*. I'm not like CeeCee, or Virginia." I paused, my throat tightening as I realized that T.J. must have admired — and unzipped — many of Virginia's luxe dresses.

T.J.'s dark brow furrowed, and he took hold of the love seat, dragging it next to my chair and sitting down.

"Oh, no. Miranda, I didn't intend to offend you," he said, leaning toward me. "I think you're pretty. I was only wondering . . . who you could let yourself become," he finished, looking satisfied with this last statement.

I opened and closed my mouth. T. J. Illingworth thought I was pretty? I was unable to fight the small glow of pleasure that filled me. God. Was that really all it took to soften me up? I was turning into such a *girl*.

"Thanks," I told T.J. again, half smiling as I met his gaze. "You know I think you're, um" — *don't say pretty!* — "very nice to look at, too."

For the thousandth time in my life, I wondered how I could be intelligent when it came to math and science and completely stupid when it came to boys.

Fortunately, T.J.'s face lit up as if I'd said the perfect thing. "Thanks," he said.

"You're welcome," I said.

I drummed my fingers on my lap. T.J. and I seemed to be adept with pleasantries.

The sound of laughter — my mother's laughter — interrupted my thoughts. I glanced over my shoulder at the open study door and saw Mom and Mr. Illingworth pass by on their way to the living room. I swallowed hard.

"Don't you feel like we're sitting at the kids' table?" I asked, looking back at T.J.

He smiled. "Yeah, I think that was pretty orchestrated." He raised his eyebrows. "On the way over here, my father wouldn't stop talking about what a good match you and I would make. And that was before he even met you!"

My heart skipped. Nervously, I started picking at my finger-nails, and then remembered my manicure and stopped. T.J. was watching me and I tugged on my ponytail, feeling ridiculously self-conscious.

"CeeCee seems to agree," I finally said, speaking to my flats. If CeeCee knew this moment was happening, she'd be doing backflips.

"I picked up on that at the Heirs party," T.J. said with a soft laugh. He was still leaning toward me, and I could smell his cologne — sophisticated and spicy, just like I'd imagined it. "People aren't too subtle, are they?" he added.

"Like my mom, back in the kitchen?" I looked at T.J. and rolled my eyes. "She's usually never so jumpy. She was acting like — like a different person," I admitted. It was sort of a relief to be able to confide in someone regarding my new, mixed-up feelings toward my mother.

"Aw, it's sweet," T.J. said. He moved his hand from where it rested on his knee to the edge of my chair. "My father used to mention your mother on and off over the years, and I think he still might carry a torch for her. I don't know what exactly happened between them, but my guess was always that she broke his heart."

My own heart was beating harder now. I remembered what Mom had said to me yesterday, about making mistakes in her youth. She must have meant Mr. Illingworth.

T.J. and I looked at each other, and I wondered if we were thinking the same thing: that, in us, our parents saw a way to somehow correct those mistakes of their past. As if T.J. and I, together, offered a second chance to get things right.

"You know what would make my dad happy again, though?" T.J. asked.

"What?" I prayed that he wouldn't say something inappropriate about my mom.

"If I found a nice girl," T.J. replied, his face looming closer until I was sure he could hear my loud heartbeat. Then, with the air of someone experimenting — in the same way I approached a test tube full of sodium bicarbonate in Chemistry lab — T.J. took my chin in his hand and put his lips on mine.

I forgot to close my eyes, so I stared, incredulous, at T.J.'s smooth, perfect earlobe as he kissed me. It was a gentlemanly kiss — closed-mouthed and soft and well choreographed. I was registering that T.J. had clearly just brushed his teeth, or eaten a mint — had he planned this, then? — when a loud *thud* came from across the room.

T.J. and I jerked back at the same time, and I glanced over at the bookshelves. The wind had knocked, of all things, *A Primer on the Legend and Lore of Selkie Island* smack onto the floor.

"I — I should pick that up," I stammered, leaping to my feet.

"Allow me," T.J. said, getting up at the same time. I was sure I was bug-eyed and blushing, but he appeared utterly unruffled.

"No, that's okay," I insisted, hurrying across the study. My head was spinning as I leaned over to retrieve the book. I couldn't help but skim the page it had fallen open on:

The island's merfolk blend in nearly seamlessly with their neighbors. However, certain oceanic markings often adorn their places of residence.

I shook my head. I'd been right; I *couldn't* touch the ridiculous book without starting to read it. I straightened up and jammed the thick volume back onto the shelf.

"Well." I heard T.J. exhale. I spun around to see him standing by the love seat, adjusting his shirt collar. "Intense, huh?" he asked, grinning at me.

I stared at him, unsure if he was referring to our kiss or to the book falling. *Had* our kiss been intense? I couldn't say. I felt too close to it, too bewildered.

"We'd better go make sure there's still some cobbler left for us," I replied. I quickly touched my hand to my lips, wondering if Mom would be able to tell what had happened, and if she would be pleased or scandalized.

Before I followed T.J. out of the study, I glanced back at the portrait of Isadora. I knew it was my imagination, but my grandmother's dark eyes seemed disapproving as she gazed down at me from her imperious perch. I sighed, feeling chastised. Isadora Beauregard Hawkins surely did not expect her granddaughter to kiss two different boys in a matter of days.

And the thing was, up until that moment, I'd never expected it of myself, either.

⥱

By the time I'd gulped down a glass of sweet tea and endured one more golf story, storm clouds were gathering in earnest. As Mom rescued the wind-tossed napkins from the porch floor, Mr. Illingworth announced that he and T.J. didn't want to overstay their welcome, anyway. Mom tried to discourage them, but I was secretly glad. I hadn't been able to make eye contact with T.J. since our moment in the study, and I craved space and quiet so I could figure out how I felt.

As we walked our guests to the door, I was surprised to see Mom extend her hand to Mr. Illingworth, who swiftly bent forward and kissed it. Their movements were so natural, it was clear they'd performed this dance many times before. My own hands were in my pockets, and Mr. Illingworth had to ask me to remove one hand so he could kiss it, which was beyond awkward. I decided to shake his hand instead. T.J. gave me a kiss on the cheek, murmured, "I'll be in touch soon," and then all the kisses were done, and the Illingworths were off.

"How'd it go?" Mom asked me the minute she shut the door. Her gray eyes were shining and her hair spilled over her shoulders. Her eagerness, her happiness, made me sort of embarrassed for her. "Did you have fun with T.J.? Do you think you'd like to see him again?"

"Mom, I don't *know*," I snapped, irritated. The whole afternoon felt jumbled in my head. I couldn't begin to parse my thoughts on T.J., or on anything — an unfamiliar feeling for me. "Leave me alone," I added, crossing my arms over my chest.

Mom put her hands on her hips. "What did you say? Since when is it permissible for you to speak to me in that tone?"

I gritted my teeth, retorts racing through my head. *Since when did we get so prim and proper? Since when do you let some guy kiss your hand?* But I didn't want to argue with Mom. We never argued. We couldn't start now.

"Sorry," I mumbled.

Mom was quiet for a moment, and then she walked toward me, her heels clicking over the compass on the floor. Her expression was suddenly solemn.

"Miranda, I'm sorry, " she said softly. "I'm being thoughtless. Here I am, going on and on about T.J. when I'm sure there's someone else on your mind."

I caught my breath. She *knew* about me and Leo?

"You're hesitant because of Greg, right?" Mom went on, looking at me closely. "It's too soon?"

"Greg?" I said, blindsided. My heart stuttered. Greg was the last person I needed thrown into the mix right now.

"I haven't said anything to you," Mom said, nodding, "because I know how you need time to yourself. But, look — I knew all along that Greg was more than a boy you tutored in physics. And when — when he stopped coming over, well, it wasn't too hard to figure out that you two must have parted ways."

I put my hands to my warm cheeks, feeling my gut tighten. "Mom, I *really* don't feel like talking about this now." *Or ever.* I stepped around my mother, heading into the living room. "Don't we need to finish cleaning up the back porch?" I added.

"Miranda, I understand it's painful," Mom said, following me through the French doors and onto the porch. Thunder rumbled ominously overhead. "You probably still have feelings for Greg, and that's why —"

"I do *not* have feelings for Greg anymore," I said, whirling around to glare at my mother. It was true; though my feelings about what had happened were knotty, even a little frightening, I didn't miss Greg. I didn't yearn for him.

Not like — the thought jolted me — not like I was yearning for Leo.

I turned away from Mom and looked out at the gray view. As always, the sight of the ocean settled me, and I imagined the life that teemed beneath the slate-colored waves. Leo had made appearances in my thoughts all day — every day since Friday — but now he was all I could think of. What was he doing? Was he thinking of me, too?

Would he care that I had kissed another boy?

Suddenly, I knew what I had to do. I knew who I had to see to make things make sense again. I wasn't sure I would find him, but I had to try.

"I'm going for a walk," I told Mom, and without waiting for her okay, turned and started down the porch steps.

"Miranda, are you insane? It's about to pour!"

"I won't be long," I called over my shoulder, my voice nearly drowned out by the wind. A fork of lightning split the sky.

"Why are you running off again?" Mom asked, hurrying down the porch steps after me. She paused on the grass.

"I need some air," I replied. "And I'm not running."

And I didn't. I walked at a steady pace until I reached the end of Glaucus Way. Then, when I knew Mom couldn't see me anymore, I broke into a run.

I ran all the way to town, where the stores had red, white, and blue HAPPY INDEPENDENCE DAY! banners strung up in their windows. People hurried to stand under awnings and pre-emptively opened umbrellas. In the green square, the women weaving grass baskets were nowhere to be seen, and mosqui-toes filled the air.

As I reached the boardwalk, I felt the first cold raindrops on my bare arms. Still, I ran down the length of the board-walk, past The Crabby Hook, past the closed marine center. Something seemed to be propelling me, something I couldn't name or understand.

When I got to the end of the boardwalk, I stepped down onto the sand and asked myself what I was doing. Though it was only five o'clock, the sky looked like midnight. The ocean was furious, lashing itself against the shore, and the palmetto trees tilted in the wind. The beach was empty; any-one sane was indoors. Maybe Mom was right; maybe I'd lost my head.

I scanned the barren dunes and churning ocean one last time before I sighed and turned away. I hugged myself and lowered my head against the wind, prepared to ascend the boardwalk steps and hopefully make it back to The Mariner before the storm.

But then I heard my name.

At first, I thought it was the call of a seagull, or the crashing of the tide.

But then it came again.

"Miranda!"

I whirled around, my heart lifting, and saw Leo walking up the sand toward me. His hair was wet, and he wore only dark blue swim trunks that sat low on his slim hips. Droplets of moisture glistened on his bare chest, and, illuminated by a flash of lightning overhead, his skin looked as luminescent as pearl. I hardly let myself believe it was him until I could see his eyes, green and sparkling and gazing right at me.

"How — where did you come from?" I shouted over the howling wind. I started toward him, too, getting sand in my flats. "Were you swimming?"

"I told you," he replied, a smile crossing his face. "You can always find me."

We stopped mere inches from each other.

"I wanted to see you," I said, although no explanation seemed necessary. "I was on the beach yesterday afternoon, but I couldn't find you, and —"

"Nighttime is usually better," Leo said. Lines of water ran down his high cheekbones, down his flat stomach. His hair looked like dark honey.

"I — I never do things like this," I told him, breathless.

I felt more cold drops strike my arms. "And it's starting to rain, and —"

"I wanted to see you, too," Leo cut in.

"Leo," I said. I didn't know what to say next, only that his name on my tongue felt right. Natural.

Then the clouds burst. Sheets of rain sluiced down, and thunder exploded, and suddenly, without warning, we were kissing.

Leo pulled me tight against him as our lips met and the wetness of the rain mingled with the wetness of his body. Somehow his skin felt as hot and flushed as mine did. I wrapped my arms around him, opening my mouth to his, running my fingers down the length of his spine. Leo dug his fingers into my hair, raking loose my ponytail, and I didn't care. I didn't care that I was getting drenched and that my bra was probably visible beneath my white T-shirt, because all that mattered was our kissing.

This was intense, I realized as we kissed and kissed in the pouring rain. This *defined* intense. My kiss with T.J. seemed faded, insignificant. Now I couldn't help but close my eyes as every thought in my head — every question — swam away.

I heard myself sigh when Leo pulled back. He pushed my sopping hair back off my face and grinned at me.

"We should really go somewhere dry," he told me, and encircled my waist with his strong arm. "You're trembling."

I was, but not because of the cold. Still, I nodded my assent and gave Leo my hand. He began leading me away from the boardwalk, toward the jagged black rocks, yet I didn't feel fear or trepidation.

"Careful," Leo said, squeezing my hand as he helped me over a big rock. The rain was as dense as a wall now. My feet slipped and slid, but I held fast to his hand, and when I reached the other side of the rock, I saw where we would shelter. There, in the sand, a collection of even larger rocks formed a grotto of sorts, complete with an overhang and craggy walls.

"How do you know about this?" I asked in awe as we wriggled through the small opening between two rocks. It was nearly pitch-black inside the grotto, and rain drummed down on the overhang. I couldn't believe we were suddenly safe from the elements.

"I grew up here," Leo replied. He led me to the driest patch of the sandy floor, then pulled me down to sit there beside him. "This is my world."

I nestled into the crook of his arm, leaning my head on his shoulder. Our hearts were pounding in equal rhythm, and we both laughed, giddy and cold. Leo lowered his head and gently nipped at my neck, which sent exquisite shivers through me.

As we sat there, cuddling close, my eyes slowly adjusted to

the darkness of our little cave. Gray mist swirled through the cracks in the rocks, and, in one shadowy corner, I could make out what looked, oddly enough, like a discarded T-shirt and a guy's zip-up hoodie. I blinked, nudging Leo.

"Do those belong to someone?" I whispered, as if fearful of waking whomever — or whatever — might have been slumbering in the grotto with us.

I felt the gentle rocking of Leo's laughter. "They're mine," he replied. "Sometimes I'll change in here before I go for a swim."

"Really?" I looked up into his face. Leaving one's belongings in a grotto seemed like essential beach behavior — so different from the protective way people guarded their things in New York. "Aren't you worried that someone might take —"

"Shh," Leo said, touching his finger to my bottom lip. "Do you hear that?" When I shook my head, he whispered, "The rain stopped."

"Already?" I asked. It did sound like the wind had died down and there was only the light pattering of drops above us.

"A summer storm," Leo said as he traced the curve of my mouth with his thumb. "Quick and powerful and then — over. It's what happens on Selkie."

I felt a twinge of disappointment. "I wasn't ready for it

to be over," I said, knowing I sounded like a child. I smiled ruefully.

"It'll rain again," Leo promised, his fingers making gentle, teasing patterns on my inner arm. We looked at each other for a long moment.

I leaned in to kiss him — I couldn't not — but then my belly rumbled. Loudly. I let out a mortified laugh, putting my hands on my stomach. My body never used to behave so willfully before.

"Hungry?" Leo asked, studying me with such fondness that I felt my embarrassment wane.

"Starved," I admitted. I realized I hadn't touched the blueberry cobbler at tea.

"Me, too," Leo said. "Should we get something to eat? We can . . . continue things later." A mischievous glint lit his eyes and I felt a rush of anticipation.

I nodded and Leo took my hands, lifting me to my feet. I watched him grab his rumpled T-shirt off the sandy ground and pull it over his head. The notion that I should contact Mom and tell her I wouldn't be home for dinner floated past me, but I didn't pursue it. I'd left my cell phone at The Mariner again, and suddenly I wanted to try on not being a good girl.

"Here, put this on," Leo said, handing me his red hoodie. I slipped my arms through the soft sleeves, thrilling at its warm, clean scent — Leo's scent. I pulled my wet hair out from under the hood and let it hang loose down my back. Then Leo and I squeezed through the rocks, abandoning our hideaway.

The beach was crisp and cool, and I took in deep lungfuls of the sweet, fresh air. The subdued ocean was lightly kissing the shore, and puddles filled the dents in the sand. The sky was a revelation — all gold and gray patches.

"It's beautiful, isn't it?" Leo said, and when I glanced at him, he was looking at me in a way that made my heart gallop.

"Very beautiful," I replied with a smile. I turned automatically toward the boardwalk and the lights of The Crabby Hook, but Leo tugged on my hand, indicating we should start in the opposite direction. Deeper into the fog.

"Hold on," I said, tugging back. "The restaurants are back there."

Leo glanced at the boardwalk, his expression dismissive. "You mean the summer restaurants. I want to take you someplace else."

Intrigue bloomed in me, but so did hesitation. I stood still, holding on to Leo's hand as his hopeful green eyes studied my face.

"Come, Miranda," Leo added. "Trust me."

Trust me. Could I? My pulse pounded. I stared at Leo, this boy I'd only just met.

"First, tell me exactly where we're going," I said, lifting my chin.

"Of course," Leo said. He tilted his head to one side, the corner of his mouth curving up. "We're going to the heart of Selkie Island."

"And where is that?" I asked, stepping closer to him.

Leo's dimples appeared in his cheeks as he smiled. "Fisherman's Village."

Nine

QUESTIONS

*B*eyond the mist, past the rocks, and up a flight of rickety wooden steps lay the ramshackle strip of pubs and shops known as Fisherman's Village. As Leo and I, our hands clasped, navigated the puddle-strewn cobblestones, I gazed around, eager to examine this slice of Leo's existence. An existence that felt a world away from the Selkie Island I'd been inhabiting.

Here, red and gold twinkle lights were twined around the oak trees, giving the area a festive vibe. None of the squat buildings were marked, and the seedy-looking alleyways called to mind pirates and smuggled treasure. I drew nearer to Leo, a little ill at ease. Almost against my will, I heard T.J.'s words in my head: *Not that a girl like you should go to Fisherman's Village.*

But I wasn't even sure what kind of girl I was anymore.

Leo, meanwhile, was in his element, introducing me to an elderly lady walking her puppy, and pointing out the local library. I began to identify bait and tackle shops, a supermarket, a post office, a bank. And I began to understand that this neighborhood was home to people who were not blown to the island by the summer winds.

By the time Leo led me to the door of a nameless rust-colored shack, I was feeling much more comfortable. The shack housed a smoky pub, where patrons were sharing waffle fries at pockmarked tables or sipping foamy beers at the bar. Most everyone was in beach gear or barefoot, and a TV blared on the wall. I smiled, thinking of how silly T.J. would look here in his button-down shirt.

"What's good?" I asked Leo as we slid into a booth and picked up our menus. My head felt hazy — maybe from hunger, or from what had happened on the beach. Or both.

"They have this great seaweed salad, kind of a local favorite," Leo said. "But I'd say it's an acquired taste." He grinned at me. His thick golden hair was starting to dry, and it fell carelessly across his forehead, begging to be swept aside. The dark green shade of his T-shirt made his eyes look even brighter.

There was something strange and wonderful about the ordinary act of sharing a meal with Leo, who was so extraordinary. The people sitting around us must have assumed we were on a date. But I felt as if Leo and I were beyond dating. We were in another category now, one that couldn't really be defined.

"How's the fried Georgia redfish with mashed potatoes?" I asked, scanning the menu. "Do you maybe want to split the crab cakes?" I was craving lusty, rich food.

"Believe it or not," Leo said, toying with the saltshaker, "I don't really eat fish or other seafood. I guess 'cause there's so much of it around all the time. . . ."

"That makes sense," I said, unzipping Leo's hoodie and shaking out my still-damp hair. Beneath the table, I slipped my feet out of my wet flats. "People get sick of what's familiar, right? In New York, the natives never gawk at the skyscrapers."

"You were gawking a little bit on the walk over here," Leo said, grinning at me. When I felt myself blush, he reached over and brushed a wet curl off my cheek. "But don't worry. It was adorable," he added, his voice full of affection.

I grinned back at Leo and felt an energy crackle in the air between us. Chemistry. Only it wasn't the kind of chemistry that could be found in a laboratory. It was, in a way, the opposite of science.

I gave a start when a waiter appeared at our booth, holding two glasses of water. With his tattoo sleeves, white beard, and white ponytail, he did bear a resemblance to the mariner in the painting, though I couldn't imagine the fictitious mariner smiling warmly.

"Leomaris!" the waiter said, pulling out his pad. "How are you?"

I paused with my glass of water halfway to my mouth. "Who?" I asked, glancing from Leo to the waiter.

Leo's ears turned red and he ducked his head. "That's my full name. Leomaris."

"Go on, tell her what it means," our waiter urged, clearly enjoying himself.

"King of the sea," Leo muttered, opening and closing his menu. His discomfort only deepened my desire to kiss him.

"I think that suits you perfectly," I said softly, meaning it. Leo glanced up at me, raising his eyebrows in a grateful way. My heart flipped over.

"Okay, okay, lovebirds, what will it be?" Our waiter chuckled.

After we'd ordered — crab cakes for me, the seaweed salad for Leo — our waiter asked Leo what his parents were up to.

"They're out on my dad's boat for the night," Leo replied, easing back in his seat and handing over his menu.

"Oh, are you worried something happened to them during the storm?" I asked, feeling my brow furrow. Leo and the waiter exchanged a glance I couldn't decipher, though I thought the waiter looked mildly amused.

"I think they're fine," Leo assured me, putting his hand on mine. "This is Miranda," he told our waiter. "She's here for the summer."

"I assumed as much," our waiter said to me, but his smile was genuine. "Should I put this all on your tab?" he asked Leo, who nodded.

I shifted in my seat, discomfort pricking me. I didn't want Leo paying for our dinner; I sensed it was more important for him to be saving his money than it was for me. But I also sensed that giving voice to that thought would wound Leo's pride.

As our waiter departed, Leo watched me fidget and he smiled wryly. "Miranda, it's cool," he said. "My family has a special deal with the pub. We're regulars."

"I can see why!" I exclaimed, perhaps a little too enthusiastically. "This place is great. All of Fisherman's Village is."

I took a sip of water, glancing at Leo over the rim of my glass. I wondered if my remark had sounded condescending, like something a summer person might say. In truth, I *was* enjoying Fisherman's Village; it had an air of friendliness that felt much more sincere than the politeness that reigned on the other side of the island.

"Besides," Leo added, as if I hadn't spoken. He was studying me in his perceptive way. "It makes me happy to treat you to something. Even if it's just crab cakes." He squeezed my hand, and warmth spread through me.

"Thank you," I murmured. Hoping to erase any offense, I leaned over the saltshaker and planted a quick kiss on his lips.

"All right," Leo said, squeezing my hand as our momentary tension receded. "I want to hear more about these skyscrapers."

As our food arrived and we devoured it, I told Leo the basics about my life in New York — my high-pressure high school, the subways, the frozen hot chocolate they served at the restaurant Serendipity — while leaving out certain details I'd decided not to dwell on. I told him about Isadora's passing, and how it had brought me and my mother to Selkie, while leaving out my mother's own ties to the island — namely, Mr. Illingworth.

Leo, wide-eyed as a little boy, was full of questions — Did I really live near the Bronx Zoo? Had I really deferred my internship at the Museum of Natural History? Did Manhattan feel like an island when you were on it? — that didn't allow me to ask any of my own.

But there was plenty of time for me to learn about Leo. As we stood to go, I thought excitedly of how much he and I could do together — visits to the marine center, barbecues, late-night swims, the Fourth of July. I had to be back in New York for my internship by the fifteenth, but maybe I could skip the internship altogether. It would probably take Mom until August to sell The Mariner, and she'd need me here.

Maybe I didn't have to go back to New York at all.

Outside, Fisherman's Village was thick with humidity and activity; people had emerged poststorm, and that particular buzz and spark of approaching night hung in the air. Leo waved to a group of rowdy, shirtless guys who were spilling out of a penny arcade. They whooped and waved back, a few of them blatantly looking me up and down. But at Leo's side, wearing his hoodie, I forgot to feel self-conscious.

When two dark-haired girls in bikini tops and jeans flip-flopped toward us, one of them sang, "He-ey, Leo!" while the other stared at me with naked curiosity. It hit me then that, among the Selkie locals, Leo must have been considered quite the catch. As Leo greeted the girls, I felt an uncharacteristic burst of possessiveness.

"So, Leomaris," I teased once the girls had passed, and he elbowed me lightly. "You're pretty popular, huh?"

"Nah," Leo laughed, lacing his fingers through mine — our touching was becoming automatic, essential. "Actually, I used to have a lot more friends than I do now."

"Me, too," I replied, and then I cleared my throat. "Why?" I asked, glancing at Leo to make sure he hadn't heard my initial response.

We started down one of the alleyways that led back to the water. The sounds of the village grew quiet behind us, and the twin scents of salt and fish rushed toward us.

"I got the job at the marine center," Leo replied, "and stopped bumming around on the beach so much. I changed." He glanced at me, his expression thoughtful. "You know, almost everyone in my life is a fisherman. My dad. My brothers. My friends' parents. I guess I decided to rebel."

Rebel. I stared ahead, toward the silvery surface of the ocean. I had never considered fighting, or even questioning, my genetic destiny: my surgeon parents, my brother the pre-med Ivy League student. My own inborn gift for science. My future — a future that surely included scalpels or test tubes — was charted and mapped.

Did it have to be?

"What's your rebellion plan?" I asked Leo as we reached the mouth of the alley.

He shrugged, the shadows in the alley slanting across his high cheekbones. "I have crazy dreams. I want to go to college, maybe in Savannah, maybe up north. As long as it's someplace on the water."

"That's not so crazy," I told him, squeezing his hand, wondering if we were both thinking that New York City was on the water.

Leo turned to look at me, and in the darkness, his expression was hard to read. "Miranda, for generations, it was basically impossible for people like my family to live anywhere other than Selkie Island."

Once again, I was aware of the gap between Leo and me — the differences in our backgrounds. Why did it have to matter?

"It's like in New York City," I said, hearing my voice go up a pitch. I felt foolish making the comparison, but I wasn't sure what else to say. "Most people who live there don't know how to drive, or even swim! They can only exist in New York, not anywhere else."

"That's . . . kind of how it is," Leo said slowly, smiling at me. "Do *you* know how to swim?"

"Me? I'm practically a fis —" I started to say. But then we emerged from the alleyway onto a spot that was familiar to me.

"The harbor!" I exclaimed. We were standing on the same dock I had stood on with Mom six days ago. Had it only been six days? I felt transformed from the Miranda I'd been then, the Miranda who hadn't met a boy named Leo.

Straight ahead of us was the wooden gateway to the island, its sign facing the still ocean; there were no incoming boats to view its cryptic warning. I squinted, half expecting to see the ferry sailing over with Sailor Hat standing at its prow.

"Uh-huh," Leo said as we strolled the length of the dock. "See those boats and trawlers?" He gestured to the small vessels that were tethered to the far end of the dock, bobbing at their moorings in the moonlight. "Some of them belong to the summer folk, and some belong to fishermen. Many mornings, you can spot the fishermen here, sitting on the dock with their poles in the water. Hence the name Fisherman's Village." He looked at me with a half smile, adding, "You took *Princess of the Deep* to Selkie, right?"

I nodded. "My mom was waiting for me right here," I recalled out loud. "Then we walked up that road," I added, pointing to the pebbly path Mom and I had climbed, "to get to our house. The Mariner." I realized then that Leo hadn't known where I was staying for the summer, though he must have guessed the neighborhood.

"An ironic shortcut," Leo said, his tone amused but slightly brittle. His bright green eyes turned solemn in the darkness. "The summer folk are closer to Fisherman's Village than most of them would want to be."

We were still holding hands, but my discomfort returned. I wanted to tell Leo that I didn't feel like I belonged among the summer folk, but I wasn't sure he would believe me. I suddenly ached to return to the grotto, where Leo and I had made our own little world, separate from the rest of Selkie Island.

"Where does *that* road lead?" I asked, changing the subject. I pointed to a dirt path we were approaching; while the pebbly path sloped up, this one curved down. A signpost stuck in it read MCCLOUD WAY.

I felt Leo relax beside me. "Funny you should ask," he replied, and cast me his brilliant smile. "It leads to my house." He paused, and added, "Would you like to see it?"

Leo's question hovered in the sultry evening air. I thought again of Mom, waiting for me back at The Mariner. I thought of how a good girl would — should — respond to Leo's invitation. Then I thought of Leo's kisses, his lips on my neck, of us having another quiet moment together.

It was already so late. I was already in so deep. Why not swim even deeper?

So I nodded and together we started down the path, both of us silent with anticipation. The question *What are you doing, Miranda?* tried to gain entry to my mind, but I wouldn't let it in.

The brick houses on the other end of the dirt path were all on stilts — because, Leo explained, of their proximity to the ocean and the threat of high tides. The beach did act as a front yard for the houses, with the tall sea grasses standing in for pruned bushes and the sea one giant, crashing pool.

Most of the houses had their lights blazing, but the house we stopped in front of was completely dark. With a jolt of nerves, I remembered Leo telling our waiter that his parents were out on a boat.

"My humble abode," Leo declared with a mock bow, but he seemed nervous, too.

I studied the red-painted front door with its gold knocker. The drainpipes that ran down the house's length ended in miniature dolphins, their mouths open to release the rainwater.

"Hey, those are cool oceanic markings," I said, then paused. *Oceanic markings* — those weren't my words. I had borrowed that phrase from somewhere else. But where?

"Check out those," Leo said, and pointed to the small carved turtles that jutted from the roof of the house like gargoyles. "Legend has it that they're good luck."

As soon as Leo said *legend*, I realized where I'd read the phrase *oceanic markings*: in *A Primer on the Legend and Lore of Selkie Island*, just that afternoon. In the section about Selkie merfolk. I smiled, ready to ask Leo if he'd grown up hearing tales about these merfolk, who supposedly — what else had the book said? — had homes close to the ocean, and liked the colors red and gold —

I froze. Red and gold. Like the colors on Leo's front door. Leo's front door, which was close to the ocean. The ocean, from which Leo had emerged earlier, as if it were perfectly normal to go swimming in a tempest. Without thinking, I glanced down at Leo's bronzed, muscular legs as if expecting to see — what?

A tail?

Oh, my God. It was official. I was going crazy.

"What's wrong?" Leo asked. He released my hand and stepped around me so that we were face-to-face. "Miranda? You're all pale."

I took a deep breath, trying to steady myself. But I was thinking about the fact that Leo didn't eat seafood, that he'd devoured that seaweed salad with gusto. I wracked my brain, trying to recall what Llewellyn Thorpe had imparted about the Selkie merfolk. I remembered something about them being nocturnal — and hadn't Leo said I'd find him more easily at night? My thoughts were adding up in a twisted kind of logic.

Leo cupped my face in his hands, staring at me. "You sure you're okay? Your cheeks are hot. Do you feel sick?"

Something *was* wrong with me. My face felt flushed. Perhaps staying out in the rain had given me a fever. Patients with high fevers sometimes had hallucinations.

"It's nothing," I finally said, and as soon as I heard my own voice, I realized how silly I was being. It was late, and I was tired. That was all. "I just had this random thought," I added, laughing a little. I wanted to tell Leo that I'd imagined him as a merman so he could laugh with me, too. But the mere word was too absurd to even say out loud. *Merman.*

"Come inside," Leo said, drawing my face closer to his. "I'll get you a drink and you can lie down."

I hesitated. There were butterflies in my stomach, as there'd been the afternoon I'd met Leo for our sea creature walk. Were these symptoms stemming from my feelings for Leo, or was it my body's way of alerting me to something? Some sort of . . . danger?

What had Sailor Hat said to me on the ferry? *Be careful of whom you meet, in and out of the water.*

When I didn't respond to his request, Leo tilted his head and gently kissed the corner of my mouth, then slid his lips over onto mine.

As before, the intensity of his kiss made my body unfurl like a petal, and I began kissing him back. But then Leo thrust one hand into my hair — loose, curly, untamed by the rain — and let the other slide down to my waist, his fingers stroking the skin between my T-shirt and capri pants.

Come inside. Lie down.

I wasn't ready for this. Was I?

Suddenly, all the questions I'd tried to block out earlier flooded my mind. Who *was* this boy I was kissing? What were his intentions? Why was I willing to go into his empty house at night? And what had happened to me, Miranda Merchant, to make me act with such abandon?

"Stop," I spoke against Leo's insistent lips. Abruptly, I broke off our kiss and took a step back. "I can't," I said. "We have to stop. I don't even *know* you."

Leo dropped his hands. His breath was coming fast, and he stared at me, his full lips parted. "Why are you freaking out?" he asked, reaching for me. I stepped back again; it must have looked as if we were performing a tense tango.

"I think we're — we're moving too fast," I replied. I felt as if I'd been underwater all evening, in a dreamworld, and I'd finally broken the surface and tasted fresh air.

"Miranda, I'm sorry, but I don't understand," Leo said, his voice hoarse and his eyes wide. "I thought you felt our connection, too. When we were on the beach earlier — and during our sea creature walk —"

"Which you totally set up," I cut in, feeling a surge of indignation. I heard a crack of thunder overhead. "Look, I found out that there was no official walk that day. Why weren't you honest with me?" I reached into the pocket of my capris and took out my extra hair band. I yanked my hair up and made a tight ponytail.

"Okay," Leo said sheepishly. He ducked his head and scratched the back of his neck. "I invented the walk so I'd have an excuse to see you again. But so what?" he added, glancing at me with a crooked smile. "You seemed shy when we spoke at the center, and I thought that would be a good way to ask you out."

"Then you admit you lied?" I asked. I was remembering the tour in the center, how Leo had glanced at the neuron on my Bronx Science T-shirt. Or had he been checking out my chest?

I studied Leo; under the night sky, he seemed to be shape-shifting into someone — something — else. A stranger. A hormone-addled local guy who thought he could take advantage of the lonely tourist girl. I thought of T.J., who would never presume to bring a girl back to his house. T.J.'s family knew my family; he wasn't a stranger at all.

"I just wanted us to get to know each other better," Leo said, frustration etched into his beautiful face. "If you'd come inside now, we could —"

"Who do you take me for?" I snapped, my city street-smarts kicking in at last. I thought of Leo's dark-haired admirers in bikini tops. "Maybe the other girls on this island all fall for that *know each other better* line," I added, "but I'm not that naïve."

Leo pushed a hand through his hair. "What other girls?" he asked, his voice full of confusion. "You know I'm not like that."

"Actually, I don't." I stared him down and, to my horror, felt my throat tighten. *No.* I could not, would not, cry. "I have absolutely no evidence," I continued, struggling to keep my voice even, "that you're any less of a creep than the majority of the male species." Speaking in scientific terms was a trick that often kept my emotions in check.

Leo knit his brows together. "You think I'm a creep?"

My chest constricted. A little while ago, I'd been making romantic plans for the two of us. How had everything turned so sour?

"Maybe this was a mistake," I said. "I shouldn't have come with you to Fisherman's Village."

Leo's expression changed. His lips came together in a line, and a muscle in his cheek jumped as understanding darkened his eyes. "A mistake," he echoed dully.

I couldn't look at him anymore. I lowered my head, studying my black flats on the hard-packed sand.

"Say no more. I get it." He inhaled sharply. "Why don't you take that shortcut back to your house, and I'll go back to mine." He didn't pose this as a question.

When I looked up, Leo was walking away from me, up the sagging porch steps. He paused before turning the knob on his red door and turned to look at me.

"I thought you were different," he said quietly.

"I am," I replied, starting to tremble.

"So am I," Leo replied, his endearing half smile returning for a second before he opened the door and let it shut behind him.

Just as Leo had predicted, it began to rain again. The drops fell slowly, stinging my cheeks and my shins. I realized I was still wearing Leo's hoodie, but my pride wouldn't allow me to follow him and return it. Instead, I pulled the hood tight over my head and turned away from his house.

Summer-induced stupidity. That was the diagnosis, I decided as I made my way up the dirt path in the pouring rain. When people went on vacation, they shed their home skins, thought they could become a new person. Leo had been a fluke, an aberration. But I had caught myself in time. There'd be no need for the two of us to meet again.

Now all I had to do was put him, our kisses, and our laughter completely out of my head. And if there was anything I was good at, besides science, it was making certain thoughts go away.

Ten

SECRETS

The Mariner stood out pale and grand against the darkness — a port in the literal storm. Hurrying through the rain, soaked to the bone, I had but two humble prayers: that the front door would be unlocked, and that Mom would either be on the phone or asleep, allowing me to sneak upstairs.

I climbed the porch steps, and as the rain battered against the life ring wreath, I pushed at the door. It gave easily under my hand, and I felt a rush of relief.

Unfortunately, Mom was standing in the middle of the entrance hall.

"Where were you?" she asked, her eyes flinty.

She hadn't changed out of her pretty pink dress, which contrasted with her furious countenance. Her hair was damp and she wore muddy flip-flops; she must have gone out to look for me. And the house smelled of burnt rice; she must have made dinner for us. Guilt flooded me.

I removed my soggy hood, listening to the rainwater drip off my body and onto the floor. I couldn't begin to imagine what kind of a wreck I looked like.

"With CeeCee." The lie leapt into my mouth.

Mom raised her eyebrows. "Really? That's funny. I just spoke to Delilah, and she told me that CeeCee had a young gentleman by the name of Bobby visiting them tonight. Somehow she failed to mention that you were there, too."

Oh, I thought, swallowing. *This is what getting in trouble feels like.*

"And don't try telling me you were with T.J.," Mom added, and I flinched automatically at his name; he'd been the last person on my mind tonight. "I called his father as well."

I'm sure you did, I thought, scowling.

"I was walking on the beach," I replied at last, speaking quickly and studying the staircase behind Mom's shoulder. "It started to rain, so I ended up in Fisherman's Village." I wondered, my heart thudding, if there was a hickey on my neck, or some other sign on me that would reveal the truth.

"Alone?" Mom pressed, narrowing her eyes at me.

When Wade was in high school and I was in middle school, he'd sworn to me that Mom was psychic; she'd always seemed to know with whom he was out breaking his curfew. I'd dismissed his theory then, but now the notion that our mother was a mind reader didn't seem too far-fetched.

"Yeah, alone," I lied again. I was becoming quite adept at it.

"Where did you get that sweatshirt?" Mom asked, lifting her chin.

Right.

My gut clenched.

"I bought it," I replied. Was this a new talent?

Mom sighed and began to pace the narrow hallway. "I know, I know," she said, shaking her head. She seemed to be speaking to herself. "It's natural for every kid to go through a rebellious phase. Your brother's seemed to last a lifetime. But somehow I always thought you'd bypass yours."

"I'm not rebelling!" I cried, forcing myself not to recall my conversation with Leo. I unzipped his hoodie and flung it onto the claw-footed chair in the corner.

"No?" Mom spun around to face me. "Then what would you call leaving for no reason — interrupting our discussion, no less — and disappearing for the next two hours without a peep?"

"I didn't have my cell phone," I said, twisting my wet hands behind my back.

Mom stopped pacing and massaged her temples. "Miranda, I asked you to come to Selkie Island so you could help me. I thought you would be the one person who wouldn't unduly stress me out. And now you're causing me the biggest stress of all!" Her voice echoed through the house.

"Well, I guess you have Delilah to confide in now," I snapped, surprised by the hurt I felt at Mom's words. "Considering you guys are so buddy-buddy and all." I pictured them in their matching head wraps on the beach. "I thought she annoyed you."

"Pardon me?" Mom snapped, looking taken aback. "It is not your place to comment or judge if I choose to reconnect with old friends."

"Like Mr. Illingworth?" I shot back.

Mom leveled me with her gaze, her expression oddly triumphant. "That's what this is about, isn't it? Mr. Illingworth and T.J.'s visit?"

"No. Whatever." I was drained. All I wanted to do was draw myself a hot bath and carry on with the business of forgetting Leo. "You said yourself that your and Mr. Illingworth's dating wasn't a big deal. Why do we need to dissect it?" *Can't you ever not be a surgeon?* I added silently.

Mom took a big breath and pressed her palms together. Her face had gone splotchy. "Miranda, there's something you should know," she said.

Fear poked at me. "Mom . . ." I began.

"Mr. Illingworth and I didn't just date," Mom said, looking

straight at me as her face grew increasingly splotchy. "When I was eighteen, we were engaged to be married."

I felt the wind knocked out of me. I stared at my mother, overcome with confusion and shock. The rainwater drip-dripped off of me.

"That's — kind of a big deal?" I managed to say, only it came out as a question.

"Yes," Mom answered, looking at her flip-flops. "It was, at the time."

"Does T.J. know? Does CeeCee?" I asked, my mind racing. "Does Dad? Does Wade?" It was fairly obvious, I realized, that Delilah did.

"I don't believe that T.J. or CeeCee know. Wade definitely does not," Mom replied softly. "Your father does, of course." Her tone was matter-of-fact.

I shook my head. "But my whole life, you never once mentioned . . ." I trailed off.

Mom stepped forward, her hands clasped together so tightly that her knuckles were white. "It never seemed practical to tell you," she said. "I never imagined you and I would end up on Selkie together, or that I'd see Teddy again. I thought that part of my life was dead and buried, Miranda."

The wind lashed against the windows and made the lace curtains dance. The past seemed to swirl around us like a ghost.

Eighteen. Mom had been eighteen and engaged. I'd be that age in two years. I tried to picture myself in a wedding gown, a diamond ring sparkling on my finger. And who would I be marrying? Greg? T.J.? Leo? I felt like laughing and crying all at once.

"Why didn't you?" I finally asked my mother. "Why didn't you marry him?" It was jarring to think that, had Mom done so, I — the specific combination of my parents' genes — would never have existed. A chill went through me.

Mom stepped up to me and put her hands on my arms, but I jerked away. "You're going to catch a cold," she said. "You should take a hot shower. We'll talk about this another time. Doctor's orders," she added with a small smile.

"I don't want to talk about it," I snapped. It was my last lie of the night. And with that, I brushed past Mom and started for the stairs, leaving small puddles in my wake.

"Miranda!" Mom barked, her voice so stern that I turned around. "I appreciate that this information was difficult to hear, but I expect you to behave yourself. No more traipsing off to Fisherman's Village. Do I make myself clear?"

"Don't worry," I said, hearing the bitterness in my tone. "I won't be setting foot in Fisherman's Village again." I fought down a tug of sadness. "But you can't keep me in here like a prisoner," I added defiantly.

Mom let out a short laugh. "You," she pronounced, folding

her arms across her chest, "are as stubborn as your grandmother."

The monster, I thought. Then I turned and pounded up the stairs. I flew into the guest room and slammed the door as hard as I could — the first time I'd done so in all my sixteen years.

<hr>

For the next two days, the weather accomplished what I'd said Mom could not. Chilly rain streaked the windows of The Mariner, trapping me inside.

Every time I glanced out at the downpour, I thought of the dolphin drainpipes on Leo's house and felt a sharp sensation in my chest. So far, my forget-about-him plan was not going too well. At night, I kept having vivid, salt-scented dreams about our grotto, only the grotto was underwater and Leo and I lived there, kissing under clouds of seaweed. Waking up became a reprieve from the gnawing sense of longing.

Though Mom and I were marooned together in the house, we stayed out of each other's way. While Mom set up downstairs, organizing the kitchen and making phone calls, I took charge of the top floor, going through the room that had once been Uncle Jim's and was now stuffed with old bicycles, rocking chairs, and more portraits of Isadora — though none as extravagant as the one hanging in the study.

At one point, Wade called my cell from L.A. "Just doing my brotherly duty and saying hi," he'd chuckled before putting Dad on the phone as well. They both sounded so California breezy, so far removed from the haunted quiet of The Mariner, that talking to them only made me more depressed. And it wasn't like I was going to tell either of them about Leo, T.J., or Mom's new quasi-boyfriend.

On the second day, I ensconced myself in Isadora's walk-in closet; back when we were still on speaking terms, Mom had mentioned that we needed to pack Isadora's clothes and ship them to a consignment shop in Savannah. I was grateful to the task for — somewhat — taking my mind off Leo and everything else. And were I a fashion lover like CeeCee, I would have been in heaven. Exquisitely crafted sundresses in different jewel tones swung from the hangers, beside shelves of white-buckled high heels, patent leather mules, straw hats with fat sashes, and tiny purses encrusted with crystals.

As I sat on the dusty closet floor, methodically wrapping each item in tissue paper, I did feel a twinge of sadness; it didn't seem right to send away these gorgeous artifacts. Though what would Mom and I do with the clothes? Wear them?

I stood to stretch my sore back. There was one rod of clothes I hadn't gone through yet, and I slid my fingers down a paisley-patterned skirt. Isadora would have looked stylish in it, I thought. A gorgeous, high-necked black lace dress with short sleeves and a short skirt caught my eye; the tag inside the collar indicated it might fit me, and I smiled, casting off the *what if* that popped into my head.

Then I noticed, wedged into the corner directly behind the dress, a big black steamer trunk. It was battered, and its giant golden clasp was in need of polishing. I figured there were more clothes inside, so I pushed away the dresses to kneel in front of it and investigate. I attempted to pry the lid open, but it wouldn't budge. I tugged on the gold-colored padlock, hoping it might give, but the trunk was locked tight.

Determination rose in me as I sat back on my heels, my skin prickling with warmth. I felt I was on the verge of a great discovery, like Alexander Fleming must have felt before he stumbled upon penicillin.

I knocked on the black lid, eliciting a hollow echo. Would Isadora have bothered to lock the trunk if it simply held dresses? Unless Isadora had nothing to do with the trunk. Unless it had been left in the house by an old pirate. I didn't want my imagination to go too far, but it seemed half plausible that there might be buried treasure inside.

Or maybe that was just Llewellyn Thorpe's influence.

Downstairs, I heard the front door opening and Mom greeting someone. Probably the repairmen coming to try and fix something, or Delilah coming over for lunch, as she had yesterday.

A key, I reasoned, patting the floor around the trunk. *Every lock has a key.* Though hiding the key right by the trunk might have been too obvious a maneuver.

"Miranda, where are you?"

I heard Mom's footsteps on the stairs, and I got to my feet, my pulse racing. I wasn't sure if Mom knew about the trunk, but somehow, I felt that I should keep it as my secret in the house for the time being — not unlike Llewellyn Thorpe's book.

I hurriedly repositioned the dresses along the rod so that they covered the trunk, and called to Mom that I was in the closet.

Mom opened the door and surveyed the dresses wrapped in their tissue-paper embraces. "You're making nice progress," she said coolly.

I nodded. I couldn't look at her without thinking of Mr. Illingworth, down on one knee. And I couldn't stop wondering if, this time, she'd accept a proposal from him. After Monday night, something between my mother and me seemed irreparable, changed.

"Come downstairs," she added, turning on her heel to go. "You have a visitor."

My heart jumped. Had Leo come to plead forgiveness? Or was T.J. dropping by, perhaps to ask me what I knew of our parents' relationship? Though Mom might have been more cheery if T.J. were here.

I wasn't sure which boy I wanted to see less — or more.

With a regretful glance down at my black tank top, gray sweat shorts, and Converse, I stepped out of the closet and followed Mom downstairs. My pulse ticked faster with each step as I envisioned Leo waiting in the foyer, his green eyes on me.

"Where have you been hiding, lady?" CeeCee cried as I entered the foyer. She was closing a white bubble umbrella and wearing a denim jacket over a pink sundress, and polka-dot Wellingtons.

"I wasn't hiding," I replied defensively, my pulse returning to its normal rate. I thought of the trunk upstairs — had it been Isadora's hiding place? And for what?

Mom waved to CeeCee and headed into the study. Impulsively, I hoped that she wouldn't pack up Llewellyn Thorpe's book. Somehow I felt I still needed it around.

CeeCee plunked her umbrella into the umbrella stand, shaking out her red waves. Then she gave me a gossip-hungry grin. "Your mother called my house Monday night looking for you!" she whispered.

I glanced at Leo's red hoodie on the claw-footed chair. I wondered how CeeCee would react if I told her that I'd been hanging out in Fisherman's Village with the townie from the marine center.

"I went for a walk and forgot my cell phone," I said nonchalantly.

"*Right,*" CeeCee said with a suggestive wink. I gulped, wondering if someone had spotted Leo and me. "Anyway," she continued with a flick of her wrist; her charm bracelet jangled. "I'm heading to the boardwalk to meet Bobby for lunch, but I thought I'd stop in and see what your plans were for tomorrow."

"Tomorrow?" I asked blankly. My mind was so full of Leo and Mom and Mr. Illingworth that I could barely make room for what day *today* was. *Wednesday,* I reminded myself. The marine center was open. So Leo was there right now. If I wanted to, I could walk to the boardwalk with CeeCee and —

No. Cease and desist.

CeeCee frowned, clearly not used to being the *less* forgetful one. "Hello? The Fourth of July?" she said. "Our nation's birthday? Ring a bell?"

"Of course," I said, feeling my face color. The Fourth, with its sparklers and picnics and summertime sense of freedom, was one of my favorite holidays.

"Every summer the island puts on an incredible fireworks show that everyone watches from the beach," CeeCee explained. "But this year Bobby said we could take out his family's boat and watch from the water! Virginia and Jacqueline and all the *guys* will be there." She gave me a meaningful look, then took a step closer to me, her rubber boots squeaking on the floor. "I know," she whispered.

My stomach twisted into a pretzel knot and my palms went cold. "Know what?"

"That you and T.J. kissed!" CeeCee's eyes gleamed. "T.J. told Bobby, and Bobby told me. You were with him Monday night, right?"

Relief and embarrassment washed over me at once. "I wasn't with T.J.," I insisted. "We're not . . . dating or anything, I mean, it was just one kiss," I fumbled, blushing deeper. "And why did he tell Bobby?" That behavior didn't strike me as particularly gentlemanly.

"Because he's into you!" CeeCee exclaimed. "He wants the world to know!"

I looked down at the compass on the floor, listening to the rain pound on the roof and weighing CeeCee's words. Maybe our less-than-sizzling kiss *had* meant a lot to T.J. And maybe he — unlike a certain local boy — saw me as more than a summer fling. It was, in some ways, as simple as a mathematical proof; when it came to the arithmetic of boys, T.J. equaled the better choice.

"Speaking of kissing," CeeCee was saying, squeezing my arm. "After dinner with my parents on Monday night, Bobby and I went up to my room and did a *lot* of it." She giggled. "And I'll have you know, Ms. Skeptic, that he is a very gifted kisser, indeed. You know those kind of make-out sessions that make you melt?"

I felt hot all over as I nodded. *Do not think of Leo,* I commanded myself.

"Was it like that with T.J.?" CeeCee pressed, giving me a sly glance.

Before I could respond truthfully — with a *no* — it hit me. That was the key! If I *did* give T.J. a chance, if I focused my attentions on him, then Leo would really recede in my thoughts. Maybe joining the heirs for the Fourth was just what I needed. And maybe I'd even talk to T.J. about our parents' history, and see what insights — if any — he might have into the weirdness.

I told CeeCee to count me in for the fireworks, and she gave me an excited kiss on the cheek before grabbing her umbrella out of the stand.

"We're meeting at the docks after sunset," she said as she opened the door. A blast of cool air swept inside. "But you're welcome to come to my house beforehand to borrow some lipstick or an outfit — if you want," she amended cautiously, raising her eyebrows at me before she scampered out into the rain.

I shut the door, considering CeeCee's offer. I picked a piece of lint off my wrinkled tank top. It was inarguable that I could use some help in the clothes department. I thought of Isadora's closet and felt a shiver down my back. Her dresses. The trunk. My heartbeat kicking up, I was starting for the stairs when I heard Mom's cell phone trill in the study.

I paused, holding my breath and wishing I hadn't been reduced to eavesdropping on my mother. It could have been Aunt Coral or Uncle Jim, but I was fairly certain that Mr. Illingworth was calling.

"Good afternoon, Mr. Phelps," I heard Mom drawl, her Southern accent dropping in for a visit. "I'm so glad you decided not to come over in this rain."

Who was Mr. Phelps? Another fiancé? I bit my lip.

"Thank you for mailing me that paperwork," Mom was saying. "I've been meaning to discuss the market value of the house with you. The interested buyer . . ."

Right. I relaxed, feeling foolish. Mr. Phelps was the lawyer who'd been handling the sale of The Mariner; Mom had mentioned his name over dinner my first night here.

"Yes," Mom said. "I've been giving a lot of thought to . . ." She lowered her voice, and as much as I strained, I could no longer make out her words.

The very air in The Mariner seemed thick with long-buried

secrets. Suddenly, I was more driven than before to find the key to Isadora's trunk, to at least unlock whatever mystery lay there.

So, leaving my mother to whisper in the study, I went upstairs to begin my quest.

Eleven

MIRRORS

There was no key.

That was the conclusion I reached the next afternoon — the Fourth of July — as I emerged from my bath. I let out a resigned sigh and wrapped myself in a towel.

Yesterday, avoiding only the rooms Mom occupied, I'd explored every nook and cranny of The Mariner, from the shelves in Isadora's closet to the cabinets in the bathroom, in hopes of catching a glint of rusted gold. But I'd come up empty.

On the bright side, I'd dreamed of keys and trunks instead of grottoes and kisses. Now all I had to do was enjoy my time with T.J. tonight, and the constant desire to see Leo again would disappear entirely.

I hoped.

Padding into my room, I heard early fireworks exploding

over Glaucus Way, followed by the cheers of impatient children. The anticipation I always felt on the Fourth swelled up in me as I walked over to the dresser.

That morning, Mom and I had taken a terse, silent walk to the gourmet market and found the town dripping in red, white, and blue. The scents of grilling meat and mesquite competed with the salt water and flowers, and the sunny skies felt like a holiday gift. It was hard to stay angry on such a day; on the way back to The Mariner, laden down with groceries, both Mom and I were more relaxed. Mom had even made a joke about the number of Confederate flags that hung alongside American ones. Still, things between us felt awkward, and there was no talk of T.J. or his father.

I pulled open each of the dresser drawers and stared dejectedly at my clothes. The hole-y skirt I'd worn to the Heirs party was out of the question, and nothing else I owned would probably be dressy enough for Bobby's boat.

My gaze strayed down to my bare feet, and then I quickly glanced up at the mirror above the dresser. My hair was in a towel turban, which made my dark eyes look big, and my skin was flushed from the heat of the bath. I remembered how Leo had looked at me after the storm. I wished I could see myself as he had, but then I reminded myself that he'd probably been faking his admiration to get me back to his house.

I peered closer at my reflection. My eyelashes were too

short, my brows too heavy, my lips too pale a pink. I recalled T.J.'s comment about The Mariner needing sprucing up, and felt a sudden surge of resolve.

If I was going to do this, I was going to do it right.

"Mom?" I called five minutes later, trotting down the stairs in jeans and a button-down shirt, my hair up in its usual pony-tail. "How do I get to CeeCee's house?"

Mom, at rest for once, was out on the back porch, reading the Tuesday Science Times section of the *New York Times*; she'd redirected our subscription to The Mariner for the month. I was grateful for that and had read an article about in vitro fertilization over breakfast. I'd been starved for science.

Mom looked up at me, pushing her sunglasses onto the top of her head. "Why the sudden urge to see Ms. Cooper?" she asked, a smile on her lips.

I told Mom about my plans with the young heirs — excising T.J.'s name, although it was certainly implied — and her face lit up. She told me that she, too, would be watching the fire-works, only from the beach with Delilah and "some friends." The unspoken implication on her end also seemed to include an Illingworth, but I was thankful that she didn't mention him by name.

Mom told me the directions to the Coopers' house and then stood up. "Hang on," she said, reaching into the pocket of her loose linen pants. "I have something for you."

And she withdrew a golden key.

My heart stopped. How on earth —

"I made you an extra one," Mom said, giving me a contrite smile. "I figured you might be out late tonight, so . . ."

I resumed normal breathing. *Okay.* It was the key to the front door, not to the trunk. And it was Mom's way of showing that my unofficial grounding was over, for now. So I thanked her, took the key, and was on my way.

The Coopers' home was a short walk from The Mariner, and though the afternoon was steamy, I'd barely broken a sweat by the time I reached Poseidon Street. The house was a smaller, better-groomed version of The Mariner, with a neatly trimmed lawn, modern-looking floor-to-ceiling windows, and a pool glimmering in the backyard. I rang the doorbell, a little worried about stopping by unannounced. Mom had assured me that people did that all the time on Selkie, but I felt I should have called CeeCee first. I was prepared to apologize to Delilah or CeeCee's dad as soon as they answered the door.

However, the door was opened by a diminutive woman in a maid's uniform who introduced herself as Althea. I was startled; I'd thought that housekeepers or butlers only answered doors in, like, nineteenth-century manors.

When I explained that I was there to visit CeeCee, Althea led me through the pastel living room. Delilah was reclining on the sofa with cucumber slices over her eyes, and when I passed by, she lifted one slice and said that she was looking forward to seeing my mother that evening. CeeCee's dad was glued to a golf game on the plasma television and looking even more walruslike than I'd remembered.

I followed Althea upstairs to CeeCee's bedroom door, which was plastered with snapshots from what had to have been last summer: CeeCee, Virginia, Jacqueline, T.J., Bobby, Macon, Rick, and the others, all equally suntanned and photogenic, all laughing and sprawled across beach towels. The sight of those photos made me wonder if I should have met CeeCee on the docks later — or better yet, spent the Fourth at The Mariner.

But then CeeCee pulled the door open — and shrieked.

"I can't believe you came!" she cried. She was clad in nothing but a beige bra and rose-trimmed panties but seemed utterly unabashed. She took my wrist and drew me into her room, which was decorated in shades of purple and smelled of her flowery perfume. After the past couple days alone in The Mariner, there was something immediately comforting about entering this bubble of femininity.

Virginia and Jacqueline, wearing colorful sundresses and licking lemon Popsicles, were lounging on what I guessed was a queen-sized bed — it was difficult to tell because it was covered in clothes. More clothes were strewn across the floor, and CeeCee's vanity was hidden beneath mountains of beauty products. An iHome blasting pop music rested precariously on a stack of pink and green paperback novels. I thought of my well-organized, orderly bedroom back in Riverdale — "freakishly neat" Linda had called it. CeeCee was on the opposite end of the freak spectrum.

"Althea, would you bring up some more Popsicles?" CeeCee demanded before shutting the door in Althea's face. I cringed, and CeeCee glanced at me, smiling. "We're so lucky that she comes out with us every summer," she remarked.

"What are you *doing* here, Miranda?" Virginia called from the bed. I turned around and saw that she looked less primped than usual; her mascara was smudged around her eyes, her turquoise halter dress was a little rumpled, and her expression was stormy.

"Don't listen to her," Jacqueline said, swatting Virginia's shoulder with her Popsicle. "She's in a *mood* because she had a fight with Rick."

"She's mullygrubbing, as my grandma might say," CeeCee giggled, walking over to her vanity. "Feeling sorry for herself."

"I didn't have a fight with Rick," Virginia countered while I struggled not to think of my fight with Leo. "He was hooking up with trampy Kay McAndrews, so we're over. The truth is, I could do much better than him. I'm out of his league."

"Well, your family has more money than his, if that's what

you mean." CeeCee laughed, and then turned to me. "Okay, wait," she said. "Why *did* you decide to come, Miranda?" She raised her eyebrows hopefully at me, as she had yesterday.

I shrugged off any lingering doubts. "CeeCee, I want you to . . ." *Make me over* sounded too definitive. Besides, I didn't believe that a person could truly be made over, metamorphosed. That kind of change only happened in nature — a pupa turning into a luna moth, a chameleon browning against a tree. "Lend me some clothes," I finished.

"I thought you'd never ask." CeeCee sighed, beaming, and Jacqueline bounced off the bed, offering to help. Virginia, though, just bit off a huge chunk of Popsicle and opened one of the magazines that was scattered across the bed.

Murmuring and clucking like mother hens, CeeCee and Jacqueline began plucking summer dresses from the floor and holding them up against me. I stood still, feeling like a lab rat.

Before leaving The Mariner, I'd considered bringing along some of Isadora's dresses, then decided that would seem sort of spooky. But as pretty as CeeCee's dresses were, none of them held the retro magic of Isadora's. I liked Isadora's clothes for the same reason I liked to shop in vintage stores: Each item had a history.

By the time Althea returned with more Popsicles, CeeCee

finally decreed a silky lavender dress with wide straps to be "the one." I didn't relish the prospect of stripping down in front of the three girls, but I managed to execute my locker-room change, pulling the dress over my head while quickly unbuttoning my shirt and wriggling out of my jeans. Once the dress was on, I saw that the price tag was still attached, and I heard myself swallow at the three boldfaced digits.

"Listen, guys," I said, fidgeting as CeeCee zipped me up and Jacqueline brought over a selection of shoes. "Let's not go overboard, okay? I still want to look like myself." I held up my hand to refuse the silver thong sandals Jacqueline held out to me; I'd worn my black flats, knowing they wouldn't be as offensive to the girls as my Converse.

"Oh, come on, Miranda," CeeCee cooed, undoing my ponytail and steering me over to the edge of the bed in one swift motion. "Live a little."

I sat down and reached out for my hair band, but CeeCee gave it to Jacqueline, who tucked it into the pocket of her orange dress.

"It's *healthy* to change up your look," Jacqueline chimed in, passing CeeCee a tall can of styling mousse.

"Exactly," CeeCee said as she pumped a dollop of mousse into her hand. Automatically, I recoiled, but CeeCee pulled me forward. "You can pretend to be someone else for a night," she added, "as if you're at a masquerade or" — her eyes brightened with inspiration — "you've had a charm put on you, like Cinderella or Ariel!"

"Who's Ariel?" I asked, forgetting to protest as CeeCee worked the mousse into my hair and Jacqueline approached me with a tube of mascara.

"Would y'all keep it down?" Virginia huffed beside me. She noisily turned the page of the magazine.

"Hello, the Little Mermaid?" CeeCee cried, rolling her eyes and fluffing my hair.

"Honestly, what were you doing between the ages of five and twelve if not watching old Disney movies?" Jacqueline asked, rolling the mascara wand over my lashes. She didn't pose the question cruelly; she truly seemed bewildered.

"Science experiments," I muttered with a shrug.

I heard Virginia snort.

"You're so weird," CeeCee said fondly, going back to her vanity to retrieve a pot of lip gloss.

Mermaid, I thought. I felt a funny little pang.

"Hey," I said, having trouble talking as CeeCee dabbed gloss on my lips, "can I ask you guys something totally insane?"

"What's up?" Jacqueline asked, holding a powder puff over my cheekbone.

I began picking at my nails — my manicure was starting to chip, anyway — but CeeCee moved my hand away.

"Do any of you know," I began, trying for nonchalance, "about something called *A Primer on the Legend and Lore of Selkie Island*?"

"No," CeeCee and Jacqueline replied at the same time, while Virginia said, "Of course." I whipped around to look at her on the bed, and CeeCee cursed over my smudged lip gloss.

"It's this book some dude wrote in the early nineteen hundreds," Virginia drawled, stretching across the bed. "It was supposedly all controversial, because he wrote it like an anthropological study, but really it was just all these superstitions."

I blinked at Virginia, realizing it was one of the first times I'd heard her speak of something not pertaining to boys.

"Oh, wait," CeeCee said, turning my chin back to her. "This sounds familiar. There's, like, a pirate ghost who haunts the island?"

Jacqueline laughed, smudging blue shadow in the gap above my eyelids. "Is that why there's that monsters sign that hangs over the harbor?"

"I think there's some stuff about a pirate who married a mermaid, and how mermaids live in the water off Siren Beach." Virginia yawned. "And maybe fish with wings or whatever. Mama used to tell me those stories when I was little."

I closed my eyes so Jacqueline could rub in the eye shadow. Did *my* mother tell me stories when I was growing up? If she'd tried to, I was sure I'd either stopped her or tuned her out.

"So the stories aren't true, right?" I asked, hoping I still sounded casual, and not as if I'd ever entertained the idea.

"Oh, please." I heard Virginia scoot off the bed and watched as she went to turn up the volume on CeeCee's iHome. "Everyone knows they're just hoaxes, like the kinds P. T. Barnum used to play on the people who went to his circuses."

"Well, yeah," I laughed, relieved but still unsettled. "I didn't *really* believe —"

"All done!" CeeCee announced, taking a step back and surveying me with a grin. "There's only *one* more thing to make it complete. . . ." She flew over to her vanity, scooped up her silver charm bracelet, and brought it over to me.

"CeeCee, I can't wear your bracelet," I said as she hooked the lobster clasp around my wrist. "What if I lose it?"

"Don't be silly," CeeCee scoffed. "I have others. Besides, a real Southern girl should sport a James Avery charm bracelet on special occasions."

"Virginia and I each have one," Jacqueline affirmed.

"I'm not a real —" I began, but then I studied the charms. There was a miniature birthday cake with diamond candles; a tiny ferryboat that resembled *Princess of the Deep*; a treble clef; a pair of ice skates.

CeeCee caught me staring, and she smiled triumphantly. "Cute, huh?" she said. "My favorite is the treble clef, even though I don't like piano lessons. My grandma gave it to me."

I nodded. To have a grandmother who gave me charms — or knit me scarves or baked me pies, or said things like "mullygrubbing" — was a foreign concept. My Merchant grandparents had died before I was born, and Isadora was . . . Isadora. Though maybe if Isadora had been in my life, she would have gifted me with a James Avery bracelet so that I, too, could be a real Southern girl. A strange thought.

"Now," CeeCee said as she took my hand and pulled me up, "you are officially ready to see yourself." She walked me over to the vanity, Jacqueline stepped aside, and I faced the large mirror.

I gasped.

I wasn't sure what kind of witchcraft CeeCee had worked, but my hair fell in soft, dark ringlets. My lips were crimson, my lashes long, and the blush on my cheeks made my skin creamy white, not sheet pale as usual. The charm bracelet looked natural on my wrist, and the lavender dress, though loose in the bust and too short — CeeCee and I had vastly different proportions — was a flattering shape. I looked . . .

"Gorgeous!" CeeCee exclaimed.

"Much, much better," Virginia remarked, coming over to join us by the mirror.

"Like a princess," Jacqueline put in.

Like Isadora, I thought.

I looked like my grandmother.

It was undeniable. The plain, hard evidence was staring at me. The Isadora in the living room photograph, in the painting, was there in the mirror. I felt my pulse pounding in my throat. Now I understood. I understood the comparisons. I really had been granted some of Isadora's genes.

Was this what Mom saw whenever she looked at me? Did she see the monster?

"Oh, no," CeeCee said, bringing her hands to her mouth. "You hate it."

I realized that my expression was as stricken as if I'd seen a ghost. I glanced away from the mirror, breaking the spell.

"No — I don't," I said, looking at CeeCee. "It's just — different."

"You'll get used to it," Jacqueline said, putting her arm across my shoulder.

"So will T.J." CeeCee giggled, clapping her hands.

My pulse pounded harder.

"Cecile LeBlanc Cooper, can you put on your outfit already?" Virginia grumbled, turning away from the mirror.

"I know you think you're Selkie royalty, but they're not going to delay the fireworks show for you."

CeeCee dressed and applied her makeup, and the four of us trooped downstairs, where Althea let us out. I was glad that Delilah was not around; her inevitable comments about how much I resembled Isadora would have freaked me out further.

The evening was warm and mosquito-filled, and the clear sky was darkening. We took the shortcut to the docks, and I couldn't help but think of Leo as we walked down the pebbly path, CeeCee and her friends stumbling in their heels. How was he spending the Fourth? Was he, too, trying to forget about me, or had he moved on already?

When the docks came into view, I found myself searching the harbor for a glimpse of dark golden hair and green eyes. Instead there were countless summer people, dressed to the nines and boarding their private boats, bottles of Champagne and wicker picnic baskets in hand.

At the far end of the harbor, though, a small fishing trawler had docked, and the men unloading the crates of fish caught my eye. The men wore plaid shirts and baggy pants, and they bantered as they worked. A large fish with gray and green scales flopped out from one of the crates — still alive, desperate to return home — and thrashed its body against the dock. My heart constricted at the sight, but then one of the fishermen, who had a thatch of thick white hair and broad shoulders, lifted the fish and tossed it back into the water. I wondered, momentarily, if I had just seen Leo's father.

"There they are," Jacqueline said.

I looked away from the fishermen to see T.J., Bobby, Macon, Rick, and Lyndon. They were standing in front of a sleek silver motorboat that was roped to the dock. They all wore sunglasses and polo shirts tucked into khakis, and Bobby held his own bottle of Champagne and wicker basket. I felt a tremor of excitement and took a breath.

"Happy Independence Day, girls!" Bobby called as CeeCee ran toward him, her arms outstretched. Jacqueline flew into Macon's embrace, and Virginia and I hung back.

I'd never seen someone do an actual double take before, but that was just what T.J. did then — he glanced at me, took off his sunglasses, blinked, and then looked again, his eyes growing enormous.

"Miranda?" he asked, his voice thick with disbelief.

I nodded, and T.J. crossed over to me, smiling broadly. Heat spread over my face, and I smiled back. Enduring the girls' makeover had been well worth this moment.

"Wow," T.J murmured as he had in The Mariner's study, taking my hands and holding me at arm's length. "Amazing. You do realize you look exactly —"

"I do," I cut him off, still slightly shaken up by the resemblance I'd seen in CeeCee's mirror.

T.J. continued to gaze at me, as satisfied as if he had created me himself. I wanted to discuss our parents with him, but he seemed far too distracted by the new and improved Miranda to talk.

Suddenly, my heart thrummed and I wondered how Leo would react if he saw me this evening. Would he make such a fuss over the change in me? I glanced back at the fishermen, who were carrying their crates toward McCloud Way, the dirt path that led to Leo's house. None of the summer folk on the dock appeared to even see them.

"Can we board?" Virginia snapped, cutting her eyes at T.J. and me. "My shoes are killing me." She *click-clack*ed toward the boat, brushing past Rick, who watched her go with a smirk. T.J. looked amused as well.

"We're waiting for a couple more passengers," Lyndon explained, and then began waving in the direction of the pebbly path, his face brightening. "And here they come!"

I turned to see two girls whom I vaguely recognized from the Heirs party. They were clattering toward us, decked out in white straw hats, white eyelet dresses, and white gloves. It was clear that they'd dressed to upstage CeeCee and her girlfriends — and they'd succeeded.

"Sallie! Kay!" CeeCee called with forced merriment. "What a . . . nice surprise."

"Ladies," T.J. intoned, dipping his head. I looked at him, wanting to laugh. Was that the only greeting in his repertoire?

Sallie and Kay merely smiled their superior smiles as Lyndon and Rick rushed forward to greet them. Without turning around, I could sense CeeCee and her friends tensing up, arching their backs like rams preparing for a battle. It crossed my mind that being part of the heirs wasn't unlike living in the wild; there was the constant threat of unknown predators who were eager to disrupt the animal kingdom.

In the style of Noah's ark, we began boarding two by two: Bobby and CeeCee led the way, followed by Macon and Jacqueline. T.J., back to his usual gallant self, took my hand and guided me over the side of the swaying vessel. Then Lyndon and Rick helped up Sallie and Kay, leaving a fuming Virginia to clamber aboard on her own. As we all crammed into the low wooden benches, I smiled, feeling a little traitorous.

The sky was almost completely dark, and the first pinpricks of stars were appearing as Bobby untied the boat from the dock. *Romantic,* I thought, aware of T.J. sitting right next to me. His cologne wafted toward me on the sea breeze. I wondered if its scent had always been so rich and pungent. Maybe he'd worn more than usual tonight.

At the rear of the boat, Bobby settled himself behind the wheel. Tiny lights on the boat's hull came on, and the engine roared to life. Everyone — even me — cheered, and Rick's shout of "Ahoy, mateys!" elicited gales of laughter from Sallie and Kay.

We sliced through the water at a speed *Princess of the Deep* could never have matched. Bobby made us bounce on the waves a bit before we joined the constellation of other boats out on the ocean. I realized that, by dint of the right genes or good fortune, I was precisely where everyone on Selkie wanted to be at this moment. And I was filled with giddiness and guilt in equal measure.

"Y'all, crack open the Veuve and help yourselves to the grub!" Bobby called over the wind as he steered. CeeCee tottered over to him and draped her arms around his neck.

"What's the Veuve?" I asked T.J., who immediately bugged out his eyes at me and started laughing.

"You're joking, right?" he asked. When I shook my head, borderline annoyed, he grabbed the Champagne bottle from where Bobby had set it on the boat's cherrywood bottom. "Veuve Clicquot is the *brand*," T.J. explained, as if I should have been born knowing that fact. Across from us, Virginia, Sallie, and Kay giggled, briefly united in their scorn.

"Right," I muttered, fiddling with one of CeeCee's charms. The bracelet made my wrist sweaty; why did Southern girls wear these things? "Of course."

"You're such a snob, T.J.," Jacqueline piped up from where she sat on Macon's lap. "You know, not everyone drinks Champagne."

"Pity," T.J. said, grinning. With a movie-perfect *pop! — If only Isadora's trunk could open with such ease,* I thought wistfully — he deftly uncorked the bottle and foam frothed out of its mouth. Everyone — except for me — cheered once more, and Virginia began removing chilled Champagne flutes from the picnic basket.

"Still good with your hands, I see," she told T.J., cocking one eyebrow at him and then looking pointedly at me.

I blushed and glanced down at the mirrorlike surface of the water. I thought I saw a flash of gold beneath the blue-black waves.

"For you, miss." T.J. grinned, handing me a filled-to-the-brim flute. Virginia and Lyndon were filling up the rest of the flutes, and Jacqueline and Macon were busy unpacking lobster rolls from the basket and passing them around.

"Thanks," I replied, and T.J. clinked his glass against mine and downed his drink. I wasn't sure that drinking on a boat at night was a great idea, but I kept the thought to myself, not wanting to sound too schoolmarmish. I watched warily as Rick took a giant swallow of Champagne and then mimed walking the plank.

"Five minutes until the show!" someone shouted from a neighboring boat, and a seagull honked overhead. Someone in another boat burst out laughing.

Figuring I might as well get into the spirit of things, I took a cautious sip of the bubbly. It tickled my throat and was more tart than I had expected. I was looking for a sturdy spot to set my glass down when my gaze landed on the orange life vests stowed beneath the bench across from me.

I tapped T.J.'s shoulder. "Shouldn't we be wearing those?" I asked, deciding not to care about the schoolmarm thing. After all, in the study the other day, T.J. had basically admitted to wanting a good girl. "Like, by law?" I added.

"Hmm?" T.J. glanced at me, midbite of his lobster roll. There was mayonnaise on the side of his mouth.

"What, and ruin our dresses?" Virginia interrupted, smoothing out the creases in her own dress. "I mean, *you* can put one on, Miranda."

"Oh, we don't need life vests," T.J. told me, the mayonnaise staying put. "The patrol isn't going to bust *anyone* tonight. And we're not even out that deep."

"There are riptides, though," Jacqueline said, handing me a

lobster roll. "If you get caught in a riptide, even if you're not in deep water, you're —"

"In deep trouble," Macon put in, nodding.

"Are you guys planning a mutiny or something?" Bobby hollered from the helm, where CeeCee was feeding him pieces of lobster roll.

"The thing about riptides is, you just have to swim parallel to the shore." T.J. shrugged. I couldn't take my eyes off the mayonnaise. "And not panic."

Jacqueline and Macon nodded in agreement as they sat back down and began to eat. I glanced at my lobster roll and realized I didn't have much of an appetite.

"I never panic," I replied truthfully. "But, um, T.J.?" I finally added. "You have something near your mouth."

Now it was T.J.'s turn to panic. "Really?" he gasped, frantically patting the wrong side of his face. "Do you have a mirror?"

"No." I knew there were some girls who carried mirrors wherever they traveled, but that was a foreign notion to me. "It's right here." I motioned to the offending spot, hesitant to touch T.J.'s strong jaw. I wasn't sure why I didn't want to touch him; we'd already kissed, after all. But our touching seemed unnatural, somehow.

"I have a mirror," Virginia said, managing to make that phrase sound suggestive. She leaned over and handed T.J. a seashell-shaped compact. Before he could open it, though, she leaned even closer and, using her napkin, wiped away the mayonnaise. She let her fingers linger near his skin longer than necessary before pulling back and smiling.

I waited for jealousy to crash over me, but no such wave came in. T.J. glanced at me sheepishly and went back to devouring his roll. I set my own roll back in the picnic basket, along with the Champagne flute, hoping it wouldn't tip over.

A great crackling sound turned everyone's faces skyward. A shower of red and blue sparks ran down the sky like a rainstorm. The show was beginning. Bobby killed the engine so that we bobbed on the water, and a hush fell over our boat — over the whole ocean. I wondered what the fish, and the turtles, and the shrimp thought of us, of the humans' strange machinations.

As bouquets of colors exploded overhead, I realized that, on the sandy shore of Siren Beach, Mom was seeing this same spectacle. And somewhere in Fisherman's Village, Leo — and maybe his family — was seeing it, too. I heard myself gasp at the startling beauty of one firework and then heard myself sigh as it faded, its smoky ghost shimmying down to earth. Fireworks were those rare things that I didn't feel the need to explain to myself; I didn't want to know how they worked, for fear of ruining the magic.

I glanced at my companions in the boat to see if they were

equally entranced, and discovered that most of them were kissing: Sallie and Lyndon; Kay and Rick; Jacqueline and Macon; CeeCee and Bobby. The light from above cast bright patterns on each couple as they pressed close together. There *was* something sexy about fireworks: the anticipation, the explosion, the release. My cheeks burned.

The only people *not* kissing were Virginia, T.J., and me. I held my breath as T.J. and I looked at each other and Virginia looked at both of us.

Okay. This was it. This was the moment when T.J. and I would share a toe-tingling kiss, and Leo would become a distant memory. I tried to bring my face close to T.J.'s, but, for the first time in maybe my whole life, my body didn't obey my brain.

Then T.J. spoke.

"I still can't believe it," he whispered, his eyes searching my face. "I told Bobby."

I furrowed my brow, confused. "What did you tell Bobby?" I whispered back.

"That you'd clean up nice," T.J. smiled. "You proved me right."

Coldness doused me, and I drew back. Was that T.J.'s version of sweet nothings?

"What else did you tell Bobby?" I asked. A firework boomed overhead, followed by three more. Applause echoed across the water, and it sounded like several couples on our boat pulled apart to gawk and gasp at the sky. But I kept my gaze on T.J., seeing the fireworks reflected in his eyes.

T.J. smiled, sliding Virginia's compact up and down his palm like a coin. "Just that I was impressed by your house and your family."

My stomach sank as the truth hit home at last. That was all T.J. cared about, wasn't it? My pedigree. My house. My face. The outward evidence of my inheritance. If I'd had no ties to his world, if I'd simply been Miranda Merchant of the New York Merchants, T. J. Illingworth wouldn't have cared a damn about me.

"What? What's wrong?" T.J. asked, blanching. I realized how transparent my emotions — when I let myself feel them — could be. "I have something in my teeth, don't I?" he asked, and promptly popped open Virginia's compact.

Another series of fireworks went off, but I still didn't look up. I watched T.J. peer into the small mirror, opening his mouth in a comical way. *Narcissus*, I thought. The guy who fell in love with his reflection and was transformed into a flower.

"It's funny," I said to T.J., raising my voice over the booming, "that you mentioned my family. Did you know that our parents were engaged?"

My bomb drop did not have its intended effect.

"Uh-huh. My father told me after we left your house," T.J. replied absently, tilting his head to get a better look at himself.

The fireworks show was reaching a crescendo, the explosions coming closer and faster now. I pressed on, determined to turn T.J. away from the mirror. "So you know that if they did get married, then we'd be, like —" *Brother and sister*, I thought. My stomach churned. I had never articulated that notion to myself before, probably because I hadn't wanted to. But maybe that was why, tonight, I hadn't been able to touch T.J.'s face or kiss him, why the idea of our being together was so off-putting.

T.J. didn't respond, but he finally tore his eyes away from the mirror and looked up at the sky. I followed his gaze. The show's grand finale was happening; fireworks were bursting in a frenzy of reds, whites, and blues. *Fireworks.* I felt myself shiver with understanding. Regardless of our parents' connection, T.J. and I didn't spark, we didn't cause a chemical reaction.

"That was *awesome*!" Bobby cried as the last firework nose-dived into the ocean, and every passenger on every boat on the water burst into rapturous applause.

I clapped, too, my palms stinging. The fireworks were done, and so was I. Freedom surged in me. Now that I'd made sense of T.J., I suddenly wanted to be as far from him as possible.

I stood and looked down at T.J., who was still applauding and grinning up at the sky, completely at peace with who he was, with his place in the world.

"T.J.," I said, hearing the firmness in my voice. "I'm not who you think I am." I knew that was a slightly ridiculous thing to say — something that the geeky guy in a movie would say to the love interest right before morphing into a superhero.

T.J. blinked up at me, but before he could ask me to explain, I turned to Virginia. She'd been shamelessly watching our interaction the whole time, gripping her Champagne flute in suspense.

"He's all yours," I told her, meaning it. Then I made my way over to the edge of the boat, passing Macon, Jacqueline, and the others. CeeCee and Bobby were still canoodling, so Bobby had made no move to restart the engine.

I looked longingly at the water. I could simply dive in. The cool sea would feel like a balm on my hot skin, and CeeCee's dress would balloon up around me. I'd duck under, paddling my feet, and then I would swim, swim, swim.

Swim to where? Not to The Mariner, I knew. But to Leo. To wherever Leo was. Why had I been struggling so hard against what was inevitable? I squinted into the night and saw the tiny red and gold lights of Fisherman's Village.

I thought back to that moment outside Leo's house. And suddenly I understood, with a crystalline clarity, why I'd pushed him away: I'd been scared. Scared of the unknown, scared of facing who Leo really was — a mythical creature, maybe, or simply the boy I was falling for. Both were equally frightening, because neither could be explained.

Unexpectedly, tears filled my eyes, and I was grateful for the post-fireworks buzz and chatter around me. My heart swelled. I didn't care what Leo was — if he was some kind of merman or a monster or just a boy from the wrong side of the island. The only thing I cared about was seeing him again. Because the thought that I might not filled me with an ache so heavy it felt like drowning.

Twelve

IMPOSSIBILITIES

I woke up determined.

It was Friday, the sun was pouring through the pink drapes, and I was going to head straight to the marine center and see Leo.

Of course, I had to wait until noon for the center to open, but when I glanced at my bedside clock, I saw that it was half past twelve.

I sat up abruptly, surprised. I hadn't slept this late since Greg's pregraduation party back in May. Last night's blur of fireworks and epiphanies had clearly taken its toll.

As I reached for my hair elastic on my wrist, I touched the cool metal of CeeCee's bracelet instead. *Right.* Though I had changed out of CeeCee's dress before collapsing into bed, I'd forgotten to remove the piece of jewelry. Now, its glinting charms were like mementos. I remembered how Bobby's boat had idled on the water for what seemed like forever, and how, when we'd finally docked, everyone had wanted to either go skinny-dipping or to Bobby's house for beers. I'd declined both and bid farewell to a confused-looking T.J., a concerned-looking CeeCee, a triumphant-looking Virginia, and the others before walking back to The Mariner.

I took off the bracelet, and in my blue whale pajama bottoms and white tank top, slipped out of bed and into the quiet hallway. The typical sounds of Mom's bustle and activity downstairs were absent. Someone was mowing a lawn across the street, but The Mariner was at rest.

I peered over the banister to the empty foyer below. Mom could have been out running errands, but intuition turned me toward her bedroom door, which was ajar. I tiptoed over and, holding my breath, peeked inside to see my mother asleep in the green canopy bed. With her hair splayed across the pillow and her features relaxed, she looked startlingly vulnerable and young. Almost like the little girl in the photograph downstairs.

I drew back, rattled. If sleeping in was rare for me, it was even rarer for Mom. I'd used my spare key to let myself in last night, so I wasn't sure what time she had gotten home. What had she been up to?

I didn't want to think about it.

As if fleeing these thoughts, I rushed into the bathroom to wash up. I turned on the faucet — the water was coming out clear now — and I was startled by my reflection in the gilt-framed mirror. My curls were wild and knotty from sleep, my eye makeup was smudged and smoky, and my lips were still a vivid red. I shook my head; a shower would be necessary before I could show my face at the marine center.

But what would I even say to Leo when I saw him? As I brushed my teeth, I pictured him standing in the aquarium room with Maurice the alligator in his hand. Would I say I was sorry for the other night? That I couldn't stop thinking about him? Or would I simply kiss him? My stomach fluttered. Perhaps that wouldn't be appropriate if there were kids around. Or perhaps Leo would make it clear that he had no interest in kissing me anymore. Considering our last interaction, that was a distinct possibility.

Filled with doubt, I turned off the water and was reaching for a hand towel when I heard knocking downstairs — a sound I'd come to recognize as a visitor at the door. Mom was right; people *did* show up unannounced on Selkie all the time. I threw a critical glance in the mirror, then figured it was probably just CeeCee coming over to grill me about my strange behavior the night before. Hopefully, it wouldn't be T.J. or Mr. Illingworth. Just to be safe, I stopped in my room to shove my feet into fuzzy white slippers.

The knocking continued as I flew downstairs. "Okay, okay," I laughed, unlocking the door. "Give me a min —"

And then I lost the power of speech.

"Hey," Leo said.

My heart whooshed up from my chest into my throat.

It seemed impossible that he was really there, standing on The Mariner's front porch in a T-shirt, shorts, and flip-flops. The afternoon breeze blew his golden hair across his forehead, and he held a bouquet of red roses in one hand.

"I know these aren't sea pansies," he said with the crooked smile that melted my core. "But they're the best I could do on short notice." He extended the roses to me, but I seemed to have lost the ability to move as well.

"How — how did you know I live here?" I asked, relieved I hadn't gone mute. My legs felt unsteady and I clung to the side of the door like it was a raft.

Leo tilted his head to one side, his bright green gaze holding mine. "You told me, remember? The Mariner's location is pretty much common knowledge on the island." He ducked his head and then glanced back up at me, his face a little flushed. "I wanted to come by sooner, but I thought you might not want to see me."

"I was on my way to see you now," I blurted, my heart pounding. I was a little frustrated that Leo had beaten me to the punch, even as happiness flooded through me at the sight of him. "I — I mean, not like this," I stammered, gesturing toward my pajamas and fighting my blush.

Leo's eyes sparkled. "I like your pants," he said. "Did you just wake up?"

"No," I lied, trying to sound indignant, but wanting more than anything to throw my arms around him. "Why aren't you at work?" I countered. I noticed that he had his LEO M. tag affixed to the front of his T-shirt.

"I asked for an early lunch break." Leo grinned. I felt the familiar crackle of energy between us. The fact that we weren't standing closer, that we weren't kissing, felt wrong.

As if he'd read my mind, Leo took a step forward, but he didn't reach for me. "Can I — come in?" he asked, his voice hesitant.

I nodded, coming to my senses, and opened the door wider. "Thank you for the roses," I said, finally accepting the bouquet. I buried my nose in the dewy, sweet-smelling petals. No boy had ever brought me flowers before. Maybe it had been Leo, not T.J., who'd been the true gentleman all along.

As Leo walked inside, he glanced around the foyer, but he didn't seem as bowled over by the house as T.J. had been. "It's nice," he said simply, smiling at me. Then his gaze fell on his red hoodie, still on the claw-footed chair. Mom had left it there as a silent challenge for me to clean up after myself.

"Oh," I said, grabbing the sweatshirt and handing it to him. "Is this what you came for?"

Leo shook his head, smiling, but he took the hoodie and tucked it under his arm.

I threw a cautious look upstairs. I hoped Mom would stay asleep for a while longer; I didn't think she'd be pleased to see an unknown boy in our house. In a whisper, I told Leo to wait for me on the back porch, and I hurried into the kitchen. My fingers quivering, I put Leo's roses in a crystal vase and poured us both glasses of ice water. Then I crept through the living room.

On the porch, I shut the French doors behind me and joined Leo on the cushioned bench, handing him a glass of water. We were close enough that I could breathe in his salty, sandy scent. The full extent of how much I had missed him walloped me. It was all I could do not to reach over and touch him, but I resisted. I still wasn't sure why Leo had come, if he was here to make amends or to tell me why we would never work.

"So . . . how's Maurice?" I asked, sipping my water.

Leo's eyes were full of mischief as he took a drink. "So-so. He keeps asking about the smart girl with the dark hair and eyes. Can't seem to forget about you."

"I know how that goes," I said softly, gripping my cold glass in both hands.

We were both quiet for a long moment as we drank our water and watched the sun glitter on the ocean. Then Leo spoke, his voice deep and thoughtful.

"It's funny," he said, setting his empty glass on the porch floor. "The views from our homes aren't so different, are they? We're both looking at the same sea."

As was often the case, there seemed to be a hidden meaning behind his words. It was as though he spoke in half riddles. I felt my heart brim over as I studied the side of his face. Once again, I thought back to our argument, how I'd told him I'd made a mistake. I knew I had to speak, to set things right, regardless of what his response would be.

"Leo, I'm so sorry —" I started, but he shook his head.

"No, *I'm* sorry," he said firmly, facing me. His green eyes were ardent. "You were right, Miranda. We *were* moving too fast."

"But I wasn't being fair," I replied. The emotion in my own voice was unfamiliar to my ears. "I think I got freaked out in that moment, because I, um, thought —" I paused, still unsure if, or how, I could articulate my crazy merman theory. Besides, Leo, sitting next to me now, seemed utterly normal. So human.

"I understand," Leo said gently. "You realized how different we are."

"Only we're not different!" I exclaimed. I set my glass

down, too, and then, giving in to my want, put my hand on his warm arm. "You said so yourself, a few seconds ago. We see the world in the same way. We both love science, and we make each other laugh, and —"

"We *are* different, Miranda," Leo interrupted again, but this time his eyes were a little sad. "Our lives are different in ways you can't even imagine."

"What do you mean?" I whispered, my pulse racing as I searched his face.

"Just that . . ." Leo pushed a hand through his hair. The muscle in his cheek jumped, as it seemed to whenever he got riled up. "Look, we were never even really introduced. We met on the beach — the great equalizer. Everything is easy on the beach. On the rest of the island, differences matter."

"Okay," I said, sitting up straighter. I took my hand off his arm and stuck it out, handshake ready. "Let's introduce ourselves, then. Let's start over."

A smile crept over Leo's face. "Okay," he said, and put his hand in mine. As always, an electric current ran through me when we touched. "My name is Leomaris Macleod, and I've lived on Selkie Island all my life. My family has been here since the town was founded. I go to the local high school in Fisherman's Village. I love science, but I also love books and music. I think I want to write a novel someday."

My throat tightened as I looked into Leo's sincere, light-filled eyes. *He's brilliant,* I realized. His was a brilliance that transcended grades or SAT scores. He was unlike any boy I had ever known.

"Your turn," Leo prompted. His tone seesawed between playful and serious.

"Miranda Merchant," I told him, shaking his hand emphatically. "I'm from New York, but my mother's family has been coming to Selkie forever. I used to think I knew exactly what I wanted in life." I paused, biting my lip. "But now, I'm not so sure."

I paused again, looking at Leo and wondering if I had the courage to say what was hovering on my tongue.

And then, suddenly, I did.

"Except for you," I said. "I am sure of you."

There was a perilous, silent instant in which neither of us breathed or spoke, only gazed at each other. Then Leo reached out and cupped my face in his hands.

"Would it be all right if I kissed you?" he asked quietly.

I grinned, took his shoulders, and pulled him toward me. I kissed him. I kissed him with all the fervor I had never felt around Greg or T.J. I kissed him the way a good girl wouldn't dare kiss someone. Leo began to kiss me back, and then he drew away, still cupping my face. I caught my breath, worried that he was still upset.

"There's something I want to tell you," he said soberly.

Suspense shot through me. What was Leo going to confess?

"There are no other girls," Leo said. "Not this summer. How could there be? Anyone but you would be ridiculous. Impossible."

"Oh," I said, feeling myself smile. I worried that my blush would burn his palms. I realized then that Leo didn't care if I was in my pajamas, or if my hair was up or down, or if I wore makeup. That fact was plain in his eyes. He moved his hands down from my face and we entwined our fingers.

"There's been no one else for me, either," I said. "I mean, there was this one guy, for a minute, that everyone else thought I should be with, but . . ." I shook my head, remembering T.J. and last night. "He wasn't for me."

"I know." Leo grinned devilishly. "Preppy summer guy with straight black hair?"

My belly flipped over. I frowned, confounded. "Wait — how did you —"

Leo shrugged, his eyes dancing. "I see things."

I rolled my eyes even as my heartbeat stuttered. I thought of the sliver of gold I'd seen in the ocean while on Bobby's boat. "You enjoy being mysterious, don't you?"

"Me?" Leo teased. "Anyway, I didn't think that guy was a serious threat. He's not your type."

I tried to feign annoyance, but I couldn't stop smiling. "So who's my type?"

Leo was still grinning playfully. "If I had to guess? Someone . . . studious."

Without wanting to, I thought of Greg — he'd been studious, all right, but he hadn't been my type. My type, if I had one at all, was sitting right beside me.

"What are you thinking?" Leo asked, watching me carefully.

Greg. I felt myself swallow. Maybe, in a way, Mom had been right; maybe what had happened with Greg was affecting me more deeply than I had ever let myself believe. I stared at Leo, trying to decide if I was ready to admit what had been brewing inside me for so long — ever since May. I took a deep breath as nervousness bloomed in me.

"Leo," I said. I spoke quietly, even though it was only the two of us and the ocean. "Remember when, outside your house, I said all guys were creeps?" He nodded, growing serious. "I didn't mean you," I said, my voice steady. "Of course I didn't. I — I guess I was talking about someone else."

"Who?" Leo asked, squeezing my hand.

"Back during the school year, I had — a boyfriend." I hesitated but Leo only nodded, so I went on. "My first-ever boyfriend. Greg. He was a senior. I tutor other kids in physics, and he was one of my students. When we started going out, it wasn't like a roller coaster or fireworks or even — I don't know — a low flame." Leo chuckled, and I smiled, feeling some of my anxiety ease. "But it was so . . . so *nice* to have someone who wanted to kiss me and spend time with me."

I blushed deeply, but I had to keep going. Now that I was ready to tell my secret, not much could stop me. It was as if a faucet had been turned on.

"I guess, at some point, he wanted to — you know — take the next step." I cleared my throat. "But I wasn't ready."

Leo nodded again, watching me closely.

"We kind of fought about it, on and off," I said, casting my memory back to the school year, to the sense of uneasiness I'd started to feel in the spring. "I didn't want to stress about it — didn't want to be the kind of girl who stressed over a guy."

"Even if you did stress over a guy, you wouldn't be that kind of girl," Leo remarked, with his crooked smile.

I squeezed his hand and continued.

"Then there was the night of Greg's pregraduation party in May. His parents let him have the apartment for the weekend. He and I had been having a tiff earlier that day, about a physics exam he'd done poorly on, and he blamed me for it." I shook my head. "I asked him why he cared, considering he'd already gotten into college. But obviously, it wasn't about the exam. I figured that out later. During the party, we kept our distance. Greg had invited half the senior class — my high school is huge — along with some of my junior friends. Including my best friend, Linda."

"Oh," Leo said.

I nodded.

"I was in the kitchen," I said, remembering the crowd of kids, the smell of beer and cigarette smoke, the pounding beat of hip-hop from the living room. "Someone needed help opening their Corona, and Linda was excellent at opening beer bottles; that was her thing. She was always cooler than me, more confident, with her scarlet-streaked hair and her eyeliner." I felt a lump start to form in my throat — tiny, inconspicuous. Smaller than a ghost shrimp. "I said I'd go look for Linda, and as I headed down the hall to the bedrooms, I realized I hadn't seen Greg in a while, either. And, you know, I've always been good at math, but I didn't put two and two together."

"Why would you?" Leo said supportively, frowning.

I remembered pushing open the door to Greg's bedroom, with its chess sets and Yankees posters and its bed on which Greg had asked, *Come on, why won't you ever take your socks off?* and implicit in that question had been another one: Why wouldn't I sleep with him?

I'm not ready, I had said.

But Greg had found someone who was.

I remembered the cold sensation I'd felt in my gut as the door opened, and I felt it again now, a plunging coldness. Like diving into a pool.

"I found Linda in Greg's bedroom," I told Leo. "She was with Greg." I swallowed, trying to force down the ever-growing lump.

Leo nodded, frowning. "Were they . . . ?"

"Not quite, but close," I said, my face flushing hotter. "I didn't even get a full picture. They were on his bed and some clothes were definitely off. But I didn't need to process more than that. I got the general essence, you know?" I heard my voice crack.

"What did you do?" Leo asked, leaning toward me.

"I said I was sorry to interrupt. And then I turned and walked away. Ran, actually — I guess I'm good at running away from upsetting things. Greg caught up with me before I could leave his apartment, said that he was sorry and he hoped I didn't hate him. I think he was expecting me to be crying" — on that unfortunate word my voice broke again — "and all hysterical, but that's not my style. I told him that I understood, and that I hoped the two of them would be very happy."

The tears were encroaching now, coming on as certain as the current.

"Miranda . . ." Leo said. He reached out his other hand to touch my face, but I looked down at the porch.

"And I didn't cry, even as I took the elevator down to the lobby and walked to the subway. I didn't cry on the way home, and I didn't cry when I got to my apartment and told my mother that I'd left the party with a stomachache. I didn't cry when Linda called me on my cell, or when *she* cried and asked me to forgive her."

"What did you say to her?" Leo asked, his tone careful. I wanted to thank him for being such a good listener — I didn't know boys could be such good listeners — but I was still afraid to look up at him.

"I told her I felt like an idiot," I replied, and the first teardrop fell and splashed down my cheek. All the shame, pain, and anger I had tamped down was bubbling to the surface. "I told her I was furious at myself for trusting her, for believing in silly things like friendship and loyalty. And I told her I never wanted to speak to her again." I swiped at my eyes uselessly, sniffling.

"And you didn't?" Leo prompted.

I shook my head, feeling the tears drip down my cheeks and land on my lips, their taste salty as seawater. "That Monday at school, I avoided not just Greg and Linda but all our friends. I clammed up. I was so afraid to show how hurt I was." I remembered, again, the coldness — the loneliness — of those weeks. Walking through the hallways clutching my books to my chest, avoiding people's glances, silent, wordless Miranda.

"And you know what?" I asked, finally looking up.

Leo raised his brows, his beautiful eyes full of empathy.

"The whole time, I didn't cry."

Then, the impossible happened. I started to cry for real, my shoulders shaking. I cried as if making up for all those swallowed-down sobs, for all those nights when I forced my mind to go elsewhere. And as much as I detested losing control in front of people, I knew I could cry in front of Leo. He wouldn't judge me or think of me differently. So I didn't resist when he pulled me into him and held me close.

"It's okay," Leo said softly, his lips on my hair. "It'll be okay."

"I'm getting your T-shirt wet," I sobbed, moving my cheek so that it wasn't pressing into his LEO M. tag.

"Shh," he said with a small laugh, and held me tighter.

I wasn't sure how long we sat there, Leo with his arms around me and me weeping into his broad chest. But soon my sobs started coming fewer and farther between, and my eyes began to feel drier. Once the tempest had passed, I drew back from Leo's embrace.

"Better?" he asked.

"Better," I affirmed, dabbing at my eyes with the back of my hand. I felt drained from my cryfest, but also somehow lighter. Free.

"You know," Leo said quietly, reaching out to caress the side of my face. "It's all right to let yourself feel things. Even if it can be damn scary sometimes."

I nodded, smiling at him gratefully. "I think I'm starting to learn that." I caught his hand and held it against my cheek. "I never thought I'd tell anyone that story. But I'm glad I told you."

"Same here," Leo said. "And I'm so sorry about what happened. That guy — Greg — he couldn't begin to deserve you." Leo smiled back at me, his dimples appearing. "Miranda, you should know that not everyone's going to hurt you. I mean, I hope you can still . . . trust people."

My heart felt full to bursting. "I trust you," I told Leo, meaning it. "I trust you." *Even if I don't totally understand you.*

Leo leaned close and kissed me. Once, twice, his mouth warm and inviting. We put our arms around each other, our kisses deepening.

"What's going on out here?"

Mom's voice sliced through the air, and I sprang away from Leo in shock. I turned my head and saw her standing in the French doors, wearing her bathrobe and a stern expression.

"I thought you were sleeping," I gasped.

Mom crossed her arms over her chest. "I can see that," she said crisply, shooting an unmistakable glare at Leo.

"Mom," I said, brushing the last tears off my cheeks. "We were just —"

Leo leapt to his feet, his face crimson. He stuck his hand out to Mom, initiating a different kind of introduction than ours had been.

"Hello, ma'am. Leo Macleod. I'm Miranda's friend. I apologize for —"

Mom didn't take his hand. She ran her eyes over him, and her disapproval couldn't have been clearer. "I think we met already. On Siren Beach?"

"That's right!" Leo exclaimed, still trying to sound positive. I twisted my hands together. I felt like throwing up.

"Leo was just coming by to, uh — get his sweatshirt," I improvised, also jumping to my feet. In the next second, I realized I had just given away my lie from the other night, and Mom narrowed her eyes at me.

"But I should be heading back to work now," Leo said, backing up toward the porch steps with his hoodie under his arm.

"That's a wise idea," Mom said, staring him down.

"Leo works at the marine center," I told Mom, as if that would somehow smooth things over.

"Are you okay?" Leo said to me as he walked backward down the steps. I could tell he wanted to come over and kiss me, but he knew better.

I nodded and then, choosing to disregard my mother, walked down the stairs after him and grabbed his hand.

"Miranda!" Mom snapped.

"I'll see you," I whispered. "As soon as I can." He had to know that Mom wouldn't keep me away.

Leo nodded. "The beach," he whispered back. "Tonight. I'm going on a fishing trip with my father this weekend, so —"

"Tonight," I confirmed. I would make it happen. "What time?"

"Anytime," Leo said, starting to smile.

That did it. I needed to put my wondering to rest. "How does that work?" I whispered. "How do you know when I'm there?"

"I just do," Leo said, his gaze holding mine. I couldn't tell if he was joking or earnest. But before I could ask, he touched my cheek, glanced over at Mom, and was gone.

I felt like I would explode. If only I'd told Leo what I'd imagined him to be — made myself speak the word *merman*. Although I was sure it was all in my head, I still wanted an explanation.

But I had bigger problems to worry about now. Namely, my mother.

I turned around with a sigh and climbed the porch steps. Mom watched me as I collected the empty water glasses and then stepped into the house, leaving the French doors open. The wind rushed in as we stood facing each other.

"Let me guess," Mom said icily. "That was who accompanied you to Fisherman's Village the other night?" Disdain colored each of her words.

I nodded, holding the glasses so tight I thought they'd break. I stared at my fluffy slippers, incongruously cheerful against the dark wood floor. I wondered if Mom could tell from my face that I'd been crying.

"Miranda," Mom said, her voice suddenly gentle. Her Southern accent had been returning more and more over the past couple days. I looked up at her, hopeful. "Tell me," she went on, her forehead creasing as she frowned. "What are you doing with a boy like that?"

Abrupt, hot anger surged in me, eclipsing my earlier sadness. I was certain there was fire in my eyes as I stared at my mother.

"I can't believe you," I said. I hadn't ever spoken to Mom this way, but I was determined not to cower. "You're just like them — like Delilah and T.J. and all the summer people you *said* you wanted nothing to do with. You never raised me to think about things like class or money and status. You never cared about who or what was appropriate for me. Now that's all you care about." I let out a shaky breath.

Mom blinked, clearly taken aback by my diatribe. "I only want what's best for you, Miranda," she replied. "Look. Your prospects with this boy are impossible. Think about it logically. We're leaving here on Sunday morning —"

"We are?" I asked, stunned. I had lost all sense of time. It was July fifth, I knew, but — "*This* Sunday?"

Mom nodded, and I felt my stomach drop. I'd known, of course, that our departure was imminent. But Mom had said nothing about it in recent days. And we still had so much sorting to do around the house . . . and . . .

And Leo. Leo.

"Have we even sold The Mariner?" I cried in confusion. "I thought we weren't going back until we found a buyer, and —"

"I have work, Miranda," Mom said firmly. "Do you know how many surgeries I've had to pass on to less capable colleagues?"

"No," I said, wondering how Mom's colleagues would react if they'd seen her sleeping in that morning.

"And you have your internship," Mom reminded me. "You knew we wouldn't be on Selkie all summer." I squinted at her, trying to discern if she was looking forward to leaving or hating that we had to go; her face betrayed nothing. "This

Leo boy," Mom continued, making my heart skip, "his world is here. But someone like T.J., someone you have other ties to —"

"Mom, I don't want to be with T.J.!" I burst out. I was too upset by her news to soften my words. "We have nothing in common, nothing real, anyway. Not to mention, dating him would be completely" — I thought of the word Jacqueline had used at the Heirs party — "*incestuous.*"

Mom raised her eyebrows, looking affronted. "You and T.J. are *not* related," she said stonily. "If that's what you're implying."

My stomach turned. "No — that's not what I meant," I said, shuddering. "But I don't understand what's so wrong about liking someone who's different from me. Isn't that human nature? Isn't that how the species survives?" I gazed at Mom, willing the scientific part of her brain to follow.

"Look," she replied, sighing. "It's also human nature to not relish the sight of your daughter making out with someone in your own house."

My blush returned, and I glanced away from her, over at the photographs on the mantel. It was funny that Mom hadn't packed them away yet.

"I'm sorry," I muttered, glancing back at Mom. "I just — on some level, I wish that you'd be glad that a boy I like actually likes me. You were right — I *have* been lonely recently." I drew a breath. Now that I'd spilled my secret to Leo, it no longer felt so heavy or so dark. "And yes, it's because of Greg. Because Greg — because he hooked up with Linda."

Mom's lips parted, and I felt a tremor of triumph at having successfully shocked her. "Linda Wu?" she asked. "*Your* Linda?"

"Well, formerly," I replied, relieved that I could smile about it.

"That's awful," Mom whispered, her forehead creasing. "Why didn't you say something to me sooner?" She stepped forward, her arms extended, but I stepped back.

"I'm telling you now," I said quietly.

"God," Mom muttered, and shook her head. "Linda! And Greg . . . he always seemed like such a nice guy."

"I know," I said. "See? You approved of him, but he wasn't so nice. Mom, Leo *is* a good guy. I know that. Can't you be happy for me?"

To my surprise, Mom was also looking at the photographs on the mantel. Her face was splotchy and a strange expression was in her eyes — regret mixed with recognition.

"Mom?" I ventured.

"I'm sorry, I suddenly have a headache," Mom said, massaging her temples. "I'm going upstairs to lie down." She walked up to me and squeezed my arm. "Miranda, I didn't mean to be insensitive. If you ever want to talk more about what happened with Greg, you know I'm here."

I nodded, but I didn't feel as if I could talk to my mother about anything at the moment. There was an emptiness in my gut. Yesterday, when Mom had given me the spare key, I'd thought we'd patched things up, that we were back on friendly ground. Now, it seemed, everything had ruptured again.

Before Mom left the living room, she glanced back at me and added, "I expect you won't be having any more strange visitors or taking any trips to Fisherman's Village today?" I could tell she was trying to come off as lighthearted, but her tone was firm.

Since she hadn't mentioned Siren Beach, I was able to nod.

As Mom went upstairs, I deposited the water glasses in the sink and fleetingly touched Leo's roses. I felt restless and jittery, almost like I'd felt my first night in The Mariner, after I'd gone for a swim. And, as I had that night, I found myself wandering down the hall, past the stairs and the mariner painting. I stopped on the threshold to the study. I hadn't been in there since my kiss with T.J., and I was surprised to see that Mom hadn't packed away any more books in the meantime. We so weren't ready to leave yet.

My thoughts roaming from Mom to Leo, I stepped into the

room. At least I'd see Leo tonight, and could tell him I was leaving. But I couldn't stop recalling Leo's parting words, or the fact that he'd been able to observe me and T.J. from an undisclosed location. I couldn't shake my growing suspicions, suspicions that seemed as insane as they were impossible.

Like any good student, I knew that the answer to most questions could be found in a book. And it was starting to become clear that my questions about Leo could be answered by only one book. So I strode over to the shelf that contained *A Primer on the Legend and Lore of Selkie Island.* Yes, the book was, as Virginia had said, no more than a collection of superstitions. But these superstitions had taken up residence in my head, and I hoped that by returning to their source, I might banish them.

I took the book off the shelf and settled into the high-backed chair. I was careful not to let too many pages slip out as I turned to the appropriate section. I put the book on my knees and started reading.

Selkie merfolk are usually recognizable by a few key features: a lush, sensitive beauty; a predilection for the colors red and gold; kindness toward visitors and explorers; and homes close to the shore. They can sometimes be spotted at night, when venturing out to swim in the waters off Siren Beach.

The island's merfolk blend in nearly seamlessly with their neighbors. However, certain oceanic markings often adorn their places of residence. Also, it is widely believed that, despite their common ancestor, Captain William McCloud, Selkie merfolk branched off into two distinct families. One branch tends to carry the surname William or Williams, and the other carries surnames that are variations on McCloud.

I lifted my hands from the book as if I'd been scalded. Goose bumps had broken out all over my arms and legs, and blood roared in my ears.

Leomaris Macleod. Macleod sounded like a variation of McCloud, didn't it? My heart was thudding. There was his lush, sensitive beauty. His nighttime swimming. The rocky grotto, where he must have always kept a pair of swim trunks to do a quick change.

It all fit. *It all fit.* Like pieces of a puzzle, clicking together.

Think of science, I commanded myself, trembling. *Think of the manatees that the sailors mistook for mermaids. Think of evolution and reproduction and the system of chemicals that make up the human body.*

And then something occurred to me, something so obvious that it filled me with instant relief. I leaned back against the chair, wanting to laugh. I might not have seen *The Little Mermaid*, but I'd absorbed enough through pop culture osmosis to know that Leo couldn't have been a merman. Of course not! Leo had been in the *water* with me. We hadn't gone swimming, but he'd gotten his feet wet on the beach walk, and in the rain. Didn't merfolk grow tails the minute water touched them?

I flipped back a page or two, recalling a tiny detail I'd read last time, something about the descendants of Caya needing to submerge in the water completely to transform. But then I slammed the book shut, refusing to go down that road. *Forget it.* I set the book on the writing desk, beside the oblong black box.

All the puzzle pieces were mere coincidences. The residents of Fisherman's Village had probably decided that the colors red and gold went nicely together, and Llewellyn Thorpe had incorporated that tidbit into his elaborate fictions. The same went for the surnames, which probably just happened to be common names on the island. My first instinct on the ferry had been correct: The legends of Selkie were just that, legends.

Still, I felt unsettled, and I knew that there was only one way I could convince myself for sure. It had to do with that most basic principle of science: experimentation. You could read and think about something forever, but nothing compared to seeing it firsthand.

I stood up, full of resolve. Tonight, I was going to prove that the boy I was crazy about — the boy who'd also made me crazy — was not a merman. I was going to get Leomaris Macleod to go swimming with me.

Thirteen

KEYS

*L*eaving the study and walking upstairs to my room, I was surprised to hear my cell phone ringing. Aside from Dad and Wade, no one had called me during my stay on Selkie. My first thought — hope — was that it was Leo, until I remembered that we'd never exchanged numbers. Was it Linda, trying to apologize again?

I snatched my cell off my nightstand. I didn't recognize the 912 area code, so I answered cautiously.

"What happened last night?" a girl with a dainty drawl demanded.

CeeCee. I sighed. I'd forgotten *she* had my number.

"What do you mean?" I asked, kicking off my slippers. In my mind, I was still downstairs with Llewellyn Thorpe's book.

"Oh, my gosh! Could you have taken off any faster?" CeeCee cried. On her side of the line, I heard the creak of what sounded like a door opening, and then the *thwack-thwack* of CeeCee's flip-flops as she walked. "Jackie and I were worried about you."

"Virginia wasn't?" I asked wryly, flopping across my unmade bed.

CeeCee was silent for a moment. "Miranda, I'm so, so sorry," she said, and her voice was truly full of regret. I was starting to grasp that CeeCee, despite her shallowness, had a good heart. Maybe I'd been the shallow one, dismissing her. "Virginia and T.J.," CeeCee continued reluctantly, "they — um — sort of, like, got together. We all went back to Bobby's house, and they —"

"CeeCee," I cut in, feeling a smile cross my face. "I thought that might happen, and I'm all right with it. Honestly. I realized last night that T.J. isn't really . . . the guy for me. You know?"

"I feel so bad!" CeeCee wailed. I heard a splashing sound in the background, followed by Jacqueline's voice. "Yeah, I'm talking to her now," CeeCee said to Jacqueline. "Miranda, can you at least come over tonight?" she then asked me hopefully. "Maybe if you saw T.J. one more time . . ." She trailed off, her tone questioning.

"Why? What's tonight?" I asked, and felt a surge of impatience thinking of Leo. I glanced out the window, willing the late afternoon sky to somehow darken faster.

"Mama told me she invited your mother and Mr. Illingworth over for a farewell dinner," CeeCee explained. "I can't believe you guys are leaving on *Sunday*."

"That makes two of us," I muttered. What I couldn't believe was that Delilah — and CeeCee — had known about my departure before I did. But that made the departure feel somehow all the more real.

I assured CeeCee that I had no desire to see T.J. again. I refrained from adding that I especially had no desire to see Mom interact with Mr. Illingworth. But I was actually a little bit giddy at the thought that Mom wouldn't be in the house come evening. That would make my escape all the easier.

"I think I'm going to pack tonight," I told CeeCee, lifting her bracelet from where I'd put it on my nightstand. "But maybe I could come over tomorrow to return your bracelet and dress?" I also did want to say good-bye to CeeCee and Jacqueline — and even Virginia if she was around. I really bore her no ill will.

"Or you could come now!" CeeCee offered, and the splashing sounds grew louder. "Jackie and I are just hanging out by the pool. Virginia's not here," she added loyally.

I pictured Jacqueline and CeeCee lounging in their bikinis and felt a pinprick of jealousy. Lucky girls. They weren't sitting around obsessing over insane things like merfolk and sea creatures. Why did I always have to be so different from everyone else?

It was all because of Llewellyn Thorpe's book, I decided with a small swell of anger. I thought of the book sitting innocently on the writing desk beside the black oblong box with the golden clasps.

I felt my brow furrow. *Wait.*

The box.

There'd been so much else to distract me in the study that I'd never bothered to wonder what the box contained; fancy writing pens or small pads of stationery would have been my guess. But now that I thought about the box, I realized that it was a clone, in miniature, of another item in the house.

The trunk in Isadora's closet.

"Miranda? Are you there?" CeeCee was saying.

My heart began pounding and I swung my feet off the bed.

"CeeCee, I'll call you later," I said distractedly, and ended the call.

Certainty raced through me as I bounded out of the room and flew downstairs. Suddenly, I felt as if everything was about to unlock before me, the secrets of Leo and of my grandmother. I reentered the study, ran over to the writing desk, and for once, ignored Llewellyn Thorpe's book.

I reached for the black box and found that its lid was,

thankfully, unlocked. And nestled against the crimson interior were, just as I'd predicted, two gold-tipped writing pens. Disappointment shot through me, but then I picked up one of the pens and stared at what had lain underneath it.

A tarnished brass key.

My thudding heartbeat started up again.

The key. It had to be.

I glanced up at the painting of Isadora. She must have loved the study, to hang her portrait here. In my ransacking of The Mariner, I had never thought to look for the key to her trunk in the most obvious place.

Clutching the key in my fist, I swept out of the room and was starting up the stairs when I almost crashed into Mom. She was in her linen pants and a boatneck top and was carrying her tote bag.

"I'm headed into town to pick up a bottle of bourbon for the Coopers," she told me, and then filled me in about the dinner that evening. "You should come, too, if you'd like," she added, giving me a contrite smile; it was obvious she still felt bad about Greg.

The key digging into my palm, I managed to say that I'd already declined CeeCee's invitation. I waited until Mom had descended the stairs and exited the house, and then I continued the rest of the way upstairs, my pulse hammering.

I dashed into Isadora's closet and pulled on the string to turn on the overhead bulb. Then I pushed past the rack of clothes I hadn't packed away, knelt before the trunk, and inserted the key.

Even though I'd been sure, I still heard myself gasp as the lock turned.

Slowly, I lifted the lid, and the smell of mothballs drifted up to greet me. The trunk contained a single dress: Cream colored and strapless, it had dusky pink flowers appliquéd along its neckline and down its full, gauzy skirt.

Bewildered, I pulled the dress out, creating a shower of dust. The gown wasn't as much my style as the lacy black dress that hung behind me, but it was inarguably beautiful. And it was definitely fancier than anything else in the closet. But that didn't explain why Isadora would have stashed it away.

Setting the dress aside, I peered back into the trunk, hoping for a clue. All that had been underneath the dress was a thick stack of envelopes, bound with a rubber band. I grabbed the stack and saw that a typed note on white paper was wrapped around the entire stack, encasing it.

Curiosity quickened my movements as I snapped off the rubber band and unfolded the letter. The date at the top was recent, only a few months before Isadora's death.

The letter read:

Dear Mrs. Hawkins:

Per the request of the deceased, one Mr. Henry Blue Williams of Selkie Island, Georgia, enclosed please find the correspondence Mr. Williams wished to bequeath to you in his last will and testament.

Sincerely,

Daryl Phelps, Esquire

I felt a shiver as I set the letter down on top of the dress. So someone — whoever Henry Blue Williams was — had granted Isadora a gift shortly before her own death. Had that inspired Isadora's subsequent generosity toward Mom? And what was this correspondence, exactly?

When I looked back at the yellowing envelopes in my hand, I gave a start; the address on each envelope was penned by Isadora herself, in her looping, elegant script. And they were all addressed to:

Henry B. Williams
5 McCloud Way
Selkie Island, Georgia

The return address on each envelope was The Mariner, and from the postmark date, I did a quick calculation: When these letters had been sent, Mom had not yet been born, and Isadora must have been in her late twenties. I tried to recall if I'd heard the name Henry Blue Williams before, but the only names familiar to me were Daryl Phelps — the lawyer Mom had been in touch with — and the street name on the envelope: McCloud Way. That was the name of the dirt path that led to Leo's house. Why had my grandmother been writing to someone in Fisherman's Village?

My fingers shaking, I flipped the first envelope in the stack over and lifted its flap to reveal the onionskin letter inside.

June 15

My beloved,

I think of you always. As I sit here, sweltering on the back porch, little C. is having a tea-party with her dolls, little J. is racing on the beach, and J.H. is storming around inside, fixing himself another gin and tonic. All of it ordinary, but when I gaze out at the deep ocean, you come to mind, and I remember how extraordinary — how magical — life can be. Thank you for teaching me that very important lesson.

Forever yours,

JBH

I put the letter down, my heart banging against my chest. I couldn't believe that people actually used such flowery, romantic language in real life. And I couldn't believe that my own grandmother had written those words — to some *guy*. Not my grandfather — that would be the *J.H.* in her letter. And *little C.* and *little J.* had to mean, respectively, Aunt Coral and Uncle Jim.

Then —

Had Isadora had an affair?

I felt like I'd just stumbled deep into history, into a part of my grandmother's life that I wasn't meant to see.

An *affair*. The idea of cheating made the back of my throat burn, made me feel ill. I thought of Linda and Greg, and then I pictured my late grandmother in her youth, lovely and coquettish. Had she really been the type to cheat on her husband, on the father of her children? Was that why my mother called her a monster?

I looked down at the curves and loops of my grandmother's handwriting — so different from my own neat, solid penmanship. As of late, I'd been feeling a growing connection to Isadora, perhaps because of our physical resemblance. But now I could feel whatever strange loyalty I'd had beginning to ebb away.

Still, determined to know more, I opened another envelope, this one postmarked a few days later.

My beloved H.,

I hate that we are kept apart by our vast and complicated differences, by your situation. It makes me want to push down the walls of my house and run reckless into the ocean. It makes me no longer want to hide our secret. If only we could spend forever on Siren Beach, far from the prying eyes of society. Tonight I will curl up in the study, read poems by T. S. Eliot, and dream about you.

Always,

IBH

I put the letter down. There were many more envelopes, but first I had to think, to collect my scattered thoughts. I sat down on the dusty floor, leaning back against the unsteady wall of dresses behind me.

I wondered if what I had read could be taken at face value. Maybe these letters, like Llewellyn Thorpe's book, were metaphoric — not meant to be literal at all. Though there was no mistaking that Isadora had referred to this man, this Henry Williams, as her "beloved." There was no denying that she'd planned to dream about him. I'd gotten C's in English, but I knew that there wasn't too much room for metaphor in those phrases.

But there were other things in the letters, other vague references that were not so easy to decipher. *I hate that we are kept apart,* Isadora had written, *by our vast and complicated differences.* Her words reminded me of what Leo had said earlier, on the porch, about the two of us.

And what did Isadora mean by Henry Williams's

"situation"? Was something wrong with him? Almost without meaning to, I glanced down at my bare feet. Webbed toes or fingers were interesting, I thought. There was something aquatic about their appearance, almost as if they were vestiges of people's ancient existence in the water.

Or maybe that's what merfolk were.

I felt my heart rate spike. There was something I'd just read in Llewellyn Thorpe's book, some small seedling of a detail that was struggling to make its way into my head. I knew it pertained to Isadora's letters, but I couldn't recall it.

I glanced back at the two envelopes I had set aside. The twin addresses stared back up at me. *Henry B. Williams. Henry B. Williams.*

Williams.

Shock coursed through me.

Oh, my God.

According to Llewellyn Thorpe, Williams was one of the surnames associated with the descendants of William McCloud. The Williamses were a separate branch of the merfolk family from the McClouds.

Which meant that, if Llewellyn Thorpe's book was in any way factual, then the man my grandmother had had an affair with had been . . .

Sweat broke out on my forehead as I got to my feet. No. It couldn't be. The book was *not* factual. Isadora must have been referring to their class differences — she living in the ivory tower of The Mariner, Henry Williams residing in Fisherman's Village.

Maybe they, too, had met on Siren Beach, the place where differences didn't matter. Maybe she'd been drawn to how free he'd seemed, how unlike everyone else in her life. I bit my lip and, glancing back, ran my hand along the black lacy dress. Maybe my grandmother and I *were* alike, alike in ways beyond our dark curls and fair skin, alike in ways I never could have imagined.

I thought about what Delilah had said, all those days ago on the beach, about history repeating itself. She'd been referring to T.J. and me as echoes of Mom and Mr. Illingworth. But now I felt that I was repeating Isadora's history, following her path like a series of steps that led down to the ocean. Maybe people didn't just inherit looks and talents and the propensity for illnesses, but they also inherited desires.

I heard the front door unlock then — Mom returning from the market. Hurriedly, I stashed the cream-colored dress and the letters back in the trunk, relocked it, and stuffed the key in the pocket of my pajama bottoms. I would come back tomorrow to finish reading. Then, acting on a sudden, sure instinct, I removed the high-necked, lacy black dress from its hanger. Holding the dress in my arms, I carried it to my room, where it would wait for nightfall.

That I made it through the rest of the afternoon was a miracle. I took a long, hot shower and then walked along our private stretch of beach, all but counting the minutes as they passed. When evening began to creep across the sky, I went back inside, where Mom, decked out in an elegant dress, was preparing to leave for dinner. As soon as she left — with a slightly suspicious glance in my direction and a reminder that I should make myself food from the fridge — I went up to my room and started to change.

Moving with all the assuredness of a chemist in a laboratory, I stepped into my black swimsuit. Then, with butterflies in my stomach, I lifted Isadora's dress from my bed. There was a small zipper on the side that I undid before pulling the dress over my head. The material was soft and scratchy at the same time, and I was surprised at how perfectly the dress adhered to my figure. The fit was as precise as if the dress had been sewn for me. A chill passed down my arms, but the fact that the dress fit seemed to be a sign that I was doing the right thing.

Finally, slipping my feet into flats, I regarded myself in the mirror above the dresser. I'd decided to leave my hair loose after my shower, and, remembering Jacqueline's actions from yesterday, I'd borrowed some of Mom's eye shadow from the bathroom cabinet and dabbed it on my lids.

I was prepared to see my resemblance to Isadora again, but what faced me in the mirror was more than resemblance. Tonight, I *was* my grandmother. It was the retro dress, to be sure, but there was something else, too — a glow to my face, a coyness in my eyes. Was it Leo — my feelings for him — that had effected this transformation?

Or was it me?

I wasn't sure if my grandmother was someone I wanted to be, but I felt as if I had no choice in the matter. The old Miranda, she of the rational head and the responsible actions, would never have snuck out of the house with her mother already upset with her. But this new Miranda — half herself, half monster — was doing the impossible. She was turning out the lights in her room and tiptoeing downstairs, not bothering to leave a note. And she was locking the front door before stepping into the embrace of the hot island night.

Fourteen

TIDES

As I stole through the darkness, glancing at the starlit ocean, I wondered if this was something Isadora had done — run under the cover of night to meet Henry by the seashore. Perhaps she'd even done so wearing this very dress. Had her pulse raced as mine was racing now, both at the anticipation of seeing her beloved and at the knowledge of her betrayal? My going to see Leo tonight was a form of cheating, after all — I was cheating on Mom, on the promise I had made her that I would be a good girl.

Grateful for the hazy light of the crescent moon, I made my way down the pebbly path to the dock. The scent of blooming jasmine mixed in with the sea air, and the boats rested quietly on the water. I decided to cut through the alley that led to Fisherman's Village, and although I was alone, I felt no trepidation. The village itself was vibrant and bustling, lit up in all its red and gold magnificence. Again, music and people flowed out from the pubs, all merriment.

This time, though, I took careful notice of how old all the buildings were. Here, even the roots of the oaks seemed to run deeper than they did on my side of the island. And, as I walked down the steps to the beach, I realized that the residents of Fisherman's Village were the true heirs of Selkie Island. I decided that I'd use that argument with Mom if she challenged me about Leo again.

On the sand, I picked my way steadily over the black rocks. Up ahead, I could see the grotto where Leo and I had waited out the storm. Flickers of light danced out from its small opening, and hope uncoiled in my chest.

I felt only a small burst of surprise when Leo emerged from the grotto, his hair damp. He wore his swim trunks and the red hoodie he'd gotten back from me. He bit his lip, grinning at me. I didn't ask him what he'd been doing in the grotto or whether he had been swimming. I only hurried toward him.

When we reached each other, Leo put his hands on my waist and lifted me, effortlessly. I felt small and light, but also somehow powerful, as our lips met. We kissed for a long time, the beach around us falling away.

"Hey," Leo said as he gently set me down. "You're absolutely beautiful."

He said this matter-of-factly, as if telling me that the

chemical formula for water was H_2O. There was no sense, as there had been with T.J., that he was studying me as if I were a painting. He was merely speaking what was on his mind. And for the first time in my life, I realized what it was to feel desired.

"Thank you," I said, standing tall before him, the wind blowing my curls back.

Leo took my hand, drawing me toward the grotto. "I wasn't sure I'd see you tonight," he said. "I was worried your mom locked you in the house."

"She tried," I replied, a little dizzy from our kissing.

Leo laughed. "Well, I'm glad I came prepared," he said as he led me through the opening of the grotto. What I saw in there made me lose my breath.

A checkered blanket was spread on the sand. Two wobbly candles were perched in each corner of the grotto, illuminating the feast in the center of the blanket: French fries in a waxed paper cone, and on two torn newspaper pages, vegetarian sushi rolls and the delicious crab cakes I'd eaten at the pub in Fisherman's Village. A decanter of red wine was balanced beside two plastic cups.

"Leo, you're unreal," I whispered — and then, considering my words, smiled.

"I'm sorry I couldn't get actual plates," Leo said, pushing a hand through his hair. "You're probably used to eating off —"

"Stop," I told him, kissing his cheek. "It's perfect."

And it was. We squeezed together on the blanket and ate by the flickering candlelight, Leo telling me about the events at the marine center that afternoon, while I told him things at home were tense. Leo let me have all the crab cakes, and I let him have the vegetarian sushi rolls. We split the fries, and Leo poured us each a cup of wine.

"I don't really drink," I told Leo, taking a small sip. The wine was tasty, though, rich with flavors. Better than the fancy Champagne I'd tried the night before.

"Me, neither," Leo said, touching his cup to mine as his dimples appeared. "But I figured this was a special occasion."

"Why?" I asked, and with a sharp twist of pain, I remembered that, because of Leo's fishing trip and my Sunday departure, tonight would be our good-bye. Leo didn't know that yet, but I felt a wave of sadness so strong that I had to put my French fry down.

"Because . . . I missed you," Leo said, his cheeks coloring.

"I missed you, too," I whispered, hoping I wouldn't burst into tears again. I took a bigger gulp of wine to swallow down the feeling.

"Hold on, what's the matter?" Leo asked right away, putting down his cup and taking my hand.

"Leo." I gazed at him, my throat tight. I wished that he wasn't always so perceptive. "I'm leaving Selkie Island this

Sunday. My mom and I, we're going back to New York." Just saying the words was heart-wrenching.

Leo's face fell, and his sea green eyes darkened. "Really?" he said after a minute, his voice deeper than it had been before. I could only nod. He took a drink of his wine, then spoke again. "I mean, I knew you weren't going to be here permanently. But I guess I didn't expect it to be so soon. . . ." He trailed off, the muscle in his cheek jumping.

"It's not *fair*," I blurted, grasping his hand and feeling a swell of frustration. "We only just found each other." I thought of what Leo had said the last time we were in the grotto, about summer storms on Selkie. Maybe he and I were meant to be nothing more than a storm — quick and intense and then over.

"I don't think it's supposed to be fair, or easy," Leo said thoughtfully. "The course of true love never did run smooth."

At the word *love*, my heart juddered. I'd always dismissed love as such a fleeting and unreliable emotion. The stuff of fairy tales, of fiction. But there was a certainty to the happiness I felt when I was with Leo. Was that love?

Instead of giving voice to my thoughts, I asked, "Who said that?"

"Who else?" Leo offered me a small smile. "Shakespeare. A *Midsummer Night's Dream*. You should read it sometime."

And for the first time, I did wonder if I should read a play, or a poem, or a novel. Maybe falling in love — if that's what was happening to me — made people want to read and listen to and see beautiful things. Though, at the moment, I felt as if Leo and I ourselves were in the middle of a midsummer night's dream, with the candlelight around us and the muffled roar of the ocean outside our rocky enclave.

Which made our impending separation all the more bittersweet.

"I just wish . . . New York and Selkie weren't so far apart," I said quietly, hearing the wobble in my voice. "I mean, do you even have e-mail? Or . . ."

"Miranda," Leo said, resting his forehead against mine. "Stop thinking about practicalities for once. And logistics. Just go with the flow. Okay?" His crooked smile was as disarming as ever.

"Okay, *dude*." I laughed, which started him laughing, too.

The next thing I knew, we were kissing. Softly at first, then with growing urgency. I felt addicted to the taste of Leo's salty, sweet mouth, the pressure of his lips against mine. *It's our last night,* I thought. I wanted to savor everything.

Still kissing me, Leo used one arm to clear away our leftovers from the blanket. I twined my arms around his neck, and together we toppled over. Again, we both burst out laughing, but then our lips were brushing once more and we couldn't stop ourselves from kissing. Our breathing grew heavier, and my skin felt hot as the Selkie sunshine. Leo put his hand on my lower back and drew me so close that I could feel the full length of him against me. I trembled. There was an intensity building within me, one I had never known before.

Without hesitation, I took Leo's hand and guided it to the zipper on my dress.

"Are you sure?" Leo whispered, breaking our kiss for a moment. His face was flushed and his green eyes were glowing in the near darkness.

"I'm sure," I said steadily.

It was then that I understood: I hadn't been ready with Greg, because Greg hadn't been right for me.

With Leo, I was ready.

I closed my eyes and drew in a deep breath as Leo pulled down my zipper and eased me out of the dress. The cool, misty air bathed my shoulders and arms. It crossed my mind that Isadora's dress would get sandy but I decided not to care. I reached up and unzipped Leo's hoodie, and he yanked his T-shirt up over his head and flung it away.

Then I felt Leo pause.

I opened my eyes and found him studying me with an amused expression.

"You're wearing a swimsuit," he observed.

Right.

My swimming plan. I'd forgotten.

I lifted my head and glanced down at myself, taking in my black bathing suit and flats. I felt a pang of embarrassment, quickly followed by a surge of resolve. As much as I wanted to be with Leo right then, I needed to go swimming with him first. I couldn't skip this experiment.

"Yes," I said, tossing my hair in the confident way CeeCee did. "I thought we could go for a dip in the ocean."

Leo furrowed his brow. "Now?"

"Sure," I said, before I could lose my nerve. I propped myself up on my elbows.

"Why?" Leo asked, sitting back on his heels.

So I can have concrete proof that you are not, in fact, a strange sea creature.

"Why not?" I countered as I sat up entirely.

"Well." Leo bit his lip in an adorable manner. "We're kind of in the middle of something, aren't we?"

I laughed, getting to my feet. "We'll come back in here after. But let's go swimming now. It'll be fun." It might have been the wine, but I did feel suddenly impulsive, and I wasn't going to let that feeling slip away.

Leo was still staring up at me like I was acting insane — which wasn't too far off the mark. "Miranda, it's really dark out," he said, standing as well.

"I thought you went swimming at night all the time," I shot back, ducking out from under the grotto.

"Yeah, but *you* don't," Leo pointed out, following me with our newspaper scraps and cups in hand. He tossed them in the trash bin a little way up the beach.

I stood on the sand in my swimsuit and flats and looked up at the sky, a navy sheath dotted with stars. The ocean crashed into the shore, its foam rippling out in a curved line. Leo came to stand beside me.

"I don't think this is a great idea," he said.

His resistance only deepened my determination.

"Oh, don't be a spoilsport," I teased, nudging him with my elbow. "How's this — I'll wade in first and test the waters, and then you can join me."

"Okay," Leo said reluctantly.

I stepped out of my flats, ready to walk to the water, but then Leo crouched beside me and put his hand on my bare ankle. My stomach tightened.

"I've been meaning to ask you," he said, looking pensive. "Why do you always hide your toes?"

"Are you trying to distract me?" I asked nervously.

"I'm serious." Leo laughed. "You have perfectly nice-looking feet."

"No, I don't," I replied, years of embarrassment rising to a crescendo inside me. "They're . . . weird. My toes were webbed when I was born. Look, you can still see the scarring from the surgery."

I pointed, a little startled that I was showing off my biggest flaw.

"Miranda," Leo said patiently, "you can't see much. But if you do look close enough, it looks, well . . . interesting."

"You mean weird," I supplied.

Leo shot me a grin, releasing my ankle. "What's so wrong with weird? I'm weird, too. We can be weird together."

Weird how? I wondered, but I didn't speak. I just leaned down to kiss the top of his head, and then I marched toward the water. The cool sand squished between my toes, and the warm ocean licked at my feet.

"It feels wonderful!" I called to Leo over my shoulder, hoping to entice him.

But he only waved, laughing. "I know!" he called back.

I stuck my tongue out at him, then turned and walked in deeper. The water climbed past my calves, my knees, my hips. I tilted my head back, feeling my hair brush my waist and the crisp air kiss my cheeks. With Leo standing not far behind me, I felt secure. Invincible.

So I ducked under.

I puffed out my cheeks and watched in wonder as my dark hair pooled out in front of me. Kicking off from the sandy bottom, I flattened myself and began to swim through the blue-gray world I had come to love so much. For a moment, I forgot to care about my Leo experiment and just relished being underwater.

When my lungs felt too full and my eyes were burning, I resurfaced. The air came as a shock, and I squealed, my hair plastered to my head and my mouth salt-stained. I spun around and waved to Leo, who now looked tiny standing on the sand. He waved back, and I felt my feet rise up on their own as I bobbed farther out.

"Come!" I called, my voice bouncing across the surf.

Leo held a hand to his ear, miming not being able to hear me. I laughed and submerged again, letting the current carry me. I swam lazily, doing a low-key breaststroke. The waves, though large, lapped lightly against me, rocking me from side to side like a mother rocking a child.

And then, suddenly, the ocean's embrace grew tighter, firmer. A force larger than me — it felt like gravity — began sucking at my feet, drawing me down. My heart stopped for a second. I noticed that the water around me had formed ripples that were a darker blue than the rest of the ocean. *A riptide,* I thought, remembering what T.J. had said on the boat. But what else had he said about riptides? Wasn't there some specific way to get out of them?

I couldn't remember.

It didn't matter; I was an experienced swimmer. I'd make it back to shore. I began to paddle hard, pushing against the strong current. But the harder I paddled, the harder the current seemed to push back. Fear gripped me, and I opened my mouth to call to Leo, but the wind snatched my words away. Water sloshed into my mouth, and I realized how deep I was floating down. I tried to wave to Leo but my arms felt very heavy, and I was working hard to slash at the water with my hands.

Stay calm, I told myself as I fought against the tide. *You're smarter than nature. You can do this.*

Something slimy wrapped itself around one of my legs. I tried to shake it off but its equally slimy twin twined itself around my other leg. I had a vision of my feet being bound, bound so tightly that I could no longer move. In my growing panic, I thought of sea serpents and krakens, of the beasts that lurked beneath the water. I'd been so wrong to dismiss those stories.

I tried to scream but I was dipping under, under. Just before I sank under the waves completely, I thought I saw Leo running toward the shore, but I couldn't be sure.

The water sucked me down. I thrashed wildly, feeling like the fish I had seen on the docks yesterday — the fish that had almost died.

No. Stop.

But I could no longer control my mind, or my body. The inevitable loomed toward me, and I felt myself begin to go limp. I was going to drown. This was how it was going to end. I was going to die a virgin. I was going to die without telling Leo I loved him. Without telling my mother what I had learned about Isadora. Without ever speaking to Linda again.

My lungs seemed to be on fire, and I could no longer fight, no longer struggle to stay afloat. I was collapsing backward, into a black blanket that swallowed me whole.

And then, just as abruptly, the blanket was gone, and I no longer felt limp or tired, and my lungs no longer burned.

I realized that someone was holding me, carrying me underwater, and I felt safe and calm. I looked up and saw that it was Leo, his golden hair streaming, his green eyes the color of the tall grasses that surrounded us. Leo. Of course! He had come to rescue me. He wouldn't have let me drown.

"Miranda," Leo said, gazing at me with tenderness. "It's okay. I'm here."

How strange that he is able to speak underwater, I thought, nodding dreamily at him, *and that I am able to hear him.* Yet it all seemed so natural.

And when Leo began to kiss me, that, too, seemed

natural. We kissed and kissed, our kisses as fluid as water. Then I glanced down, amazed at the speed at which we were swimming. And I saw — was it? — the briefest blur of red and gold.

Was this what it was like with Isadora and Henry? I wondered. Was this how she had seen him for the first time?

"I know," I said into Leo's ear as we swam past schools of brilliantly colored fish. "I know about you now."

"Shh," he said, cradling me close.

"I don't want to leave," I whispered, and Leo kissed me again. He kept on kissing me, drawing back and then looking at me from a great distance before kissing me once more. I wanted to kiss him back, but I couldn't quite move my lips.

And then the heaviness descended again, and I closed my eyes.

"Miranda? Miranda, can you hear me?"

Leo's voice was coming from very far away.

"Miranda, I know you can hear me. Miranda?"

Why was his tone so pleading, so frantic? I wanted to tell him not to worry, that I wouldn't ever tell his secret.

If only I could speak. Or open my eyes.

It was quiet around us; I could hear the rushing of the

ocean, and the slow rise and fall of Leo's breath. I felt the grit of sand between my teeth, and my body was completely drenched, waterlogged. Had Leo taken me to some sort of hiding place underwater?

I parted my lips — why were they so cracked? — to ask where we were, but instead I coughed, a wracking cough that shook my whole body. *I caught a cold,* I thought. *From swimming for so long.* I coughed again, and somehow felt more awake.

"Miranda?"

I managed to open my eyes and saw Leo hovering over me, soaking wet and bare chested. Was I lying down?

"Thank God," Leo muttered, gazing at me as if he could never look anywhere else. "You're okay. You're okay." He repeated this like a mantra.

I blinked at the dark rocks above Leo's head and realized that we were inside the grotto. Not under the sea. And I *was* lying on the ground, but there was something soft and dry beneath me. The checkered blanket? I tried to turn my head to see, but my neck ached.

"Careful," Leo murmured, scooting closer to me. "Don't move."

His own movement gave me the chance to run my eyes down his body. I saw, with a pang of disappointment, that only his tanned, muscular legs extended from his wet swim trunks. Of course. He would no longer have his tail out of water. But earlier, his tail had been there. I had seen it. I had *felt* it.

"You — your" — *tail*, I wanted to say, but my voice, croaky like a frog's, wouldn't cooperate with me.

"Don't," Leo said, moving my sopping hair out of my eyes. "You have to rest."

"What — what happened?" My voice still came out hoarse. I coughed again, feeling feeble and frail. How could it be? Only moments ago, I'd been happily gliding beneath the waves in Leo's arms. Dimly, I looked down at *my* arms and saw that Leo had wrapped me in his red hoodie.

Leo frowned. "You had . . . an accident. Do you remember? You got caught in a riptide, and it pulled you under."

A riptide. The word seemed faintly familiar, but my mind felt too cloudy to chase the memory down.

"You started panicking and you swallowed a lot of water," Leo went on, brushing what felt like sand off my forehead. "If I hadn't swum out to you in time . . . you could have . . ." His Adam's apple bobbed up and down. He didn't finish. He didn't need to.

"You saved my life," I whispered, regaining my voice. I reached my trembling, wet hands up to touch Leo's lips, wondering if I could ever repay him.

"It was my pleasure," Leo replied, his tone slightly playful but his face serious.

Everything came back to me then in a rush of clarity — the way the water had seemed to suck me down, and how hard I'd fought against the current.

"The sea serpents," I rasped, struggling to sit up, wanting Leo to understand. "The — the sharp-toothed sea serpents. They . . . tried to pull me down."

I motioned to my bare legs, which were spattered with drops of water and streaks of mud and sand. There were also long scratches in my calves — where I'd been bitten, no doubt. *Oh, my God.* How was I even alive?

Leo stared at me for a long moment, frowning. He seemed to be questing for the right words, and finally he spoke softly.

"Miranda, you had seaweed around your legs when I pulled you out. That's what you must have felt. Strands of seaweed."

Seaweed? Yes, I had seen seaweed when I'd gone under-water, but what I'd felt had been much fiercer. "But — but what are those cuts from?" I demanded, pointing.

"Rocks," Leo said, lightly caressing one of the scratches. "The ocean floor gets really rocky in the spot where you were. When you sank, you must have cut yourself."

I looked back at Leo, trying to process his logical explanation. Was he right? I had been so certain, in that moment, of the sea serpents' existence. As certain as I had been about Leo's underwater transformation.

The wind whispered through the grotto. Our candles had long been extinguished. I was sitting up now, my wet hair hanging down my back, and Leo and I were facing each other, our knees pressed together and our faces inches apart. I had to try to ask him.

"I — when you swam out to get me . . ." I began haltingly. Now that I was coming to my senses, my heart began to pump harder. "Underwater . . . you looked . . . I could have sworn I saw . . ." I bit my lip, trying to read Leo's reaction in his gaze.

There was a second — a millisecond — of joy in Leo's eyes, of relief and excitement. But it was so quick, so fleeting, that I might very well have conjured it. Then Leo cupped my cheek in his warm hand, studying me with concern.

"You were unconscious when I got to you," he murmured. "I was so scared. I took you in my arms and managed to swim back to shore with you, one-armed. As I was carrying you toward the grotto, you started to say things I couldn't really make out, but one of the things you said was, 'I don't want to leave.'"

"I remember that," I whispered, grabbing Leo's arms and holding on tight. "And then you kissed me," I added.

Leo's mouth curved up in that indelible crooked smile. "I didn't kiss you. I was giving you mouth-to-mouth resuscitation. It probably just seemed like a kiss to you." As if to demonstrate a true kiss, Leo drew my face toward his and touched his lips to mine.

His kiss, however brief, sent pleasure racing through me. But I couldn't get over the fact that Leo and I had seemingly switched roles — suddenly, he was the one with explanations for everything while I was willing to follow the tide.

Had it all been a hallucination, a dream? Or had I, in that suspended state before I lost consciousness, seen what was true, what Leo had tried to hide?

Would I ever know?

And then it occurred to me that maybe I didn't need to know. Maybe some things didn't require an explanation.

"Are you feeling strong enough to stand?" Leo asked as I rubbed my cold, bare legs. "We should get you home."

Home. Where Mom waited. Even if she would sleep through my return, I would have to tell her about what had happened in the morning — there would be no hiding the scratches on me or whatever other side effects I bore from my accident. I let out a sigh as deep as the ocean.

Slowly, Leo helped me to my feet, and he gently guided my feet back into my flats. My legs wobbly, I watched as Leo pulled his T-shirt on and then picked up Isadora's dress. He shook it out before balling it up and tucking it under his arm. He offered to carry me, but I refused, wanting to see if I could walk all right. And I could, only with an unsteady gait. As a compromise, Leo wrapped his arm tight around my waist and told me to hoist most of my weight onto him.

As we slipped out of the grotto, I was thankful for the cover of night. I knew we must have made a strange sight, me in my swimsuit and Leo's hoodie, wet and shaken. And Leo in his swim trunks and bare feet, holding my dress and holding me up.

Silently, we crossed the beach toward the docks and made our limping, careful way up the pebbly path to Triton's Pass. Before I knew it, we had reached the thick oak trees and hanging Spanish moss of Glaucus Way.

"I think I'm okay here," I told Leo, coming to a standstill. I felt so secure in his arms — as secure as I had felt underwater — but I knew that if Mom happened to see him again, he'd endure a wrath worse than that of the kraken. I reached for Isadora's dress; I'd stashed my door key inside the skirt pocket. "I can walk the rest of the way, and I'll just let myself into the house —"

Leo gave me a *you've got to be kidding* look before wordlessly releasing my waist and then scooping me up into his arms. There was no room for argument as he carried me down Glaucus Way, toward the looming specter of The Mariner.

I felt distinctly old-world glamorous — almost like a

Southern damsel from the Civil War era — as Leo carried me up the porch steps. He retrieved the key from the dress pocket and inserted it into the lock.

"I want an explanation!"

I heard Mom's furious voice first so at least I was prepared for the sight of her, standing in the foyer. Pale-faced, she was wearing her dress from dinner, holding her cell phone in one hand and a flashlight in the other. And at her side was Mr. Illingworth, looking less polished than usual in jeans and an untucked button-down shirt.

Leo and I stood frozen.

"What happened?" Mom demanded, looking wildly from Leo to me. "I — was about to call the police. Or go look for you. I called Teddy first. How — what — I —"

For the first time in my life — and maybe hers — Mom was at a loss for words.

"Did he hurt you?" she finally asked, rushing up to me.

I was so confused that I simply stared at her — and then I realized she was talking about Leo. I shook my head vehemently, but I did wriggle out of Leo's grip and he, understanding, let me drop slowly to the floor.

Mom turned to Leo, her eyes fiery. "If you so much as laid a hand on my daughter, so help me, I will —"

"Amelia." I was surprised to hear Mr. Illingworth's voice. He sounded gruff, and worried. "Let them explain."

I shot a thankful look at T.J.'s father, then faced my mother. "Mom," I managed to say. "Listen to me. Leo saved my life."

My mother's cell phone fell from her grip and clattered to the wooden floor, landing on the compass. She studied me, my battered, soaking wet figure. Leo stood by my side, his body tensed, not speaking or moving.

"I almost drowned," I added, for clarification. Speaking that phrase gave it a sudden, frightening realness, but I still didn't feel afraid. I was with Leo. I'd been with Leo the whole time, whether his transformation had been real or imagined. He'd been with me.

"What were you *doing*?" Mom asked, putting a hand to her head. "I came home late from Delilah's, past one o'clock, and when I saw your bedroom door wide open, I thought you'd run off and —"

"I went for a swim," I replied truthfully. "I left to go meet Leo on the beach. When I went in the water, I —" I thought once more of the sea serpents, of everything I had believed back on the beach.

Leo cleared his throat. "She got caught in a riptide," he said, stepping forward.

Mr. Illingworth took a step forward, too. "Those are very common around here, Amelia," he put in, and gave Leo an *I'm on your side* nod.

"It was lucky that I was there to swim out and bring her back to shore," Leo said, looking at Mom in his impassioned, earnest way. "I'm so sorry, ma'am. I hope you know I mean your daughter no harm. Quite the opposite, actually."

Mom didn't speak. I could practically see her mind working over everything, her natural inclination not to trust people being won over by the impossibility of Leo and me, before her. Together.

"I know you don't," she finally told Leo, her tone resigned. "I know you don't."

Mr. Illingworth came forward and extended his hand to Leo. "You were very brave, young man," he said.

I blinked at Mr. Illingworth, as if seeing him for the first time. Maybe he was a good match for Mom, in a way; he could be calm in those few moments when she wasn't.

While Leo, looking as surprised as I felt, shook Mr. Illingworth's hand, I saw Mom's gaze land on the dress under Leo's arm. Her eyes widened, and she looked at me.

"Isn't that," she began, a question in her voice, "one of Isadora's? Why . . ."

"It fit," I said, by way of explanation. I was too tired to say more.

Mom nodded dazedly and she accepted the dress from Leo. She studied the bunched material in her hands, then gave Leo a meaningful look.

"Thank you," she said quietly.

Something — some inner reserve of strength — had been keeping me together during our interaction, but just then I felt myself weaken with relief. Mom, seeing this, announced that she was going to walk Mr. Illingworth out, and then she'd be back to tend to me. Mr. Illingworth told me he was glad I was all right, and then he and Mom stepped out the front door, murmuring together.

Leo and I turned to each other, and I caught my breath.

This was it — the briefest of windows in which we could say our good-byes. I no longer heard the whirring of the ceiling fans, and the dwindling night seemed to hold its breath as he and I stood in the dim foyer. An idea came to me.

"Maybe," I began, my voice plaintive, "I can stay here on Selkie. With you." I took his hand. "I'm sure there's room for another intern at the marine center, right?" After all, I couldn't see myself at the Museum of Natural History now, among the dinosaur bones and data charts, pretending I didn't know deeper secrets. "And I could even — maybe — help you out on your dad's fishing boat."

I realized how ridiculous my offer sounded. But the thought of parting with Leo felt as impossible as what I'd seen underwater.

"Miranda," he said tenderly. He reached out to stroke my

hair, his fingers getting tangled in my sandy curls. "You know that wouldn't work. You have to go home."

"I know," I replied as tears blurred my vision. "A girl can dream, I guess." Not that I'd ever been a dreamer before.

Leo's own eyes were very bright, and he swallowed a few times before speaking again. "I wanted to thank you," he said.

"Me?" I asked, shaking my head. "For what? I didn't rescue you."

"For giving me a chance," Leo said, and the mischievous expression I'd come to love crossed his face. "I know I wasn't always straightforward with you." His cheeks colored a little.

I smiled through my tears. "It's okay."

Suddenly, I remembered a quotation of my own, one I had learned back at the beginning of the school year, in physics class. I decided to tell it to Leo then.

"The most beautiful thing we can experience is the mysterious," I said.

Leo raised one eyebrow, and his thumb traced my mouth in a way that made me shiver. "That's true," he replied. "Who said that?"

"Who else?" I smiled. "A scientist. Einstein."

Leomaris Macleod and I leaned toward each other and kissed, soft and sweet. Then we hugged, and I breathed in his fresh smell, tried to memorize the warmth of his body, the firmness of his chest against mine. When we parted, I gave him back his hoodie for the second time. I couldn't believe I was letting him go. I watched, my heart racing, as he walked to the door. Before he opened it and stepped out into the night, he glanced over his shoulder and smiled at me.

"Hey, Miranda?" he said.

I waited for him to quote Shakespeare. To tell me that he was a merman. To actually say the word *good-bye*.

"Remember, on the beach walk, when we talked about happy endings?" he asked.

"I do," I said quietly. I wouldn't forget anything about Leo.

"We'll get ours," Leo said. "Soon."

And then he was gone.

I wiped my tears with the back of my hand, still feeling the ghost of Leo's lips on my mouth, hearing his voice whisper in my ear. I wanted him to come back, but I also felt tired and achy, wrung out. Slowly I settled down on the staircase's bottom step. I knew Mom would come back any minute, but before she did, I wanted to sit still and imagine Leo. I imagined him walking down the pebbly path and across the dock as the sun began to peer over the ocean. And I imagined him back on the beach, diving into the water, his body moving gracefully with the current. Returning home.

Fifteen

TRUTHS

After the bath and the cup of hot tea Mom insisted on, I crawled into bed and fell asleep instantly. And for the first time since arriving on Selkie, I slept without dreaming.

I awoke to bright daylight coming through the pink curtains and a delicious smell wafting under my door. The smell was both exotic and familiar — cinnamon and bay leaf and ginger and something else I couldn't name — and it made my stomach growl.

I was still sore, which became painfully apparent as I turned my head to see the clock; it was two in the afternoon. But I no longer felt shaky and fragile, even though the prior night's events seemed as close and as real as ever. I could still recall the terror I'd felt before sinking underwater. I could still feel Leo's arms around me.

Thinking of Leo, wondering if he was already on his fishing trip, I carefully eased myself out of bed. Pulling up my pajama bottoms, I noted that the scratches on my legs were, thanks to Mom's application of Neosporin, starting to heal. I hobbled downstairs, the mouthwatering scent growing stronger.

I found Mom in the kitchen, standing at the counter and surrounded by ingredients. There was a bowl containing scrubbed red potatoes sitting beside freshly shucked ears of corn and a cutting board laden with pink shrimp. A large silver pot full of water was bubbling away on the stove.

When I entered, Mom turned to me, and I saw that her eyes were red with tears. I felt a tremor of alarm, remembering how she'd told me the news of Isadora's death. Then I noticed that she was in the process of chopping an onion.

"You're up," Mom said, setting her knife down and coming toward me. She wiped her hands on her apron and regarded me cautiously. "How are you feeling?"

"Much better," I replied. "I needed the sleep." I smiled cautiously at Mom; she didn't seem angry now, and she hadn't last night, when she'd returned from bidding farewell to Mr. Illingworth. But she hadn't mentioned Leo. I nodded toward the pot, knowing that if my thoughts lingered on Leo, *I'd* start crying. "What are you making?"

"Low-country boil," Mom replied, turning back to her

ingredients. "I thought you could use some hearty regional cuisine. This is an old classic. My mother used to make it, and so did my grandmother before her."

"It smells amazing," I said, joining my mother at the counter and surveying the various potions she had going at once. "What do you put in it?"

"Everything." Mom laughed, and I realized what joy cooking brought her. "Potatoes, corn, sausage, shrimp. Oh, and Old Bay seasoning — that must be what you're smelling. That gives the boil its extra kick." Mom glanced at me sideways and said, casually, "Do you want to watch?"

"Actually," I said, suddenly curious and eager to throw myself into an activity that felt real and solid, "can I . . . help?"

Within minutes, I was learning how to peel and devein shrimp and I was, to my surprise, not remotely grossed out. There was something satisfying about working with my hands, something almost scientific about the process. Mom and I worked side by side in perfect rhythm — like two surgeons, I thought — with Mom passing me a knife and me handing her an ear of corn at different intervals.

When all the ingredients were prepared and could be added to the pot, I watched in near awe as they cooked, each element breaking down, influencing the other. The potatoes grew redder, the shrimp paler, the corn a bright sunshine yellow. Cooking, I realized, was not unlike chemistry. Both arts were, ultimately, about change.

By the time the boil was done and Mom and I could eat, I had almost forgotten about the animosity that had existed between us over the past few days. Cooking had bonded us again, and we smiled at each other as Mom cracked open a cold beer for herself (the first I'd ever seen her with) and I spooned our portions into Isadora's china bowls. Then we sat down across from each other at the round kitchen table.

We began eating in friendly silence; the smoky boil, with its mix of flavors and textures, tasted as heavenly as it smelled. Between this and grits, I was taking quite a liking to Southern cuisine. When I complimented Mom on the dish, she grinned and said graciously, "I had an excellent sous-chef."

"So you used to eat this growing up?" I asked around a mouthful of red potatoes. The steam rising from the food seemed to be the very breath of the past. In it, I could taste nostalgia and memory and history — both my mother's and Selkie Island's.

Mom nodded, nibbling on an ear of corn. "All the time. Isadora — well, I know I'm not one to lavish praise on her, but she made a mean low-country boil." Mom got a far-off look in her gray eyes, and I flashed onto an image of her, young and sitting at this table with Isadora, the two of them eating the mess of corn and sausage and shrimp. I felt the same chill I had felt yesterday when I'd discovered the letters in the black trunk.

I cleared my throat and wiped my hands on a napkin. I simply had to tell Mom what I'd found in Isadora's closet — she'd discover it anyway once we started packing everything up.

"Mom?" I began, a little nervous. "Speaking of Isadora . . ."

Mom sighed, putting down her demolished corncob. "Miranda. I know what you're going to ask me," she said.

My stomach jumped. "You do?" Once again, I thought of Wade's psychic-mom theory.

Mom nodded and gazed at me solemnly. "And it's high time I told you why your grandmother and I were estranged."

Oh.

I nodded, new curiosity flaring up in me.

Mom took a sip of beer, then looked at me. "It's a long story," she warned.

"That's fine," I said. I had nowhere to go, and stories were starting to grow on me.

"It all started before my eighteenth birthday," Mom began. "My seventeenth year was tumultuous. My father passed away from a heart attack, and Isadora decided that we shouldn't come to Selkie Island anymore. She threw all her energies into planning my debutante ball. And my wedding."

"You were a debutante?" I asked Mom, smiling.

Mom rolled her eyes, her cheeks coloring slightly. "I never quite made it that far, but yes, that was the plan. In Savannah society — high society — when a girl turns seventeen or eighteen, she has her 'coming out' at a ball, or a cotillion. Cotillions are very lavish affairs, almost akin to weddings. And long ago, the debutante tradition had much to do with a girl being of marrying age. Of course, Isadora made sure that I had the double whammy. Once I turned eighteen in April, Theodore Illingworth and I were to be married that summer. There would be no college for me, and Teddy and I would move into the carriage house on the Illingworths' Savannah property."

"How did you even meet Mr. Illingworth?" I asked, wanting to fill in the holes. I thought of him in our foyer last night, how different he had seemed to me in that moment. "How long did you date?"

Mom shrugged, fussing with the label on her beer bottle. "We grew up in the same neighborhood in Savannah, Ardsley Park, and we both summered here on Selkie. We were both the youngest in our families. As far as our mothers were concerned, it was a no-brainer that we'd end up together." Mom was quiet for a moment, studying her beer bottle, and then glanced up at me. "But I didn't love him," she said softly.

What about now? I wanted to ask. Still, I kept the question to myself, knowing Mom had more to say.

"Don't get me wrong," she sighed. "For a time, I *was* happy with Teddy. He was a true gentleman, and he treated me very well. But he didn't quite understand my interest in science and medicine. I think he found me a little strange." She smiled knowingly at me. "And by my eighteenth birthday, I was fed up. I hated how my whole life had been mapped out for me, every last detail. I hated how predictable everything had become, how all my friends dated all my other friends, how all the girls wore the same sandals every summer, attended the same parties on the boardwalk. I began to resent the rigid structures of my life — the rules that were to be followed at all times."

The way Mom was speaking made me think of how I had unleashed my story on Leo yesterday — again, a faucet, a shower spout, came to mind. The memories and old truths were pouring out of my mother at last.

"I had other interests and desires," Mom said, meeting my gaze. "I had told Isadora, at an early age, that I wanted to be a doctor and she had chucked me under my chin and told me I could marry one. That was Isadora to a tee — she was whip smart, you see, but she had long ago made peace with her station in life. And she saw no reason why I shouldn't follow her lead. Isadora always played by the rules."

No, she didn't, I thought, but I didn't speak.

"Without telling my mother, I had applied to college — and not just any college, but to a college up north," Mom continued.

"Yale," I filled in for her, and she nodded.

"Y is for Yankee," she said with a smile. "Isadora had very little regard for Yankees. She was one of those Southern women who referred to the Civil War as the War of Northern Aggression. Her youngest daughter going off to study in the wilds of Connecticut — there couldn't be a worse fate.

"So I told her. I received my acceptance letter from Yale on the day before the cotillion, and I marched over to my mother and told her. I told her I was sick of it all, the closed-mindedness, the lack of opportunities. I had my acceptance letter in one hand, and in the other I held my debutante ball gown. And I handed the gown to Isadora. I told her I had no use for it anymore. I told her to call off the ball. And the wedding."

"What did she say?" I asked, trying to envision the showdown.

"She was horrified, of course," Mom said, looking a little pleased and regretful. "We had a terrible argument. She told me I was going through a rebellious phase, that I'd come to my senses. I didn't, obviously."

"Is that when you stopped speaking?" I asked, leaning toward my mother.

"That was the beginning of the end," Mom said, tracing a circle on her icy beer bottle. "When I went on to Yale, and met your father, and eventually married him — that's when the real rupture happened." Mom smiled, her expression suddenly fond. "Your father," she added, looking at me, "was unlike anyone I had ever met. He was brash and loud and he broke rules all the time. Of course, that's probably what led to our divorce. If I'd been speaking to Isadora at the time, I'm sure she would haven't been able to resist chortling, *I told you so.*"

"Isadora didn't approve of Dad, huh?" I asked, smiling, too. Just thinking of my father — my funny, blunt, Yankee father, not a merman at all — filled me with a comforting sense of normalcy.

"Are you kidding?" Mom laughed. "My senior year, I dared to bring him home for winter break, and the fights Isadora and I had about him are legendary."

Mom paused, eying me, and I wondered if she was thinking — as I was — of our recent fights. I remembered how, yesterday, she'd cut herself off in the middle of scolding me about Leo. How she'd glanced at the photos on the mantel. Had she been thinking of herself and Isadora having a similar argument about an inappropriate boy?

Had Mom realized — the most frightening realization — that she was turning into her own mother?

"I think," Mom went on, putting her chin in her hand, "that Isadora just couldn't accept how far I'd strayed from her and from everything she believed in." Mom chuckled, shaking her head. "You know, Coral told me that Isadora even hung on to my debutante gown for safekeeping, as if I was going to change my mind someday."

Something stirred in me, a lightninglike realization.

"What did your dress look like?" I asked, and Mom raised her eyebrows, understandably thrown by my question. "CeeCee's influence," I deadpanned, hoping that explanation would be enough.

"It was quite pretty," Mom replied, her eyes misting over again. "It was cream colored, with these small pink roses trailing down the side. It actually broke my heart to give the dress up, but I knew I had to stand strong." Mom shrugged, not aware of the way I was gaping at her.

My heart and my mind were racing. The dress in the trunk was Mom's debutante ball gown. Isadora *had* hung on to it for all these years. But why had she hidden it? And why did it share a hiding place with her letters from Henry Williams?

Mom was saying something else about Isadora's reaction, but my thoughts were on those letters. Even though so much had happened since I'd read them yesterday, they were still fresh in my mind. And, as I had done with the passages in Llewellyn Thorpe's book, I started piecing fragments together, fragments that I had seen but hadn't quite absorbed.

Like the fact that Isadora had written those letters about a year before Mom had been born.

Like the fact that — *oh, my God* — Henry Williams was, according to the address on the envelopes, and to Daryl Phelps's letter, Henry *B.* Williams.

Henry *Blue* Williams.

Mom's name was Amelia Blue. That was what people had always called her until she got to college, she'd said. Before she'd decided that just plain *Amelia* was easier. That was what people on Selkie Island called her now.

I could barely catch my breath. Had Isadora named her youngest daughter Amelia Blue as a tribute to the man she'd loved? Or had she given her that name because Henry Blue Williams had been Mom's . . .

"Miranda?" Mom asked, and I realized that she'd stopped talking — and that I had pushed back my chair and was hugging myself. I could feel how huge my eyes were, and there was gooseflesh on my arms. Mom stared at me with naked concern, and repeated my name.

"Mom," I burst out. "Isadora kept your debutante gown. It's in a trunk in her closet upstairs. Along with these —

letters. Letters that Isadora wrote to a man named Henry Blue Williams."

I waited for my mother to ask me what on earth I was talking about. But instead, her face grew pale and her eyebrows came together.

"They wrote letters?" she asked softly.

"You know about him?" I asked, a shiver going down my back.

Mom nodded slowly, pressing her fingers to her temples. Then she looked at me, fear and hesitation in her eyes.

"Mom, tell me," I pleaded. I already felt I knew what was coming.

"You see," Mom said, and she surprised me by reaching across the table to put her hand on top of mine, "a lot of truths came out in those fights I had with Isadora. During one argument, I lost my patience and lashed out at her, saying that her dramatics had driven my father to an early grave. And she told me" — Mom paused, and took a big breath — "she told me that my real father wasn't Jeremiah Hawkins but a man named Henry Blue Williams. She didn't say where he was from, and I didn't want to know the details. I wasn't even sure if she was lying or not — Isadora loved to spin fanciful tales."

"I think he must have been from Selkie Island," I said, my heart hammering. "A local." *And quite possibly a merman.*

Which meant that Mom —

Which meant that I —

My head swam. The kitchen began to take on a hazy, otherworldly quality. Was *that* why Leo had been drawn to me? Why I loved the ocean? Why my toes were webbed? I knew Mom wasn't a mermaid — I'd seen her swim enough times to know that — but maybe the traits got watered down through the generations. Or maybe my own children would be . . .

I couldn't think. The basics of my life seemed altered and thrown into question. After all, our families — our ancestors — are our identities. Biology is destiny.

I'm not who you think I am, I had said to T.J. the last time I'd seen him. Maybe I wasn't who *I'd* thought I was, either.

"That — you know, that makes sense," Mom said quietly, pulling me out of the quicksand of my thoughts. Her eyes were tear-filled and her bottom lip was trembling, but the sight didn't frighten me now. "My God. All this time, I had no idea — none at all — why Isadora left The Mariner to me. Yes, I loved Selkie Island, but so did Coral and Jim, and she never quarreled with them like she did with me. But . . ."

"Maybe this house is your birthright in a different way," I offered, feeling choked up as well. *And maybe Isadora wasn't such a monster after all.* I didn't dare utter those words, although I could tell, from the look dawning in Mom's eyes, that she was starting to think that, too.

"You know something, my love?" Mom squeezed my hand. "You're too smart for your own good." She let out a big sigh, then dabbed at her cheeks with a napkin. "I'd like to see those letters sometime," she added softly, glancing up at me.

I nodded, suddenly looking forward to sharing that discovery with my mother. Maybe there was even more in those letters that would teach me things. "I mean, we have to pack them up soon, don't we?"

"Oh," Mom said, smiling at me. She set down her napkin and sighed. "That was the other thing I meant to tell you."

"What?" I asked, feeling a new twinge of nervousness. I wasn't sure how many more revelations I could handle.

"I've been giving it a lot of thought, and I've decided not to sell the house," Mom said. "We're keeping The Mariner."

"We are?" I gasped. It was true that the signs had been there: Mom suddenly losing interest in packing and organizing; the conversation I'd overheard between her and Daryl Phelps. "Why did you change your mind?" I blurted, and offered the first thing that came to *my* mind. "Is it because of Mr. Illingworth?"

Mom looked at me, startled, and then she blushed — a full-on blush that, for some reason, made me grin. "In part," she said, glancing down at her half-eaten food. "In part because of Delilah and the other friends I've reconnected with here. It's funny how people change in life, Miranda. I was so *certain* about things when I was your age. I had such strong opinions about the kind of people that Teddy and Delilah and my mother were. I wrote them off. Now . . . after so many years . . . well, some people are worth a second chance."

Like Linda, I thought, surprising myself.

"Like Leo," Mom said, doubling my surprise.

I blinked at her, overwhelmed.

Mom smiled at me, her eyes beseeching. "I know I was a little harsh with him," she told me. "I'll have to apologize to him the next time."

The next time. Relief and disbelief hit me like a wall of water, so powerful that I caught my breath. There *was* going to be a next time. If Mom and I were keeping the house, that meant we'd be back on Selkie Island.

I was going to see Leo again.

And that realization, more than anything else, was what made me get up, walk around the table, and give my mother a hug.

"I'm glad," I told her. "I'm glad we're keeping the house." I was even okay with the idea of her spending time with Mr. Illingworth again. I really was.

Mom hugged me back, tight, tighter than she'd ever hugged me before. I wondered if Mom wished she could reverse time and hug Isadora in the same way. I was pretty sure they had never embraced over their unfinished low-country boils.

"The house still needs repairs, though," Mom said, releasing me with a pat on the arm. "If we're going to be spending summers here, we're going to need Internet. And the study needs a new coat of paint and all that. But it will be nice. A fresh start."

I nodded, listening to the ocean swish onto the shore and then recede. It struck me then how much the past — not just the past but history and family — was like the ocean tide. It was always the same ocean, but the waves made it fresh and new each time.

Mom and I spent the rest of the evening packing the belongings we'd brought with us to Selkie. There were also a few additions; when I showed Mom Isadora's trunk, she grew teary-eyed again, both at the sight of her debutante gown and the letters. She decided to pack up everything, saying it would be best if we went over the letters together, at our own pace, at home in Riverdale. And the gown, she said, could use a good dry cleaning in the city. The same went for the dress I'd worn last night, and Mom said I was welcome to any of Isadora's other dresses. "I bet you'd look very pretty in her style of clothes," she'd said, regarding me affectionately, and I was pleased.

There was one more dress to deal with; as night fell, I

walked CeeCee's lavender dress and her charm bracelet over to her house. After all my intense talk with Mom, I was actually ready for a dose of CeeCee's lightness. Althea, answering the door, told me that CeeCee was in her room and that the Coopers were out for the evening. Jacqueline, Althea informed me as she waved me upstairs, was out with a young man — Macon, I presumed.

I knocked on CeeCee's door, but she must have not heard me over the music blaring inside, so I slowly turned the knob, hoping I wasn't overstepping my bounds.

"Are you decent?" I asked, pretending to cover my eyes.

"Oh, my gosh!" CeeCee cried, spinning away from her mirror. "Miranda! Don't come in!"

She was wearing a short, ruffled nightie, and nothing seemed strange — until I noticed that she had a strip of white paper stuck to her chin. I glanced at her vanity, at the small tub of hot wax and the tongue depressors that sat there.

"I — I get these little hairs on my chin sometimes," CeeCee told me unnecessarily, her face flaming. "I've been meaning to get electrolysis, but — I — I should have locked the door." Her hands were trembling as she ripped the cloth from her chin in one motion.

"CeeCee, it's okay," I said, biting down on my lip to keep from giggling at her dramatic reaction. "It's not a big deal."

"Miranda, you cannot tell *anyone*," CeeCee told me fiercely, slamming her door as I laid her dress and bracelet down on the bed. "It would ruin me."

I turned to face her; there was an angry red mark on her chin, and her eyes were full of shame. "What are you talking about?" I asked, shaking my head. "You're not the first girl who's had to wax her chin. I think it's pretty common."

"It's embarrassing," CeeCee sputtered. "It's a problem I have — I totally got it from my dad's side of the family — they're all *so* hairy." She shuddered, then walked over to her bed, clearing aside clothes and magazines so she could sit. She motioned for me to sit beside her. "I really wish you hadn't seen me doing this," she said quietly.

I was thrown by how different she seemed from the typically chipper CeeCee. I sat down next to her, studying her pretty face. "Why?" I asked. "I'm, like, the *last* person you should be ashamed in front of." I glanced down at my feet, encased in Converse.

"Please." CeeCee rolled her big blue eyes at me. "You're perfect, Miranda. You're always so — I don't know — in control and stuff. It's totally intimidating."

I was blindsided by her words. "You're joking, right?" I exclaimed. "That's basically how I feel about *you* and your friends," I admitted with a shrug. "You must not realize how you girls come off to other people."

CeeCee smirked. "Virginia and Jackie? Give me a break. Gin has a total inferiority complex — why do you think she's always desperate for boy attention? And Jackie's getting better, but she had major eating issues for a while there. She was all roly-poly a few years ago, and she hates it when anyone brings that up."

I felt like CeeCee was speaking a foreign language. "That's crazy," I told her, trying to process everything.

"This is all top-secret, of course," CeeCee said quickly, giving me a piercing look.

"Of course," I echoed, clasping my hands in my lap. CeeCee looked so forlorn that I could only think of one way to cheer her up. "I have a secret, too," I said, glancing back down at my sneakers.

"Ooh, what?" CeeCee whispered, inching closer to me. I could already feel her brightening. "I won't tell the girls, I swear."

"Do you remember that guy in the marine center?" I said, smiling as I glanced back up at CeeCee. "The one who was giving the tour?"

"Sort of," CeeCee said, looking confused. "He was cute?"

I nodded, feeling my smile widen and my heartbeat pick up. "We kind of, um, had, like, a thing."

"Shut *up*!" CeeCee squealed, bouncing up and down on the bed. "How? When? Oh, my gosh — a local boy? That is so naughty of you, Miranda!" She gazed at me with something like admiration.

"Not really," I laughed, blushing.

"Don't worry," CeeCee told me in a conspiratorial whisper. "Your secret's safe with me."

I wasn't sure how sincere that promise was, but I didn't really care. I didn't want Leo to be a secret.

Except for what I had seen, or thought I had seen, underwater — that, I knew, would belong only between me and Leo.

I stood to go, and CeeCee gave me back my jeans and shirt from the other night, along with a quick hug. She'd, naturally, learned last night that Mom wasn't selling The Mariner, so she said she couldn't wait for us to hang out again soon.

"Oh, and I forgot!" CeeCee added as I was leaving. She reached out to touch my hair, beaming. "I really like your new look."

I thanked CeeCee, realizing how comfortable I felt with my hair loose while wearing a standard outfit of vintage jeans and Converse. It was a nice balance.

Walking home from CeeCee's house, my thoughts turned back to Leo. I wished he wasn't out on his dad's boat, that there was some way I could let him know the good news about my being able to return to Selkie. I knew I could call the marine center and leave a message for him, and I was sure he had to have e-mail or a cell phone. But, as always was the case when Leo was in his world and I was in mine, those two worlds seemed very hard to bridge.

The next morning, though, as Mom and I walked onto the hot, sun-soaked dock with our bags full of old letters and old dresses, I glanced around hopefully — first toward the fog of Fisherman's Village, and then at the glimmering blue ahead. Deep down, I was sure that, in his half-magic way, Leo had to know what had transpired and would show up at the last minute on his father's boat to tell me how glad he was. But I didn't see him.

Back on Glaucus Way, The Mariner was locked up, Llewellyn Thorpe's book was still on the shelf in the study, everything was in its place. Yet I felt unsettled, unsteady, as if I were already on the boat.

Mom joined the line of passengers waiting for the ferry — among them the little blond boy and his parents who'd made the trip over with me — but I stood still on the wooden slats. I shielded my eyes from the glare, imagining Leo on his father's boat and hoping to catch sight of a fishing trawler.

There was nothing.

Maybe Leo wasn't really on a fishing trip, I thought, remembering our moment underwater. Maybe Selkie mermen needed to return to the ocean for a few days, as a kind of maintenance. I smiled, realizing that was the sort of detail Llewellyn Thorpe would have put in his book.

The ocean seemed so ordinary today, so itself — the swells and dips, the way it caressed the dock — that it was hard to believe in the unbelievable. I peered into its murky depths, trying to make sense of everything the water could contain.

When I glanced up again, there was a white speck on the horizon, and my heart sprang into my throat. But as the speck grew larger and larger, I realized it was *Princess of the Deep*. A sense of disappointment overwhelmed me, and for the first time since Leo and I had argued outside his house, I doubted him. I gave a sigh that made Mom glance at me over the tops of her sunglasses.

Letting out its familiar belch, the pretty ferry began to dock. The boat seemed much smaller to my eyes than it had a few weeks ago; *had I grown?* I wondered.

It seemed so strange that our time on Selkie was over for now, that in a few hours we'd be back to the firm reality of New York. And I'd be starting my internship, and maybe — maybe — thinking about calling Linda. But what I now knew about Mom, and what she knew about me, would follow us.

As the waiting passengers surged forward, Mom took my arm and steered me toward the gangplank. My throat welling with emotion, I glanced over my shoulder, still hoping to catch a glimpse of Leo's golden hair.

"Come on, Miranda," Mom said in her businesslike way. "Don't dawdle." The closer we got to the ferryboat — the closer to the mainland — the more she seemed to be returning to her old self, the accomplished surgeon.

Fighting tears, I stepped up to the gangplank and was fiercely studying my Converse when a gravelly male voice said, "We meet again, sweet pea."

Even before I lifted my head, I knew that it was Sailor Hat. He looked unchanged, wearing the same clothes he had worn last time. His sailor hat, too, was at the same jaunty angle.

"It's Miranda," I told him brusquely, blinking back my tears. I did not want him to see me crying. It was safer to return to the old dance we had performed.

"Well, looks like you survived, Miranda," Sailor Hat said, smiling at me as he tore my ticket in two.

On the one hand, I was not remotely in the mood for Sailor Hat's ribbing. On the other hand, I now had a new appreciation for everything he had told me.

"I guess," I said nonchalantly, but he was watching me in a quizzical way.

Maybe he knows, I realized with a rush of inspiration. He couldn't have known exactly what had happened to me during my stay, but he might have had answers about Leo. About the sea serpents. About Henry Blue Williams.

"Miranda," Mom said from behind me, giving me a gentle nudge. She was clearly aggravated that I was standing there exchanging pleasantries with this old man.

"No need to be sad," Sailor Hat said as I finally walked past him and up the gangplank. "You want to know the true legend of Selkie Island?" he called after me.

I turned and looked at him. I nodded.

"The island stays with you," he said. "Always. Even if you leave it behind. But one never really leaves Selkie behind. If you've been here once, you'll be back."

Mom had obviously heard him, and he'd obviously made an impression because she cleared her throat a few times, and, once he'd torn her ticket, she caught up to me and whispered, "Who *is* that guy?"

"I'm not sure," I replied, smiling. I suddenly felt light, as light as a bird skimming the water.

Without conferring first, Mom and I seemed to agree that the upper level was where we wanted to be. We climbed the winding metal staircase, and we positioned ourselves by the railing. As the wind blew my curls across my face, I inhaled the salty air and held it in my lungs. Then I looked one more time down into the sea.

And I saw something.

A movement, a flash, a glimpse that was familiar. It could have been a dolphin. A turtle. Or a sea serpent. Or really anything at all. But the sight of it, like Sailor Hat's words, made my spirits rise.

"See you soon," I murmured. Then, touching a hand to my lips, I threw a kiss down to the water.

Mom watched me, wearing an understanding smile. "Thinking of someone?" she asked. When I nodded, looking up at her, she put her arm across my shoulder. "He's a nice boy," she said. "A very nice boy."

"Thanks, Mom," I said as the ferryboat honked its horn. "I think so, too."

We slid away from the harbor, and my legs felt steady this time. I thought again of sailors — fearful, excited, half mad, their minds filled with krakens and mermaids. It was easy to go a little mad out on the ocean, I thought, with no specific chart or guide other than the sky. But madness could be lovely sometimes.

The ferryboat turned its great bulk, aiming its nose toward the opposite shore, but I spun around and watched Selkie Island: the trees and the houses and the boardwalk. I watched the land for as long as I could, until it disappeared behind its shawl of mist, and until I had it fixed in my mind — unchanged, mysterious, and beautiful.

ACKNOWLEDGMENTS

My deepest thanks to those who have been my ports in the storm:

My magnificent editor and mentor, Abby McAden, for restoring my sanity when necessary. Morgan Matson, Cheryl Weisman, Becky Terhune, Sheila Marie Everett, and the whole fantastic team at Scholastic, for helping this book come together. Jaynie Saunders Tiller and Chad Tiller (for the mullygrubs); Joshua Gee (for believing in merfolk); Lisa Ann Sandell; Siobhan McGowan; Marni Meyer; Adah Nuchi; Robert Flax; Jennifer Clark; Elizabeth Harty; Martha Kelehan; Emily Smith; Nicole Weitzner; Jon Gemma; and especially Daniel Treiman, for the friendship, support, advice, and love (and a special thanks to those who have tried, with interesting results, to teach me how to swim).

Of course my family — my brilliant sister, brother-in-law, and nephew, and my patient and wise parents, for forever reading and listening and soothing.

And to the memory of Ann Reit, and most especially to Craig Walker, without whom none of this would have ever been possible. You will always be remembered and loved.

The Year My Sister
Got Lucky

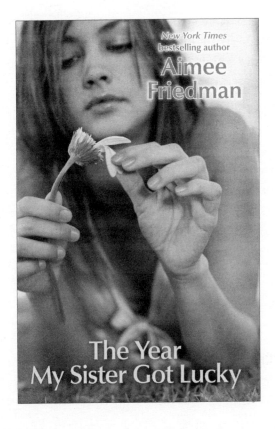

"Katie, you're being overdramatic." Michaela closes her eyes and her long lashes rest against her cheeks. I want to ask her what's wrong with being overdramatic, but it's clear she's trying to distract me, and I can't allow that to happen. Silently, I get to my feet and begin to cross our tiny room, sidestepping Michaela's boxy pink toe shoes, which lie in a tangle on the carpet. I duck to avoid the low shelf that holds our hand-painted Russian nesting dolls, and then plunk down onto Michaela's bed. Her sheets feel crisp and neat, unlike mine.

"Katie!" Michaela bolts upright. "Get off!" She nudges me — hard — with her foot. It's a foot made strong from years of ballet training, so I know better than to mess with it. "What are you doing?"

I shrug, but scoot back. We sit on opposite ends of the bed, facing each other. "This way, you can't ignore me," I explain.

Michaela groans. "We have to get up early for dance tomorrow and —"

"I'm not going to fall asleep anyway so —"

"— Svetlana has been *on* me about nailing my pirouettes and —"

"— you'd better tell me whatever it is that's bugging you because —"

"— if I'm zonked in the morning it will be all your fault —"

"— since when do we keep things from each other?"

It's that last question that quiets Michaela. She holds my gaze, and I think we are both holding our breaths. Sometimes when I'm staring right at Michaela, I get the creeped-out sensation that I'm looking at *myself*. We don't have the same eyes, but I guess it's the expression in them that's the same: a look that our mom calls "penetrating." I'm not sure what that means exactly, but right now, I do feel as if Michaela is boring into me with her gaze, trying to read me, or maybe to read herself. Outside, a garbage truck is huffing and puffing, and I can hear our dad's rumbly snores from the next room.

"Okay," Michaela says, and her voice is less than a whisper, a feather of a whisper. I can smell her breath — minty and toothpaste-y — and see the faint shimmer of sweat on her upper lip. "Promise you won't tell Mom and Dad?"

I knew it!

"I promise, I promise. Can I guess?" Michaela half smiles, half shrugs, so I pounce. "It's about dance, isn't it?" Leave it to Michaela to have nightmares about pirouettes.

Michaela slowly shakes her head from side to side. "Not really. Sort of. No."

I lean back on my hands, wracking my brain. School is a distant memory in August, and we're not close enough to September for Michaela's coming senior year to be an issue.

And then a wild thought occurs to me.

My pulse flutters at the base of my throat. No. Impossible. But it *could* be. What else would keep my levelheaded sister up at night other than . . .

"A *boy*?" I whisper in shock. "You're thinking about a boy." I feel my stomach drop.

Boys. Such strange, alien creatures. Take the boys in my junior high, for example. They all chew with their mouths open, get into scuffling fights in gym class, and look at the floor whenever girls speak to them. Horrible. Sofia Pappas, who is sixteen, swears up and down that boys get cuter once they hit high school — *and* that kissing them feels nice — but

I'm doubtful. After all, Michaela, who is seventeen and knows better, has never promised anything of the sort.

True, Michaela has only kissed one boy: Jason Rosenthal, the only boy in her dance class last year. Jason had wavy dark hair and a goofy smile, and was good at the big jumps. One afternoon, when I was home sick with a cold, Jason walked Michaela to the subway and kissed her just as the train was roaring in. The next day, he dropped out of dance school after some guys in his neighborhood found his tights in his bookbag and gave him a purple-black eye. Michaela never heard from Jason again, but she didn't seem to mind much. She's not the type to get all mopey and obsessive over boys — unless you count Ethan Stiefel, the so-gorgeous-it-hurts principal dancer of the American Ballet Theater. Michaela has a poster of him, leaping through the air, over her bed. Sometimes the two of us will lie back on Michaela's pillows and stare up at Ethan, wondering why we don't know any guys as perfect as him.

"Is Jason Rosenthal back?" I ask, studying Michaela's surprised face.

When she doesn't respond right away, dread seeps through me. So *that* explains why my sister's been avoiding me in favor of Sofia. Last year, whenever Michaela tried to talk to me about Jason, I'd swat the subject away like it was a mosquito.

"You can tell me, Michaela," I press on, trying to be brave. "It's okay — I promise I won't get weird or —"

"It's not about Jason," Michaela says flatly. "Or any boy."

Oh.

Before I can feel the full force of my relief, Michaela speaks again.

"We're moving," she says.

To Do List:
Read all the Point books!

♡ 📖 ♡

Airhead
Being Nikki
Runaway
By **Meg Cabot**

Wish
By **Alexandra Bullen**

Top 8
By **Katie Finn**

Sea Change
The Year My Sister Got Lucky
South Beach
French Kiss
Hollywood Hills
By **Aimee Friedman**

Ruined
By **Paula Morris**

Possessed
By **Kate Cann**

Suite Scarlett
Scarlett Fever
By **Maureen Johnson**

The Lonely Hearts Club
By **Elizabeth Eulberg**

Wherever Nina Lies
By **Lynn Weingarten**

Girls In Love
Summer Girls
Summer Boys
Next Summer
After Summer
Last Summer
By **Hailey Abbott**

Point
www.thisispoint.com